NOT
Colored

CRYSTAL JACKSON

BAIT-CAL
PUBLISHING

ISBN: 978-0-9859619-8-5

Acknowledgments

I must first and foremost acknowledge my grandmother Veda James, who was my hero. I strived to be as strong and intelligent as her. I thank her for saving all the photos and sharing so many stories with me.

I also want to acknowledge my father, Lionel "Frenchy" Grandison. Without him, I could not have filled in the missing pieces to this story. I love and miss you, Dad.

Special thanks to my friends and family that gave me constructive feedback; Chanelle Grandison, Scherri Scott, Romelle Craig, Dominque Topps, and Veronica Wright.

And finally, my brother Lon Grandison. Without him, my ideas would remain just that, ideas. I can write a good book, but he made it great. Without his guidance and logical thinking, I would be all over the place.

About the Author

Crystal Jackson is an author, historian, and filmmaker who has embarked on preserving and sharing the 1500-year history of Pacoima, one of Los Angeles' oldest towns. Her critically acclaimed first book, "The Entrance: Pacoima's Story," was a 670-page encyclopedia of history about her hometown. She also produced and directed a film, "PacoimaStories: Land of Dreams," which drew rave reviews at the Pan African Film Festival and earned her a "Best Feature Documentary" nomination.

"Not Colored" is her first fiction novel, in a series based on her grandmother, the first woman to work in LAPD's detective unit. Jackson attended California State University, Northridge majoring in journalism.

Author's Note

The Black experience is not monolithic. Like all other cultures, every family has a unique story, and this book is a true testament to that fact.

This historical novel is based on generations of stories passed down by my great-grandmother, grandmother, and mother. However, what makes it truly special is sharing images that uniquely bring this tale to life.

I remember the aroma of kerosene filtering my great grandmother Edna's house while sitting glued listening to old stories. My imagination ran wild, wondering what life was like back in those days. I asked a thousand questions taking notes in my mind. Edna told me about retrieving her three children after a nasty divorce in the 1920s. She described her triumph with humor and grace, creating a childhood memory I never forgot. Yet, at the same time, an air of sadness was present when speaking of the mother she never met, who died during Edna's birth. I remember asking her mom's name, and she softly replied, "Adeline Southern." My great-grandmother was the most wholesome person I ever knew and is the matriarch of this story.

However, her daughter, Veda, my grandmother, inspired this book. As a child, I saw the respect she commanded while working for the Los Angeles Police Department. She was a no-nonsense woman of color whose great memory helped solve many homicide cases. Yet breaking barriers in a world of misogyny and racism came with countless nightmares that I didn't understand until much later.

I watched her struggle to sleep and discovered that demons lurked behind her success. Her photographic mind processed graphic crime scenes and froze the images deep within her in ways most of us could never understand. Searching through my memories, I compiled the police stories she told me, the marriages, and how she raised her children, which enhanced my respect for this exceptional lady. After digging deeper, I realized her strength was present from the very beginning.

Following the breadcrumbs, it was my gossipy mother who shared with me many of Veda's most intimate secrets. I strolled down memory lane to recall those conversations and further connect the dots of my grandmother's story. My mom once shared how Veda stood face to face with a gun at her head after her husband returned home on leave from the military, never flinching as her life was threatened. She told the story as if it was normal, but it was not, and I remember it well. She also told me how fantastic Veda sang, but I never heard her sing anything, which was confusing. A photo of her singing at the Dunbar Hotel never made sense until I learned it was music legends Count Basie and T-Bone Walker on stage with her. This blew my mind. Between family recounts and photos, everything came together.

I feared these generational stories would be lost forever because this unique maternal linage would end with my daughter Tara, who has Down Syndrome and will never have children. Consequently, my unrelenting desire to ensure the stories of these great women are told is mainly because of Tara. There are names and historical events my readers will recognize. My eternal hope is that it will stand the test of time and show that everyone has a place in history, or should I say "her-story."

Chapter 1:

Isn't She Lovely?

It was 1918 and sweat dripped down 22-year-old Edna's face as she endured the birth of her second child. The pain came and went, leaving her dreading the next contraction and praying it would ease up soon. She bowed her head and said a prayer as she knew that was usually the answer.

Edna reflected on the heated journey she withstood before going into labor, traveling from Arkansas to Los Angeles during the worst flu pandemic in history. The Spanish flu had people dying daily, but Edna had faith that would not be her fate. If she survived that carriage ride with a toddler in hand, she felt she could do anything.

The bumpy road had made her nausea worse, but she never complained to her husband. She had to grin and bear it until they reached California, and the tortuous journey could end. Although automobiles were getting popular, they still traveled by horse and carriage.

Lying on the bed, she noticed lace doilies on a chair next to the dresser as she felt the contractions coming sooner. The midwife wore a long dress, a face mask, and a bonnet. Her kind eyes put Edna at ease as she went through another strong one. Edna's husband, Rufus, sat outside the bedroom with their daughter Lolita waiting for the birth to conclude.

Rufus Durr was a tall man with deep-set eyes. His bronze skin and silky black hair highlighted his Native American ancestry, but he was colored, just Like everyone else. His mother, Gertrude, and Father Jake had two other children that didn't survive. They spoiled Rufus rotten and were upset when he did not follow them to Detroit, from Sherman, Texas. Instead, Rufus and Edna left for Little Rock, where there was kinfolk.

Gertrude had counted the months from when Edna and Rufus married on July 15, 1915, to Lolita's birth on January 9, 1916. Edna, Gertrude thought, was not the woman for her precious son. But she was determined to have grandchildren and be a part of their lives, and Edna could accommodate that.

Born on a Texas farm in 1895, Edna's life had a tragic start. Her mother died during her birth, leaving her father, Wesley Green, with six children and a newborn. Heartbreak would hit again when her baby sister died later that year, leaving Wesley devastated and their home somber.

Wesley was born in 1859 during America's slavery era. His parents, originally from Virginia, were sold to a plantation in Arkansas where they produced twenty children for their slave owner's inventory. Shortly after Wesley's birth, some of the family was sold and relocated to Madison, Texas. After two years of the bloody civil war, Abraham Lincoln signed the Emancipation Proclamation ending slavery. On January 1, 1863, freedom was legally theirs; however, authorities did not inform the Texas family until two years later.

After the death of Edna's mother, he found himself in a difficult situation. He spent his days tending to the farm and in the fields. A lot fell on his oldest daughter Annabelle, who was 10 when Edna was born, and she took on most of the maternal duties.

However, her mother's twin sister Hattie stepped in to help. She later gave birth to two more of Wesley's kids making the total seven. After he died in 1910, Hattie left for Houston and took the youngest with her. They were never heard from again. In 1914, five of the siblings packed and headed for Los Angeles, while 19-year-old Edna took off with her love Rufus to Arkansas, where they married.

The September heat intensified the birthing experience as Edna was going on 8 hours of intense labor. She was of the Christian Science faith, which did not believe in doctors; instead, it was healing by prayer. Edna read Mary Baker Eddy's literature about channeling spiritual healing through God's divine laws. It was that faith that guided Edna throughout her entire life.

She would read the Christian Science Monitor, Mary Baker Eddy books, or the Bible whenever feeling ill. It never failed her. But giving birth did not allow for reading, so intense prayer would have to do. The midwife examined Edna's vagina and could see the head crowning. Edna's sister, Esma, was in the room holding Edna's hand as the midwife told Edna to push. Edna felt the urge as she screamed from the immense pain. Out came the baby after three solid, forceful thrusts, and Edna could finally breathe again.

"It's a girl," the midwife said with joy.

"A girl?" Edna asked. "Are you sure?"

"She's beautiful, congratulations!"

Edna did not share that cheerful sentiment. She had hoped to give Rufus a son to carry on his name. Having a girl meant more kids. While Edna was fond of kids, she had expected to break the color line and be someone special. Although her introverted ways and traditional upbringing clarified the limitations of being a colored woman, she secretly dreamed of being much more. During moments of solitude, her imagination placed her race as white, with no restrictions. In those moments, she twisted her thin hair, proud it was not kinky, and made a point to stay out of the sun so as not to get darker. When outside, she always wore a sun hat. Edna was a beautiful, dainty woman with caramel-colored skin and almond-shaped eyes. Her lips were plump and even on both the top and bottom. There was a perfect arch on the upper lip. Her hair was dark with a thin, ultra-fine texture. She loved twisting it in two buns on the side but mostly wore it pulled back.

The tiny baby cried fiercely as the midwife handed her to Edna. The white film was still on her with blood from the birth, dripping. As Edna held the wailing infant, Esma took a wet towel and wiped her off. The midwife proceeded to push on Edna's stomach to help release the after birth. Edna then tried to breastfeed, but the baby would not latch. This child was different than Lolita, who was so easy and manageable. She ate immediately and made having a newborn enjoyable. Edna assumed all babies would be like Lolita, who they called Lita, but boy was she wrong.

"She's lovely," Esma said. "I'll go get Rufus and Lita."

"Wait, Esma! Give me a minute," Edna pleaded.

Esma ignored Edna and went to get Rufus and share the news. Esma was a blessing, but it was her oldest sister Annabel who she wanted most. Annabel was like a mother and Edna's thoughts dwelled on wshing she was there. Annabelle had never seen Lita because she was born in Arkansas. Lita wouldn't even go to her when they first arrived in Los Angeles. She clung relentlessly to Edna and Rufus when Edna's family came around. Since they were staying with Esma, Lita eventually warmed up to her.

Two-year-old Lita was eager to see her little sister. Rufus, however, found it hard to hide his disappointment. He went into the bedroom and could see the exhaustion on Edna's face. But when he looked at the 6-pound little girl, he was mesmerized. She was beautiful with perfect cheeks, perfect lips, and big, gorgeous eyes that were alert and attentive. She had stopped crying and looked like she was trying to communicate but didn't have the words, or did she? Rufus immediately saw there was something different about her, and so did Edna.

Quickly overcome with his new offspring, Rufus extinguished his disappointment relatively fast. He bent over and kissed Edna on the forehead.

"I can't wait for my mother to see her," he immediately proclaimed. "She's gonna be thrilled."

His statement sent off red alarm bells to Edna. She had just reunited with her siblings in Los Angeles. She loved being around them and knew the others would come once word got out. Edna didn't want to leave Los Angeles, but Rufus clearly wanted to move to Detroit soon, and Edna could not deny him.

The baby, refusing to latch and eat right away, baffled Edna. It took a day before she finally ate. When it ultimately happened, her baby fed with ease. It was like she did it on purpose, Edna thought briefly.

Edna never had a mother and felt somewhat responsible for her death. As a child, the family tried to protect Edna from the truth about her mother's passing. However, when she was ten, her father divulged everything after a night of excessive drinking. His inability to cope with his grief led him to many nights of intoxication.

Buried deep in Edna's prized possessions was a picture of her mother. Many nights she spent starring at that picture, wondering who Adeline Southern Green was. She tried hard to bury the feelings of guilt that often overcame her when she thought about her mom. Edna pondered what she smelled like or how her voice sounded and frequently asked why God made this happen? Yet, it was God that always gave her strength.

During Edna's upbringing, she called her aunt just "Hattie." Her other mother figure Annabel was her sister. Thus, Edna associated a mother figure with the first name. No one in Edna's life was called mother, mama, or mom, and that's the way it was for her, and she was okay with that. So, her kids were going to call her Edna no matter what anyone said.

Her other siblings came to Esma's house to see the baby, all wearing facemasks because of the pandemic. Edna looked through a baby name book she got as a gift when Lita was born. When she looked at the infant's precious face, she saw the eyes of an old soul that seemed to understand everything going on around her. Veda was a Hindu name meaning "knowledge and wisdom," which was perfect, and that was the name Edna wanted. Veda Delois Durr was her choice; now, would Rufus agree?

"I like the name Veda," Edna revealed two days after she was born. "It means knowledge and wisdom. What do you think?"

"As long as you give me a son to name Rufus, I don't care what you name her," he said callously.

Rufus' parents were Jake and Gertrude Durr. Jake was from the Cherokee Nation and known to wear an Indian headdress. Gertrude was of full-African descent. The death of their first two children left her devastated. She later gave birth to their third child, Rufus, who became her pride and joy.

Rufus could not wait to get to Detroit with his two daughters. Edna, on the other hand, was dreading it. She insisted they ride by train and not horse and carriage. Travel would take two months by buggy or eight hours by train, and with the Spanish Flu pandemic, it could be deadly. Nevertheless, Rufus wasted no time getting the train tickets.

Veda was just six months old, and Edna was having morning sickness once again. However, she did not tell Rufus until they got to Detroit and ultimately got settled. Rufus noticed she did not have her period for a while but said nothing.

It was a quiet afternoon in the Durr's apartment. Jake and Gertrude were tending to the girls while Rufus and Edna were sitting outside on the deck.

"Rufus, I have something to tell you," Edna nervously divulged.

"What's that?" Rufus asked.

"I'm having another baby," she explained.

"It's about time you told me."

"You knew?"

"You've been clean for a long time. Of course, I knew."

Edna was relieved and sad at the same time. Although now Rufus knew for sure she was pregnant, Gertrude was another matter. She made no qualms about how she felt about Edna. Gertrude felt Edna had taken her son away. She continually put Edna down, and Rufus never defended her, which made life miserable.

She understood Gertrude had lost two of her babies, a type of pain Edna could not even imagine. The pain would be unbearable. But that was Gertrude's issue, and it wasn't going to be hers.

Despite the conflict, Edna enjoyed raising her kids. Veda walked at only nine months while touching everything within reach and exploring objects with intensity. Edna always had to keep an eye on her. Being told to stop was only a momentary delay. She would always go back to finish her exploration.

Veda was 15 months old when her little brother Rufus Jr. was born. Edna wanted to call him Pete instead of junior. No one seemed to complain about that. Edna did not know she could feel so much love for her son. Lolita was obedient and passive, Veda was defiant and bossy, but Pete stole a part of Edna's heart she never knew existed. She recognized early it would be hard for her not to play favorites, but clearly, he was hers.

They had been in Detroit for barely two years, and Gertrude's dislike of Edna was becoming intolerable. At every turn, she undermined her parenting and seemed to want Edna gone. Edna felt Gertrude would even put her out if she thought she could get away with it.

Watching the relationship between Rufus and his mother disturbed Edna as well. Their bond seemed strange and unnatural. She could not put her finger on it, but her gut told her something was wrong. She had doubts about Gertrude's mental state. Those doubts became a reality when she walked into the kitchen and heard Gertrude talking to herself.

"My babies need me. That hussy needs to go. She's in the way of me being their mama. She's got to go," Gertrude said under her breath in an eerie tone while staring at the window.

Edna was shocked at what she just heard. She really does want her gone and wanted her children. Edna quietly backed out, horrified at the thought. She immediately went to the bedroom where Rufus was.

"Rufus, I overheard your mother talking to herself. She wants our children."

"Don't be silly. She just loves them."

"It's more than that. She wants me gone."

"Now you're sounding like the crazy one."

"I'm beginning to think you're in on this with her," Edna railed. "Is that why you brought me here so she could take my kids?"

"Woman, you can take that nonsense somewhere else."

Edna was at a loss. She sat down in the living room, wondering what she got herself into and confused about what to think. She had no allies and felt all alone in this battle. Her mind began to wonder about what happened to Gertrude's other two kids. No one ever said how they died, and she had a bizarre relationship with Rufus, often more like husband and wife than mother and son. They always huddled together seeming like they were in their own world. Edna decided then that Lita, Veda, and Pete would stay in her sight from that point on.

Edna and Rufus were in the living room watching the kids play a few weeks after the Gertrude incident. Edna was knitting, and Rufus was listening to the radio. Veda pushed Lolita down for cause and effect, which she regularly did to get the adults' reactions.

"Veda, don't push your sister," Edna reprimanded.

"Now, now, pretty Veda, that's not nice." Rufus chided, infuriating Edna.

"You shouldn't do that, Rufus. She is never going to learn to behave herself. You must be tough with her and not give her a compliment when she gets in trouble!"

"Well, if you stopped gloating over Pete and gave her a little attention, she wouldn't always be like this."

Edna felt her blood pressure rise. How could he bring up Pete, a baby, when the dialogue is Veda's behavior?

"I'm not gloating over him. He's a baby, for goodness' sake," Edna exclaimed.

"You've been gloating ever since he was born. He gets more attention than I do."

"Well, maybe he deserves it more than you."

As the argument continued, Gertrude walked into the room. Edna knew whose side she would take, as always.

"Edna, you really shouldn't talk to your husband like that," Gertrude scolded. "Didn't your mother teach you how to treat a man? Oops, I forgot your mother died giving birth to you. I probably would have died too."

Edna was horrified, angry, and shocked at what Gertrude just said. It was downright cruel. Edna looked down at the bible sitting on the end table next to her. In her mind, she asked God what to do. Whatever it was, she could not be weak and decided to say her piece. Everything had been building up to this. She had reached the limit, especially after overhearing Gertrude plotting against her.

"Gertrude, that was a mean, mean thing to say to me," Edna said forcefully. "But I get it. God took your two babies from you for a reason. You are not fit, you do not pray, you're mean, and have a heart full of hate! God does not like hate. As bad as you treat me, I refuse to hate you, but these are my children, and no one will tell me how to raise them. God is with me, and I hope you find God too."

"Edna, you will not talk to her like that," Rufus exploded.

"What? I'm not going to let her talk to me like that! She's crazy and wants my children. I believe you're helping her," Edna shouted, looking him in the eye.

"If you feel like that, then I think it's time for you to go."

"So, you're choosing her over me, over us?"

Edna could not fight back the tears. She grabbed her handbag and looked at the kids.

"Come on, kids."

"No. They are staying here."

"I'm not leaving here without them."

"You can either walk out the door, or I'll throw you out. It's your choice," Rufus said with evil in his eyes.

"I am not leaving without my kids."

Rufus grabbed Edna, and they began a struggle. Edna reached for the kids who were crying as they saw this unfold. He grabbed her arms and began dragging her towards the door. Edna hit the cocktail table in the struggle, knocking off the photos with a loud crashing sound.

"Edna," Veda called out.

Rufus reached for the door, swinging it open with one hand and gripping Edna in the other.

"My kids, give me my kids!" Edna yelled as Rufus threw her out the door, shoving her to the ground.

Rufus slammed the door and turned around. The first thing he saw was his mother standing there with a smirk on her face. Then he turned and looked at his kids. Pete and Lita were crying hysterically; however, Veda seemed calm, not taking her eyes off her father. She watched every move he made, never saying a word.

Edna slowly picked herself up. Barely able to see through the tears, she began to walk through the courtyard. Then she felt a hand on her shoulder.

"Mrs. Durr," a voice said. Edna turned around, and it was an older lady with uncombed hair who lived in the complex. Edna looked at her but could not speak.

"I seen what dat man did to you," she said, concerned. "Let me tell you something, you needs to get custody of yo kids. Ms. Gertrude is touched in the head. She kilt her kids. She told me herself. It was an accident, but she's responsible jus da same. Don't let her raise yo kids. I knows somebody who can help you, and I'll help you too. Come wit me, I'll get you da numba," the lady continued.

Edna got the number and thanked the lady but knew she could not stay. Not knowing where to go, Edna ended up at the church. While there, she saw one of the choir ladies who offered her a place to stay until she worked things out.

She cried that whole night but woke up determined to get her kids back. As it turned out, the number she got from the lady was a lawyer willing to help her.

The Durr's were financially stable, and Edna knew this would be a brutal fight, but 1921 would become the year of her independence.

Michigan had 86⁣ divorces that year, but it was not easy for a woman to get one. Edna filed the papers on May 31, 1921, and it took a long eight months for finalization. In the meantime, Edna did laundry for money until the legal process was complete. Finally, on January 5, 1922, Lita's birthday, the court granted Edna's divorce. She got full custody of her three children based on extreme cruelty. Now all she had to do was pick them up and head for California. With her divorce decree in hand and the train tickets purchased, she went off to the Durrs' apartment for her kids.

Edna knocked on the door, nervous about how this encounter would go. She then pounded harder until Gertrude appeared.

"What do you want?" she said with a wicked look on her face.

"You know what I want, Gertrude. I came to get my kids," Edna replied boldly.

"Over my dead body."

"I have my papers Custody was granted to me."

"They aren't here, Edna," Gertrude belted out and closed the door.

Upset at what just transpired, Edna departed. There is no way Gertrude would prevail in this. Luckily, there was a police station down the street. As she entered the building, she felt invisible. The white officers acted like she was not there. She went to a desk and asked if someone could help her. A fat man with his oversized cap pointed her to another counter. Edna went there only to get told she belonged in another department. They were not rude but unhelpful. Edna stopped, bent her head down, and prayed for an answer. Just then, an officer approached her.

"Are you okay?" he asked.

"No. I'm trying to get my children back."

"Did someone kidnap them?" he asked, sounding concerned.

"Well, kind of. I just got custody, and now my husband, I mean ex-husband, is hiding them from me," she explained.

"Do you have your court documents?"

Edna reached in her purse and pulled out the divorce decree. She looked at the ceiling to thank God as she handed him the papers.

"Let's go. I'll help you find them."

The officer had a kind smile and gave Edna a good feeling. He was a nice-looking white man that impressed her with the respect he gave. Although she got along well with most Caucasians, some could be cold and soulless. However, this man was gentle and friendly. He made small talk as they walked to the apartment complex.

"Your name is Edna Durr? I noticed that on the papers."

"Yes," Edna replied.

"Mrs. Durr, what are your children's names?"

"Lolita, Veda, and Pete."

"Two girls and a boy. Nice names. What happened to your marriage if you don't mind me asking?"

Edna was hesitant in divulging too much information, but she felt comfortable with him for some reason.

"My mother-in-law hates me. Need I say more?"

"Do you have any idea where they could be?" he inquired.

"They have to be somewhere near the apartment."

There were two multi-story masonry apartment buildings on Sherman Street. Edna watched as a 1920 'Model A' slowly cruised down the road. Papa Jake, who also lived with them, worked as a machine operator at an auto manufacturer. He got Rufus a job there helping with odd duties. Edna knew they would both be at work this time of day, so Gertrude was the main obstacle.

As they passed the first complex, Edna heard a girl's voice saying "stop it" while laughing. She knew it was Lita, instantly. She looked up where the sound came from and saw an open window.

"I'm sorry, what was your name?" Edna asked.

"Thomas. Officer Thomas Williams."

"That voice is Lita's, Officer Williams. I know it anywhere."

"Let's go check it out. Is this where they live?"

Edna had no idea why they would be in this particular building because it wasn't where they lived.

"No. The Durrs live in the next building, but that was Lita's voice."

Edna and the officer walked up the stairs into the building. Inside was a courtyard with colored kids playing. Edna hoped to see one of hers out there, but she didn't. They climbed the stairs to the second floor. The officer adjusted his hat as he knocked on the door. His peacock jacket with buttons on the front made him look intimidating. He pounded again, and a colored man opened it with a scared look on his face.

"Good afternoon, sir. Do you have any children here?"

It was apparent children were in his unit. They could hear them playing in the background. The middle-aged man had a button-up cotton shirt and wrinkled pants. He had uncombed hair, and his eyes bulged as he looked at the officer.

"Uh yes sah," he said.

"Can I see them?"

"Yes sah."

He opened the door wide enough to see the kids. Edna stayed back as not to ruin things, but her heart was beating like crazy. Officer Williams saw Lita, who looked a bit timid when she noticed him.

"Come here, sweetie," he said.

Lita looked frightened. She had been in awkward positions before when questioned. She was asked a lot about her nationality because of her straight black hair and high cheekbones. Her look was more Native American than the rest of the kids, and Lita became very self-conscious about it.

"What's your name?" Officer Williams asked her nicely.

"I'm colored Lolita," the six-year-old instinctively blurted out. Officer Williams thought that was hilarious while trying to keep a serious face. Edna peaked her head in to look, drawing the attention of four-year-old Veda, who saw her first.

"Edna!!!" she screamed running up with a big smile on her face. Edna hugged Veda, then looked up to see 2-year-old Pete just standing there. She walked over to pick him up, but he didn't seem sure who she was.

"It's me, baby, Edna."

"Edna," Pete said as he smiled.

Before she knew it, Edna was gleefully hugging her three children.

"Let's go, guys."

"Where's daddy?" Lita asked

Edna did not know if they would understand the whole story. She knew they loved their father and grandparents, but this was in their best interest. There was no time to explain. She could tell them when they got older.

"Your father is staying here. We are going to see Aunt Esma in Los Angeles. You guys want to ride on a train?" Edna asked.

Both Lita and Veda screamed, "yes!!" Pete was too young to understand. They left the building with nothing, and Edna would be starting over from scratch.

Veda was excited she was going to ride a train. However, she was also obsessed with their new friend, the police officer. His uniform, oversized hat, and billy club fascinated her, but she did not know what that mole on his neck was. It looked like a big giant raisin.

As they got to the street, Veda grabbed Officer William's hand. Edna had Pete in her arms, along with Lita by her side, as they walked to the train station. Veda smiled at the officer, studying every detail of him, including his silver wedding ring. Noticing how observant she was, Officer Williams smiled back at her. Veda's white lace dress, white knee-high socks, and bow headband accented her charm.

"What's your name?" Veda asked.

"Officer Williams," he replied. "Can you remember that?"

"I can remember everything," Veda boldly said as they proceeded to the streetcar that would take them to the station.

"Mrs. Durr, I can accompany you all the way if you want. The Michigan Central Station can be pretty rough, and you have three little ones to watch after."

"Yes, yes," Veda exclaimed.

"That is so nice of you," Edna said.

They boarded the streetcar and took a twenty-minute ride to the train depot. When they arrived at the station, there was a massive office tower with 13 stories and two mezzanine levels. It had a roof height of 230 feet and was the tallest rail station in the world. Edna hoped this was the last time she ever saw this dreary, intimidating station.

"I'm so glad you came with me. I would have been lost," Edna confided to Officer Williams.

"I'm glad I came too. You have a kind face, and you deserve happiness. So, what's waiting for you in Los Angeles?" he curiously asked.

"My family is there, and right now, that's what I need."

"I've thought about moving west, but my job keeps me here. I guess it's not that bad — getting to meet nice people like you."

"They're lucky to have you," Edna said. "Can I ask a small favor? Can you watch Pete for me while I go to the restroom with the girls? I have to find the colored facilities."

"Sure, they are on the backside of the building. Right over there. For the life of me, I don't get this separate but equal."

As Edna passed Pete's hand to officer Williams, he had to let go of Vedas, which irritated the four-year-old. Both adults noticed people staring. Officer Williams seemed unphased by the attention while Edna felt slightly self-conscious.

Something about Edna fascinated him. Was it her beauty or perhaps her inner strength? He wasn't sure, but he wanted to know more, and he was happy to help out. The kids seemed to like him too. As Edna took off with the girls, Officer Williams picked up Pete, who didn't seem to mind. Little Pete was adorable with his cap on as he looked curiously at this stranger.

"Hey bud, your mom and sisters will be right back. We're gonna hang out here for a second."

Pete looked at him and said nothing.

"You're going to see your family in Los Angeles. Doesn't that make you happy?"

Pete continued to look at him, showing no emotion, so Officer Williams put an extensive animated look on his face.

"Hey, you're about to go on a choo-choo train! It's gonna be fun. Are you excited?"

There was still no reaction from Pete, only a stare. Realizing he had a tough audience, Williams then changed tactics.

"I see you don't talk much, but that sure is a neat hat you have on."

Pete paused for a moment, looked at the police hat on the officer's head, and smiled as he reached up to touch it.

"Yea, my hat's pretty neat too," officer Williams said as he broke out laughing. Pete let out a hardy laugh as well. Williams was relieved he made headway.

When the girls returned from the restroom, Veda immediately took Officer Williams's hand, causing him to give Pete back to Edna.

"Looks like you two got along," Edna said as she looked at Pete, who was still smiling.

Just then, the loudspeaker announced, "Track 4 is now boarding."

"That's me," Edna said, looking at the officer. "Come on, girls. I guess this is goodbye."

Williams looked down at Veda, who was still holding his hand. He admired her spirit and bent down to talk to her.

"You make sure you take care of your mother."

"I will. You be sure to catch all the bad guys," Veda replied.

"I will," he said winking at her.

Her intense eyes with the big bow in her hair melted him. Veda gave him a warm hug. He then stood up straight and looked Edna in the eye.

"Mrs. Durr, have a safe trip. You have wonderful kids," he said with sincerity.

"Bless your heart. I don't know how to thank you. You have been such a big help to me. I could not have got my kids without you. I'm eternally grateful," Edna said, realizing how handsome this man who helped her was.

"My pleasure."

Williams thought Edna was beautiful as well as they parted ways.

Edna and the kids headed to where the colored people were waiting. There were a lot of men with suits and hats and a hand full of women. Edna felt out of place since she wasn't dressed in her best and wasn't wearing a nice hat. Officer Williams went off to the side where he could watch. Veda looked in his direction and waved. He couldn't believe she was only four. He lost sight of them as they merged with the other passengers, who all toted their luggage. The steam trumpet sounded off, warning people the locomotive would be departing soon. Edna was off to Los Angeles to start her new life as a single parent.

The Durr family took this portrait in 1920 while in Detroit. Pictured from the left are Lita, Rufus, Edna, Veda, and baby Pete.

1915 photo taken in Sherman, TX shows Edna (Green) and her siblings. From the left, Birdie, Edna, Wesley Jr, James (Bubs), Esma, and Annabelle

1918 photo of Edna, Lita, and baby Veda in Los Angeles before moving to Detroit

When Edna finally reached Los Angeles, there was a sigh of relief. The atmosphere was peaceful and serene. Although Detroit and LA were both big cities, somehow, Edna felt a connection to California. It was meant for her. The smell of the ocean gave a sense of freedom and invincibility she never felt before. She could not wait to take her kids to see the humongous blue sea once they got older. However, many beaches were still segregated, and she had to find out which areas allowed coloreds. Her sisters were sure to know.

In the meantime, Edna was staying with Esma. It was a little cramped there, so she thought it would be temporary. The Greens kept everything immaculate. Beds made every day; dishes washed right after meals; floors swept and mopped regularly was how Wesley ran his house when they were growing up. It was second nature to Edna.

Esma was three years older than Edna, and they were close. Her small two-bedroom house on 33rd Avenue was one of two areas in Los Angeles where coloreds could live in 1922. It had land, but the structure was barely 700 square feet. The front porch, however, was huge. She and the kids barely fit in the extra bedroom, but they made it work. The house had running water, but it wasn't heated. She would have to boil it for baths but occasionally they bathed in cold water.

Edna knew she would have to figure things out fast. She found odd jobs when they first arrived, however, they ended up living there for a couple of years.

The blessing for coloreds was the availability of work, particularly for women. White families wanted their homes and laundry cleaned. Esma worked for a lady who had a sister in Eagle Rock who needed help. She owned a 2-bedroom duplex available for a live-in housekeeper. Edna jumped on that offer. Her brother James, who they called Bubs, was a World War I veteran who loved touting his military uniform. He owned a Ford Model T and drove them just south of Glendale to Eagle Rock for her interview.

Mrs. Johnson was a down-to-earth white woman who wore her dark hair up in a bun. They hit it off right away. Mrs. Johnson loved the look of lace just like Edna. She was also thrilled that Edna knew how to crochet and offered to pay her for items. Learning to knit from Aunt Hattie, who also taught her to sew, Edna was incredibly good at it and added special signature touches that made her creations unique.

So now Edna had a cozy place of her own, a good job, and a good beginning. The only problem was Eagle Rock was not color friendly, so she had to tread carefully, and so did her kids. Mrs. Johnson warned her about how bad it was and not to go out after dark.

They had a lovely yard and plenty of cool toys that the kids had to share. Edna bought them a pair of metal skates with adjustable straps for Christmas. They were so excited and took turns as they rode on the bumpy sidewalk. Edna also got them a pedal car to share, but it seemed more for Pete. While Edna worked, the girls would watch Pete. Veda was always adventurous and sought competition and challenges. She would tussle with Pete all the time, burning off his 5-year-old boy testosterone. Lita was seldom up for it. Her favorite pastime, combing her doll's blonde hair, was an obsession that consumed her for hours.

One day they were all outside while Edna was working. Veda and Pete were playing a game where Veda would hit him and take off. Pete would catch her and reciprocate. The activity went on for a while until Pete got bored. Then the black pedal car caught his attention, and he walked over to take a ride. Tilting his page boy cap up, Pete pedaled through the dirt and rocks while making car noises. Veda had no interest in dolls, so she headed over to him because it seemed like he was enjoying himself.

"Can you get out, Pete?"

"I'm in it now. Wait till I'm done." Pete said defiantly. He knew he had to stand up to her, or she would run all over him.

"No. Get out now. I need it to be a police car, so I can get the bad guys."

"What bad guys?"

"There's plenty around. They could be hiding."

"Hiding where?"

"You never know. Now get out."

"No!!!"

Veda realized she had to use a different tactic. She could have just pulled him out and taken the car, but after their hit-and-run game, she realized she had a better solution. Veda approached Lita, who almost always did what she said.

"Come on, Lita. Let's go inside and leave Pete out here by himself."

"We really should watch him," Lita protested.

"He'll be fine. Let's go. BYE PETE!!!"

They both went up the porch and inside. Pete ignored them at first and rolled a little in his car. He looked around and saw a vehicle pass the house slowly. Pete was usually brave, but Veda was always his insurance. Something told him to go inside. It was a combination of loneliness and fear of the big world without his sister's protection. He got out of the car, bowed his head down, and headed inside, shuffling his feet in the dirt.

"Edna said you two are supposed to watch me," he said while entering the house.

"We are watching you. Did you put the car up?" Veda gloated, proud her plan worked.

"No," Pete said.

Just then, they heard a knock at the door. Veda looked at Lita and shrugged her shoulders.

"Who is it?" she yelled.

"It's me. Junior."

Junior was their 7-year- old cousin. His mother, Lucille, was Edna's niece and big sister Annabel's only daughter. Lucille, who sometimes worked at the Johnson's house, was beautiful and could pass as white. Their kids were the same age, and all hung out together. When Junior came to the door, he looked through the mailbox slot but did not see anyone. Veda could not resist the opportunity to tease him.

"Nobody's home!" Veda yelled, hiding from Junior's view.

Meant as a joke, Veda waited for his reply. But to her surprise, Junior said "OK" and walked away. The three kids ran to the window and saw Junior heading down the driveway. Veda and Pete fell out laughing; however, Lita did not see the humor.

"Veda, why did you do that?" Lita asked.

"It was funny."

It was at that moment they heard another knock. Assuming it was Junior returning, Veda swung open the door. The word "Junior" halfway came out of her mouth when a tall white man appeared standing before her. Veda's jaw dropped.

"Hi, Little girl. Is your mommy home?" he asked.

Veda studied him carefully. He looked a little different, a little older, but she recognized him. His face was cleanly shaven now with no mustache. She looked for his wedding ring, but it wasn't there.

"Why do you want to know?" she asked.

"Are you kids alone?"

Alarm bells went off with Lita. Why was this man asking these questions? Now was her moment to play big sister, but Veda beat her to it.

"We don't give out that information. But I must tell you that I know who you are," Veda said.

"Veda, we aren't supposed to talk to anyone. Shut the door." Lita finally yelled out.

Completely disobeying what Edna always taught them, Veda was confident she had things under control and felt she could trust this man, a dangerous supposition for a seven-year-old.

"You know who I am?" the man asked.

But Lita was frightened. She felt the situation was out of control with a stranger.

"Veda, he could try to kidnap us. Shut the door!" she yelled hysterically.

As calm as a whip, Veda never flinched. Instead, she tried to calm Lita down before she had a cardiac arrest.

"He's a police officer, Lita. I never forget a face. He helped Edna find us in Detroit. This is the officer that got us from old man Ray's house. Don't you remember? Look at his mole."

Impressed with her memory of him, the man smiled.

"Yes, I did—my goodness, Veda, you were only 4 when I met you. I came by to see your mom, and I wanted to know how you guys were doing."

"How did you know where we lived, Officer Williams?"

"You remember my name?"

"Of course, where's your uniform?" Veda asked as she checked out his attire.

"I just moved to the area. I don't wear a uniform anymore."

By this time, Lita was dumbfounded and was still struggling to remember him. After all, she was only six back then.

"You're colored Lolita," the man said looking at her.

She hadn't used those words in years, but something felt familiar.

"Is your mother home?"

Lita did not reply and looked at Veda, who was quick to answer.

"Officer Williams, you know you shouldn't ask children questions like that, don't you?"

"You must be around what, seven?"

"Around? Yes, I'm seven, but I want to know one thing. Where is your ring? Did you lose it?"

Veda was intrigued by Officer Williams. He looked so different without his peacoat and hat, but he still had that police officer persona.

"Uh, no. It's a long story. You don't miss a thing, do you? You guys look like you're doing fine. I just wanted to check on how things were going."

"Well, Mr. Williams. It's kind of you to check on us. Yes, everything is fine. If you want to see my mother, you can come back later. We should not be talking to you without her here."

"OK. I will," Williams replied.

Despite Lita getting a little hysterical, which was her nature, Veda thought she handled things well. Her skill at analyzing situations was exceptional, and she instinctively never panicked. Edna constantly reminded her she was only a child, but Veda never felt like one. As Mr. Williams was turning to leave, Edna walked upholding a large paper bag.

"Oh my. Whatever are you doing here?" Edna asked, looking down at her checkered dress and apron, while nervously patting down any loose flyaway hairs.

"Well, I just moved out this way, and I was thinking about you. I thought I'd look you up and see how you're doing."

"Come on in," Edna said to him; feeling pleased, he took the time out to check on her. She remembered how sweet Officer Williams was to her. Edna thought they had a connection that day in Detroit but dismissed it because of his race.

Although her experience with whites mainly was positive, the evil they were capable of Edna knew all too well. She remembered when her father farmed from dusk till dawn in Texas, and the landholder often chastised him. They called him names more times than she could count, and he rarely ever received his deserved pay. But it was the landowner's wife who taught him to read and do basic math to avoid getting cheated. That kindness inspired him to send all his kids to school instead of forcing them to work the fields as everyone else did. He chose to work harder so his children could get an education. His downfall was when he got home; alcohol was his escape. He would drink till he passed out, then get up the following day and work 15 hours only to repeat the same routine. The only time he spent with the kids was Sunday when they went to church.

Edna walked into the house and put the bag on the dining room table.

"I brought dinner home from the Johnsons. There's fried chicken and some goodies."

It wasn't uncommon for Edna to bring food home from the big house. The Johnsons raised chickens, which Edna would pluck, cut up and cook. Sometimes she had to kill them too, but Mr. Johnson mostly did that. It was nice not always having to cook twice.

She invited Officer Williams to have a seat as she gave each of the kids a kiss on the forehead.

"Is everything OK?" she asked.

Veda took the initiative to answer as usual. She could read Edna well and saw a glow in her eyes when she looked at Officer Williams. Veda remembered them talking back in Detroit when they were walking to the train station. Edna was a little giddy and different. She never acted that way around their dad. She mostly defended herself.

"Yes. Everything is under control. Junior came by but didn't stay," Veda said.

Edna couldn't remember Officer William's name. She didn't want to offend him by asking since he remembered hers. But she had to bite the bullet and ask.

"I'm sorry. This is embarrassing, but I don't remember your name."

He began to answer when Veda seized on the opportunity. One of Veda's biggest thrills was to demonstrate her knowledge. It wasn't so much being a showboat but being proud of what she knew.

"His name is Thomas Williams," Veda blurted out. "Officer Thomas Williams."

"Veda! Your manners. He can answer."

Edna always found herself correcting her kids for manners. But Veda was persistent with this one.

"So, Mr. Williams, what are you doing in Los Angeles?"

Edna let this go because she, too, wanted to know the answer.

"I'm a detective here. Do you know that is?"

Veda precisely knew what a detective was. Of course, she did. That was borderline insulting.

"Oh, So you're still in law enforcement. You're not helping women in distress anymore?"

With that, Edna had to inject herself. Veda was taking this conversation too far.

"OK Veda. That's enough," Edna interjected.

Officer Williams saw Veda's uniqueness and welcomed her questions. It crossed his mind how far she could go in if she were not colored and how unfair life can be. But there was a gleam within her, a sense of self that he rarely saw in people. This little girl knew who she was and spoke freely to a white person, rare in 1925.

"Oh no. That's OK," Officer Williams said.

"OK, you guys go clean-up for dinner."

As the kids left to wash up, Edna turned to him.

"So, what brings you here?"

"I just transferred to this city, and I remembered you said you were coming to Los Angeles. I hoped that I would find you in the phone book and there you were. You made an impression on me. I've been wondering how things turned out for you."

"How could a colored woman make an impression on you?"

"Colored woman? I don't see you as colored. I see you as a woman."

"I spent many nights wondering why you helped me. Why me?"

"Honestly, I don't know. I looked into your eyes, and I just felt compelled to help you. I haven't stopped thinking about you since."

The kids returned and went over to the dining room table, except for Veda, who went to the couch where Edna and Mr. Williams were sitting. Lita got the plates and pulled the food out of the bag, then she and Pete sat down and waited. Veda still wanted to engage Officer Williams but did not want to get in trouble.

"Mr. Williams, would you like to join us for dinner?" Veda asked.

Edna looked at Veda, then back at Mr. Williams.

"Oh no thank you, Veda. I'm just staying for a minute."

"So, Mr. Williams, what's the story with your ring? Are you divorced?" Veda asked as she sat next to him with her hand under her chin, looking him in the eye and waiting intensely for his response.

"Veda!!" Edna exclaimed.

"No. No. It's OK. My wife passed away, so I felt the need to start a new life. I applied at LAPD, and here I am," Williams explained. "I like it here."

"I'm so sorry to hear that," Edna said.

Again, Veda's curiosity peaked. 'Did someone kill her? Did she have cancer like Aunt Birdie?' Before she could think how to phrase the question, it just came out.

"How did she die?"

Edna was horrified once more with Veda's directness. Before she could respond, Veda went for broke.

"You never know. She could have been killed," Veda belted out.

Edna was now beyond angry and embarrassed with Veda. She could not have said anything worse.

"Veda!" Edna shouted. "That is enough. You know better than that!! I am so sorry, Mr. Williams. I really am. I can't apologize enough."

More impressed with Veda than ever, Williams knew he had to defuse this situation. He did not want anything to take that fire from Veda. She was on point, so direct, so intuitive. If she had so much talent at this age, how far could she go as an adult?

"No need to apologize. She is a bright little girl. Mrs. Durr, your daughter is special," he said as he turned to Veda.

"Veda, she wasn't killed. She had cancer. But that's good thinking on your part. Keep thinking like that and asking questions. If you don't ask, you won't know the answer."

"And you can't analyze the reaction either," Veda added.

Once more, she blew Williams away. He did not want Veda to get into any more trouble with her mother, so he decided it was time to leave. This experience confirmed what he always thought about this family. They were remarkable. He wished others could see what he did, but he knew they couldn't or wouldn't.

"Well, I'll let you get to your dinner. I'm glad to see you're doing good. I hope you don't mind if I check on you from time to time. You have your hands full with that one. She's unique. Most young people can't comprehend what she can. As a matter of fact, most adults probably can't either," he said. "And from now on, please, please call me Tom."

"And you call me Edna," she said with a smile.

Williams left, and Edna just shook her head at Veda. After that, they all sat down at the table and prayed, then placed their food on the plates.

"You said Junior came by?" Edna asked.

Pete was dying to tell her what Veda did. He knew he could be a thorn in her side sometimes, but she deserved it. She was always doing things to him, like the time she locked him outside in his underwear. Lita didn't help him either. She was too passive and didn't want to face the wrath of Veda.

"Yeah, he knocked on the door, but Veda said no one was home, and he left," Pete explained.

Edna chuckled.

"He left? You guys know he can be a little slow. Was that nice, Veda?"

"Yeah, I know. I was gonna send Pete to get him, but Officer Williams showed up. I wasn't trying to be mean. Honestly, I didn't think he would believe me."

Veda had a hard time understanding people with no common sense. By the time she was nine, she had begun to realize that others did not think like her. It was hard, though, because things seemed so simple, yet many struggled.

Officer Williams continued to visit Edna and the kids. He only came inside occasionally, but his car was in the neighborhood a lot. One Friday evening, Veda was looking out the window and saw Edna sitting in his black vehicle. She had a smile on her face, but Veda could not figure out what they were saying. The two seemed to be getting close. His car was a 1925 Ford model T coupe and was shiny black with big rectangular windows. Tom was behind the oversized steering wheel, and Edna was next to him.

"You know you don't have to keep giving me a ride to the market. I can manage," Edna said.

"I know. I want to."

"You know people in my neighborhood are talking. This is a sundown town. I've been lucky not to have any problems."

"Have you ever had problems?"

"Not really, but they are still out there. I'm not naïve. I know we have a connection, and I love seeing you, but there's no room for us to grow."

Tom had to dig down deep to explain his attraction to her and how he had fallen in love. But he knew he could not put her through the chaos of an interracial relationship, fully aware of how cruel white folks could be.

"Edna, for some reason I have never seen color. My father hated coloreds, but I had a Mamie who raised me for my mother. She nursed me, changed my diaper, taught me to walk, while her kids were home raising each other. She told me I could be different if I wanted. My father would come in and be so demeaning and mean to her. It was like he resented my attachment to her. Mamie would say to me, 'live with love, Thomas. Don't see color.' I guess what she told me stuck. I just can't see it. That's why I can see you for who you are."

"Who am I?" Edna asked.

"You are an honest, loving, thoughtful woman. I do not think you could lie if someone paid you to. Please forgive me if I am out of line, but you are so damned beautiful."

Edna was caught a little off guard and blushed a bit.

"I want to be more than just friends, but I know that can't happen," he added.

Tom paused, wanting to say so much more, but felt he could not. Not yet. But he loved her kind ways and black hair with a loose curl which gave her so much class. He liked how she wore lace and her feminine charm. He admired that she was soft-spoken and had a cute chuckle when she found something funny.

"What was your wife like?" Edna asked.

"Nothing like you. We grew up together, and she just didn't want to be a spinster. In my hometown, the worst thing in the world was an unmarried woman. My parents convinced me to take her as my wife and start a family."

"Do you have children?"

"No. My wife never got pregnant and was sick most of our marriage, until she died," he explained. "So, how old were you when you got married?"

"That's a good question, Tom. I got married at 18 and had strict moral values, and really loved him. I have never spoken of this before, but I was with child before the marriage, and I've been praying for God's forgiveness ever since. But lord, did he test me with my ex-husband and mother-in-law."

"You told me she was the reason for your divorce when I first met you."

"Well, after Veda was born here in Los Angeles, we went to Detroit and that's where everything fell apart. I don't think Rufus ever touched me after we got there. His mother had lost two children, and he was the only one who survived. She went crazy and wanted my kids. I lived a nightmare for three years."

"She was that crazy?"

"Worse. I thought she wanted me dead. Thank God for some good people who helped after he put me out."

"Wow. You went through a lot, and you're still a sweet person."

"God teaches us to forgive our enemies. I got my children back legally, and thanks to you, physically. They never even talk about him or his mother. So, when I think about life after marriage, I'm blessed."

"You're amazing," Tom said. "I really want to kiss you."

Edna smiled, not even remembering what it was like to kiss someone. He leaned over and placed his lips on hers passionately. It was a passion that Edna never felt before. She could feel his hand trembling as he embraced her, and her heart began beating faster than she ever thought it could as she got lightheaded and dizzy. It felt so natural to be with him.

As the kiss ended, they gazed into each other's eyes, not wanting that moment to end.

"I love you, Edna."

"I love you too, Tom."

Veda had been watching and could not believe they were kissing. She decided to go outside and be nosy. The car was impressive, with a rectangle body sitting on four rather large wheels. Model T automobiles were now in mass production and had become affordable to the average person. It was exciting for

Veda to be around cars. Her Uncle Bubs had one too. As she approached, they both saw her. Tom rolled his window down.

"Hi, Mr. Williams," she said. "You like Edna, huh?"

"I do. And hello to you, Ms. Veda."

"I knew it. What are you going to do about it?"

Tom looked at Edna and did not know what to say. They had just expressed their feelings for each other, and the moment was awkward. He looked back at the nine-year-old.

"Veda. Remember this. Live with love, don't see color."

Veda tried to absorb what he just said, but it didn't quite compute.

"You mean I'm not colored?"

"No, that's not what I mean."

Edna realized Veda was being Veda, and it was time to go. She got out of the car and bid her farewell to Tom feeling tingly inside. Having her soul disrupted and turned upside down was a first for Edna. She smiled to herself and bit her lip as she thought about that kiss. She felt like she was walking on air. Veda was still standing by the driver's window, and Tom had a final word for her.

"Veda, what I mean is you can break any barrier you want if you just believe in yourself."

"You mean I can be a detective?"

"I think you would make a great detective," Tom said gleefully. "You guys have a wonderful night."

Tom gave Veda the inspiration she very much needed. But she, too, inspired him. He didn't know what to do about Edna. The hell they would face if this went to the next level was more than he was willing to put her through. Neither she nor the kids should have to face that ugliness. He knew that for sure.

Arrival back to Los Angeles (From back-left) Bubs, Edna and Esma, unknown (Front-left) Veda, Pete, Lita

Pete in Eagle Rock playing with his toy car

Edna during the 1920's while working at the Johnson's house caring for their son

At school, the Durrs were the only colored kids. Lita avoided most negative comments because she looked like a Native American Indian. They did not know what to call her, so she was pretty much left alone. Occasionally, "injin" would pop up, but Lita ignored it. Pete was a prime target, a colored male mocked by the white establishment. They called Pete names and picked on him from day one.

On the other hand, Veda blended right in, not seeing herself as different and never intimidated. When she started school, teachers were amazed at her knowledge. Veda could read and comprehend better than any previous student. With her perfect diction, inquisitive nature, and maturity, she was their favorite. They called on her to help pass out supplies and papers while the other kids played and acted childishly.

School at times became tricky because it was too easy.

While internalizing Mr. Williams' advice, Veda's intellectual abilities presented unique childhood challenges. By the fourth grade, she found herself often in trouble, being sent to the principal's office once a week, usually for having a smart mouth. However, in Veda's mind, she was only correcting the teacher and there was nothing wrong with that. Nevertheless, Edna receiving a call from the school became commonplace.

Despite the disciplinary issues, Veda excelled as a student and wanted recognition for her grades. The school presented annual awards for top student honors and was about to announce the fourth grade. The big day was sunny and warm as Veda picked out her favorite outfit. It was a beautiful white dress with layers of lace around it that Edna had sewed for her, a headband, and a matching bow along with her lucky knee-high socks.

While walking to school, thoughts ran through Veda's mind of what she would say to the other kids after winning the award. She was confident about her academic performance but had angered her teacher, Mrs. Griffin, several times during the school year and hoped that would not be a problem. Regardless, Veda felt she had this award in the bag.

Mrs. Griffin was standing by the desk when Veda arrived at her classroom. She was a white woman in her thirties wearing a long dress, a scarf around her neck, and hair in a bun. Veda took a seat and patiently waited for morning announcements by the principal Mr. Beck.

"Good morning, everybody. Please stand for the pledge of allegiance," the voice said. "Cross your heart. Ready, begin."

Veda cited the pledge with all the other students, but her mind kept drifting to the award. She had scored "A"s on all her assignments. No one else had accomplished that, and Veda knew the grades of all her classmates. There was one smart girl, Jackie Cotton, with whom Veda routinely competed. But Veda knew Jackie received only a "B" plus on two tests.

"Good morn...ing again, everybody," Mr. Beck's voice chimed. "My first announcement is a problem we have been having with bullying. So, we want to remind everyone that bullying will not be tolerated. Do not bully your classmates, and for those who display kindness to others, we are giving good citizenship awards. Lunch today is hamburgers, so get your lunch money out and give it to your teacher if you're buying today. Now, the moment you've been waiting for—our student of the year is..."

Veda just knew it was going to be her. She visualized her reaction as being humble and surprised. Her heart was beating so fast as Mr. Beck drug it out. Why was he taking so long? she thought. Then he said it.

"Jackie Cotton. Congratulations!!"

Veda's heart sank. She was the best, the smartest, and could run circles around Jackie Cotton. After all, her memory was way better. She knew all of Jackie's grades, what she wore to school last Friday, and even remembered what Jackie brought for show and tell in kindergarten, for God's sake. How could she not get student of the year?

While stewing over her loss, Mrs. Griffin began class. It was something Veda knew a lot about, history. She attempted to refocus.

"Can anyone tell me what year Christopher Columbus discovered America?" Mrs. Griffin began.

Veda had just read a book about Christopher Columbus that she checked out at the library. Eagle Rock had a man who opened one in the back of his grocery store. He had many books, so sometimes, she would stop there with Pete and Lita on the way home. She had read *Christopher Columbus, The First Voyage to America*. Veda fiercely raised her hand, but Mrs. Griffin bypassed her and called on Charles.

"Do you know the answer, Charles?"

"1492," he replied

"1492 is correct, Charles."

Veda immediately raised her hand again with a sense of urgency. Mrs. Griffin couldn't ignore her.

"Yes, Veda."

"Mrs. Griffin. He landed on the islands in 1492 but didn't hit the Americas until 1493."

"Well, if you look in the textbook on your desk, it says Christopher Columbus discovered America in 1492, and that's the date we all observe."

"But that's not correct. The book I read said 1493. So, what makes this book right and that book wrong?"

"That's enough, Veda," Mrs. Griffin adamantly expressed, "Christopher Columbus discovered America in 1492."

"But!" Veda protested.

"That's enough, Veda." snapped Mrs. Griffin, cutting her off.

"Can't you explain why?"

"Veda, do you want to get sent to the principals' office...again?"

Feeling defeated, Veda hung her head. To top it off, she noticed Charles with a smirk on his face. As lunch hour came around, the glorious day Veda planned had fallen to pieces. She felt cheated, thought her teacher unfair, and was upset about it.

Veda ate lunch with Lita then went to the playground. She looked for Pete to make sure he was OK. He was having a tough time being the only colored boy in school. Veda knew that very well and always protected him.

Still struggling with her morning disaster, she noticed Pete with four boys surrounding him. Recognizing trouble, she ran over immediately.

"Chocolate boy. I need a slave," one of the boys said.

"I ain't no slave!" Pete replied, defending himself, trying to be brave.

Jimmy Tristan, a school bully, was escalating the encounter.

"You are what I say you are," Jimmy barked.

As Veda approached, her blood began to boil.

"What's going on here?"

"Who wants to know?" Jimmy defiantly responded.

Jimmy was big for his age and appeared unkempt. Veda noticed he had swirls of hair going in the opposite direction, which she found unusual.

"Me..... What do you think you're doing?"

"What are you gonna do about it?" he snarled.

"Look, I'm already having a bad day, so I'm gonna give you one chance to leave my brother alone, or I'm going to whoop your butt."

A taunting response came from the boys.

"Oooh. She's calling you out — a girl too. You gonna let a nigger girl talk to you like that?" one of the boys said.

"I'm an American girl, and I tell you what, if I win, you leave my brother alone. If I lose, I do your homework. How's that?"

Veda knew the school's punishment for fighting and that Edna would kill her. But none of that mattered. She could deliver, and this was the perfect opportunity to release her frustration. Being a good fighter, she had never lost to a girl or boy.

Jimmy looked at Veda, noticing how short and tiny she was. There was no way she could beat him. He would quickly demolish her. It was going to be a cakewalk for him, he thought.

"You're skinny, you're a girl, and you're a nigger. You ain't got a chance." Jimmy boasted.

With an eerie air of confidence that eluded Jimmy, Veda was ready. She knew the moves and had the skills.

"Let's do this," Veda said.

Jimmy did not want to get caught fighting again. He was always in trouble, so he planned to get it over with fast and easy. He suggested they go behind the classroom building, and Veda was just fine with that. However, Pete knew Jimmy had seriously underestimated Veda and what was coming.

Pete had witnessed Veda in action and knew how tactical she fought. He remembered her bout with Patty Shaw, the biggest girl in school. Patty had challenged Veda, then ran up on her. Veda strategically stepped back and extended her leg, causing Patty to run into her foot. Clutching her stomach, Patty bent over in tears. Pete remembered Veda seemed disappointed that the fight ended so quickly. Moreover, no girl dared challenge Veda again.

"Oh boy, he's in for it," Pete mumbled under his breath, shaking his head, knowing how this would end regardless of how big Jimmy was.

Veda and Jimmy walked behind the building. After they turned the corner, the boys could not contain their curiosity. They had to see this for themselves.

"I expect my math homework done first." Jimmy confidently blurted before the fight began.

Veda sized Jimmy up. He was big but slow. While he had the strength, she was fast. Uncle Bubs taught her to punch in the face first and blind them. Without eyes, you can't see. If you have no vision, you can't win. Jimmy came towards her. She went straight for the eyes with a punch. He didn't even have time to block it.

As he reached for his eye, she tripped him, and he fell. Veda began punching his face. Jimmy never got a clean hit in. He was in tears almost as fast as Patty Shaw.

The boys were yelling, "fight...fight...fight!!" Veda knew her time was short before the noon guard got there. She saw his nose begin to bleed, so she got up. The last thing she needed was blood on her white dress. Her knee got scratched, but she suffered no actual injuries. In her book, the fight was over. She brushed herself off and turned to the other boys.

"Anyone else?"

The boys looked at their friend lying on the ground with a bloody nose. They all then looked at Veda and shook their heads "no."

"That's what I thought. I'm sure you boys won't bother my brother again. And if you tell, well, you know what folks think about losing fights to girls. It's not pretty."

Mission accomplished. Veda and Pete left before any adults arrived. Veda made it back to class proud of herself. While she was at her desk, Mr. Beck came into the room and handed Mrs. Griffin a note. Mrs. Griffin looked directly at Veda.

"Veda Durr, gather your things."

Veda smiled and gathered her books and sweater. Going to the principal's office wasn't unusual, but mainly because the teacher sent her there. This time the man himself came to get her. She headed out the door with a snide attitude.

When she got inside his office, she immediately noticed his military certificate was missing from the shelf. Veda's photographic memory held images of almost everything she saw and read. Faces and names stayed with her too.

"Mr. Beck. What happened to your Army award that was on the wall?" she asked while taking a seat at his desk.

Mr. Beck enjoyed being principal and interacting with the students. Veda was one of the kids he knew very well. Dressed in his typical white, long-sleeved shirt and tie, he looked at her through his thin metal glasses, with circle-shaped lenses.

"Veda, we are here to discuss this fight."

"What fight?"

"Veeeda," he groaned.

"I got into a little scuffle. You said this morning no bullying and some kids were not being good citizens and bullying my brother. You said it just today, Mr. Beck".

"Then you should tell a teacher, Veda."

"I'm not allowed to be a tattletale, plus that's not what you said in your announcement."

Veda started looking around the office to see what she could use as a distraction. The USC diploma stood out.

"You graduated from USC? That's amazing. What was your major, Mr. Beck?"

"Veda, they said you beat up Jimmy."

Veda realized her distraction wasn't working, so she reverted to common sense.

"Now, look at me I'm short and little. How could I possibly beat up a big kid like Jimmy? Are you kidding me? He would clobber me, Mr. Beck I think someone is pulling the wool over your eyes. A little thing like me beating up Jimmy? That's laughable."

Mr. Beck thought about it and saw Veda's point. He had questioned that himself. How could she? He then saw a scratch on her knee and asked about it.

"How did you get that?" he said, pointing.

"Oh, my mother bought us skates for Christmas," she said, thinking quickly. "Me and my brother and sister have to share them, but the ground is bumpy. I took a spill. It's a kid thing."

Mr. Beck felt perplexed. Of course, this little girl couldn't beat up Jimmy. However, that was not his only concern. He wondered if he could make this extremely bright student understand how things worked.

"Veda... On the shelf behind you, tell me what's on it without looking?"

Veda loved to show off her exceptional memory, and this was her opportunity to impress Mr. Beck. Maybe if she did well, she would have a better chance at the award next year.

"Sure, Mr. Beck. Your family photo with your wife, son Johnny, daughter Mary, and baby Emily, a picture of you in World War I, probably around 1916 I'm guessing, because my uncle Bubs has a photo just like that. There is a wedding picture of you and your beautiful wife, but I never learned her name."

"Mrs. Beck," he said with a serious face.

"Oh, well Mrs. Beck is in two pictures. There is a clock and a beautiful painting of a lady in a white chiffon dress. Your army certificate is gone, but your USC diploma is front and center. I think that's about it."

"Now, I want you to turn around and look at the wall."

Veda turned around, pleased she got everything right.

"Do you see anything that you missed?"

"No."

"Exactly. Not many kids nor adults can do that."

Veda paused and thought about what Mr. Beck was saying.

"Yeah, but I still didn't get student of the year, so what difference does it make?"

"Is that why you were fighting?"

"I told you, it was a scuffle."

"Veda, with your grades and knowledge, maybe you should have got it. But you don't always have to be combative to prove yourself."

A combination of relief and anger ran through this 10-year-old's mind.

"All I know is I'm the smartest in my grade and should have won."

"I understand how you feel. Life is not always fair. But you do not have to prove yourself to everyone all the time. Pick and choose your battles, Veda, and you will go far. Angering teachers is not the way to go."

"I didn't mean to anger anyone."

"I'm sure you didn't, but a good lesson is to know when to put up and when to shut up. You are special and have a gift. You need to use it wisely. Just know this, some people don't like smart colored girls, especially if they fight. Now get back to class."

They both looked at each other.

"I understand, Mr. Beck, but it was a scuffle," added Veda. "You are the second person that called me special. I'm not exactly sure what that means but thank you. Are you going to call my mother?"

"Your mother is a good God-fearing woman. I had to call her once this week, so I won't trouble her. Just behave yourself and remember everything I said."

Heading back to class, Veda thought about the discussion and analyzed why the award went to Jackie. Things did not add up.

Maybe Mr. Beck was right, and she was too combative, or could it be Mrs. Grant did not like smart colored girls? Maybe her teacher did not like her at all. That would explain getting overlooked when raising her hand and frequently being sent to the office. The smile she gave every day may not have been real, Veda thought. Edna always said people's actions mattered more than words.

Mr. Beck gave Veda much to consider. He was impressed with her recollection abilities and said most adults could not do what she could. However, her memory came naturally. She always played a card game called Concentration with Lita, which required laying them all face down on the floor. You would turn one card up and then another. If they matched, you took them. If not, you had to remember where the matching card was on your next turn. Veda beat Lita every time. She tried to get Pete to play, but he had no interest, so she just played by herself when she was bored.

After arriving back to class, Veda sat and observed Mrs. Grant. She listened to her words and noticed the teacher never even looked at her. Veda raised her hand several times to answer questions, but as usual was not called on, even if she was the only student with their hand up. All her other teachers seemed fair, but now she felt different about Mrs. Grant.

When school was out, the three Durr children walked home. The streets were quiet with an occasional car passing by. Lita was curious about how Veda survived the day.

"How on earth did you get them to leave Pete alone AND not call Edna for you fighting?"

"You have to understand human nature and Caucasian people. Both can be complicated. You have to pick and choose your battles and can't always be combative."

"What are you talking about? Where do you get this stuff?" Lita asked.

"She's a half breed—part devil, part girl, that's what I say," Pete added.

Veda instinctively punched Pete in the arm.

"I'm what you call ...extraordinary," Veda added.

"Ex...what?"

"I'll teach you when you're a bit older."

Just then, two white boys ran past them, yelling, "Nigger!!!"

"You need to go punch them, Veda, not me."

At the dinner table that night, there was concern on Edna's face. She held her head down in prayer as they sat at the table, eating dinner. But Veda sensed something different in Edna's demeanor as she passed the mashed potatoes to Lita.

"Veda, I hear you had more trouble today," Edna said in a somber voice.

Veda instantly thought Pete or Lita told on her.

"Who said?" Veda asked. "I had to close a few deals today, that's all."

"Well, the deals you keep closing are creating problems. Some parents complained to Mrs. Grant. She called me today."

"I had that covered. The boys think they will get embarrassed, and that's a fate worse than death. They won't touch either of us," Veda tried to explain.

"One of the boys got a black eye. You don't understand racial conflict, Veda. You may have the boys scared, but their parents aren't. I pretty much kept it from you, but Caucasians don't like getting challenged, especially by a colored girl or woman. They can and will hurt you."

"Everyone likes challenges."

"No Veda, only you like to challenge everything."

Veda saw the seriousness in Edna's face and just stared into her eyes for a moment. She had a worried look, and Veda thought again about what Mr. Beck said. Then, after a brief silence, Pete playfully chimed in.

"Yeah Veda, only you like to challenge everything."

"I was only defending you," Veda snapped at Pete.

"Well, we are going to have to move from this area now. I was lucky to get this cottage on the Johnsons' land, but it's not going to work out anymore. Esma has a bigger house now, so we are moving there."

"I don't understand why we can't still live here. Caucasians let coloreds live on their land during slavery," Veda said.

"Veda! We don't talk about slavery. Caucasians have been good to us. My father was born during slavery, and it was a Caucasian woman that taught him to read. But it's time to go. We do not have a choice."

Veda refused to drop the subject.

"We have been treated good because of how we talk and our education. That's why I plan to go to college. But I still don't get why exactly we have to move? What did Mrs. Grant say? You should talk to Mr. Beck."

By now, Edna was getting exasperated. She knew there was another reason they had to move but did not want to bring it up. When she got home earlier that day, she received an anonymous call that frightened her. A man's voice said, "There will be no race mixing in Eagle Rock," and then a click. She had to protect her children.

"Because I don't want Pete, or you hurt."

That did not make sense to Veda. Edna always taught them to defend themselves. This day went quickly, from bad to worse. Now she would never get a chance to win that award.

"Are you sure this doesn't have to do with anything else?"

"Veda, eat your dinner. There is nothing more to say."

Although Edna could not admit it, Veda was right. The truth was, word had gotten out about her and Tom. The neighbors were well-aware of the time they were spending together. Veda's incident was the spark needed to light the fuse. With Veda fighting and Edna's friendship with Tom, things were getting out of hand. It was time to move.

After the kids went to bed, Edna called Tom to tell him the bad news.

"Hi, Tom."

"Hey beautiful, how was your day?"

"Not good."

"Why?"

"We have to move."

"Really, why? The Johnson's need their place back?"

"I wish it were that simple. Unfortunately, we've been seen together too often, and people are talking. It's getting ugly around here."

"Did anyone try to hurt you? I'll take care of that."

Choosing not to tell Tom about the phone call, Edna decided to focus on Veda's situation and not make things worse.

"It's Veda too. She got into a fight today, and things spiraled downhill. It's just not safe anymore so, I must say goodbye to you, Tom."

He was silent while processing the painful words Edna just uttered.

"Are you still there?"

"I don't want to say goodbye, Edna. I love you. You are the brightest part of my life."

"Oh, I love you too, Tom. This hurts, but it has to be done."

"Sometimes, I just loathe my people. Why do they have to be so hateful?"

"This is the world we live in that God created. Don't have ill feelings. That won't help anyone. Some things just aren't meant to be."

"So, where will you go?"

"To my sisters for a while and then we'll see."

After hanging up, Edna wondered if she would ever feel love like that again. Their magical kisses still lingered. She thought about what he said to Veda about seeing love, not color. But this world was not going to let them see love because color was all it saw. So maybe this move was for the best. Edna knew how ugly this could get and how it would affect the kids. She went to bed that night, realizing what a broken heart felt like, and shed some tears at the thought of never seeing Tom again.

Edna often wore stylish hats to protect her skin from the sun, shown here posing in front of a log cabin with a bulldog next to her

After completing grammar school, Veda began attending McKinley Junior High, whose demographics were evenly mixed. The school first opened in 1889 under the name East Vernon School but changed to McKinley's name in 1912. There was a combination of many races, Japanese, white, Black, and Mexican, which was unusual because Los Angeles had implemented a master plan to segregate races.

During her tenure in junior high, Veda thrived. She participated in numerous school activities and still received straight "A" s in all her classes. Now, fully aware that memory was her most significant asset, she also learned to use charm and wit to achieve the desired result.

Living with Aunt Esma and Uncle Bubs at 1622 ½ Lake Shore Ave was fun. Esma had a son Don, who kept them entertained. But when they moved to Jefferson Blvd in 1932, Veda remembered how much better it was to have their own house. She could finally have some privacy.

Their new home was a quaint 3-bedroom, one-bath, 1179 square foot house built in 1905. Edna was thrilled to have her own place again, and Veda felt an elevated status living there. It had a lovely size porch with aluminum shades over each window, which gave it charm.

McKinley Junior High was a 25-minute walk straight down Avalon. Veda joined the Girls Glee Club and landed a leading role in one of the plays where they saluted the Navy. Lita was in it too.

"Everyone is talking about you playing the lead," Lita said.

"Well, not everyone is small like me and looks like a toddler."

"You don't look like a toddler!"

"Lita! I'm just kidding. But I'm sure I got the role because I'm short. But watch me nail it," Veda said enthusiastically.

"You have a great voice. Not too many can sing those low notes like you."

"I know. Now I have to practice, so Joe Bridges will notice me."

"You like him, don't you?"

"Well, he's the smartest of all the colored guys."

"Yeah, and he's kinda cute too," Lita said giddily.

"This play will be better than last year's," Veda proclaimed." I don't know what the whites are doing yet, but ours is going to be the best. I am personally sewing my own outfit."

"What? You're not wearing the navy shirt and pants like the rest of us?"

"Are you kidding me? I'm wearing a short skirt, shiny top and maybe a cape or wrap. I'm not sure yet."

"Don't you have to ask Mrs. Anderson?"

"Nah. I'm just going to make it. But I need Edna to get me the material."

Veda managed to pull it off without a glitch. She was the star of the 1933 winter play at McKinley Junior High. People talked about it for months, including local talent agents. She even landed the lead role in the spring play but was gravely disappointed because a 6.4 magnitude earthquake damaged the school's auditorium forcing the play's cancellation.

In 1933, Veda starred in the annual school play at McKinley Junior High

When the time for high school arrived, everything changed. Although Jefferson High School was just a mile down the street, only a 22-minute walk, Edna was a stickler for education and wanted the kids to have the best. Belmont High, predominately white, was over an hour's walk and closer to the Wilshire district. Luckily, the city had just completed a trolly car route that shortened the commute. Edna also worked for several white families in that area.

The first to attend Belmont was Lita, being one of only ten colored students enrolled. However, by the time Veda arrived, that number had tripled. The entire school had about 500 students.

Veda's best friend was Clare Middleton, who she had known since grammar school. When Edna enrolled Veda at Belmont, Clare signed up too.

Each morning, Edna would get up at 5:00 am, along with the girls, and catch the trolley with them down Main St., before parting way for work.

Both Veda and Clare were stunning. Extremely popular, they had those movie-star looks, like Pearl Bailey or Dorothy Dandridge, and knew it. To top it off, they were brilliant, although in different ways. Veda's perfect diction and education helped her blend in with all races. Her unique facial features and shoulder-length hair sometimes lent a middle eastern look, and she always dressed well.

Clare's hair was a little thicker, and she liked to wear it up. Her oval eyes, light brown skin, and perfectly shaped lips made her appealing to the guys. The two teens loved to wear shorts at home, which sometimes angered Edna because they were too revealing in her eyes. But Veda liked pushing the envelope with most things in her life.

Belmont High was a fantastic experience for Veda. She felt comfortable, even empowered at times, and was well-respected. Clare, more or less, was the same. One day they were sitting outside at the lunch table like any other day. The weather was warm, and the sky bright blue.

"So, are you gonna try out for the play? I heard they're having auditions," Clare asked.

"I haven't even thought about it. What play are they doing? They always want me to be a housekeeper or something lame like that. Not my style."

The girls laughed. Of course, no one could ever see Veda as a housekeeper, but in the '30s, that was the only character available for coloreds. Veda didn't see herself like that, ever.

"You mean you're not colored enough."

"I don't even talk like a colored girl. Plus, I'd rather play a non-racial role."

"You mean like a lioness?" Clare laughed. Veda broke into laughter too. They both thought it would be an ironically fitting role for Veda.

"There are no housekeepers in this play, but it does have a lion." Clare teased.

"What's the play?"

"Wizard of Oz Musical. It's going to be the biggest high school event in the city, and you're the best singer."

Just then, Romie Craig walked by. New to Belmont High, he was the most gorgeous boy they had ever seen. With fair skin, wavy hair parted to the side, and perfect facial features, his looks were irresistible. In addition, his teeth were pearly white when he smiled, giving him a special glow. Jefferson High had kicked him out for fighting, and Belmont wasn't thrilled to admit him but eventually did. He was determined to finish his senior year, despite his struggles with reading.

Suddenly, a scuffle broke out between Walter, a darker-skinned boy, and Max, who was light. Walter, who wore a wool cap, was constantly teased because of his large nostrils and thick lips. He was tired of it, but his mother gave him a Catholic school or Belmont choice, and Walter chose the latter. However, fighting among his own was something he never expected. Max just embarrassed him horribly, calling him out in front of the white boys, which made him angry. When confronted, Max said, "fuck you," and the fight began. Standing nearby was Romie, who was no stranger to fisticuffs.

As Max and Walter started throwing blows, Romie intervened.

"Man, Walter, don't do dis," Romie pleaded. "We all gotta stick togetha. We caint fall apart now. They lookin' at chu."

Romie saw the lunch guard heading in their direction. He knew they could all get kicked out of school. Romie put his arm around Max and started laughing.

"Man, go wit me on dis. The guard is comin'," he whispered.

Romie was good at charming people and quick-witted. So finessing would be a breeze for him as the guard approached.

"What's goin on here with you boys?" the guard bellowed.

"Oh, nothin. We just playin' around." Romie explained. "These cats play too much."

"Y'all looked upset," said the guard.

"Heck naw!! We aite."

"You boys behave," he warned, then walked away.

Walter was still upset with Max as they parted ways. Romie looked over and noticed Veda sitting with Clare. He loved these two beautiful girls. As a matter of fact, Romie loved all beautiful girls. Knowing they were the most gorgeous in the school of any color, he couldn't decide which one was prettier.

"Hey, ladies!"

Both Clare and Veda smiled, each having a crush on Romie. He had the perfect body and a charismatic personality.

"You handled that well, Romie," Veda said

"Yeah. I didn't know you had that in you," Clare added.

"Well...You know," Romie said while shrugging his shoulders and smiling, showing his pearly teeth. "So, what's goin on with the two most beautiful girls at Belmont High?"

"Nothing but school and more school," Veda replied.

"Sounds borin'. Y'all gotta have some fun."

"So, what do you do for fun?" Clare asked Romie in a sexy tone.

"Besides breaking up fights?" Veda added.

"I tries to entertain beautiful gals. Dats what I do's."

"Sounds like a first-class gigolo to me," Veda chimed in.

"Nawww. I'm just me," Romie said, not even sure he knew what gigolo meant.

Recognizing he was a lady's man and good at it, Veda kept trying to find something intriguing to say, but it never seemed to come out right. She knew this encounter would get rehashed in her mind and later think of something better she could have said. Moreover, every word he spoke would linger forever in her psyche.

Clare was feeling a little left out of this back and forth with Veda and Romie. She, too, was in awe of him — after all, who wouldn't be? He had that "It" factor. Clare had to think of something to say, so she made it a little more personal.

"Isn't Shalana your sister?" Clare asked.

"Yeah."

"You look just like her."

Popping his collar and throwing out his charm, Romie bent over to Clare and suavely whispered, "Naw. She looks like me," and winked at her.

Clare's heart throbbed as a chill ran up her spine. He was scoring colossal points in her teenage mind.

"Well, ladies. Y'all have a great day," Romie said as he walked away.

Both Veda and Clare were in la-la land as they watched him leave. They both looked at each other and spoke at the same time.

"Oh my gosh! He is so cute!"

"Those eyes," Veca uttered.

Both girls were relishing in the magic of Romie Craig when the tower bell rang, signifying it was time to return to class. Veda wasn't sure she would be able to concentrate. She replayed the conversation that took place while sitting in class. How could she be different to make him want her? That's where Veda's mind was going, and so was Clare's.

All day Saturday, Veda was sewing her and Clare's Easter dresses. Most of the community went to either a Baptist or Catholic church. Veda went to neither because of their Christian Science faith, and Edna made sure the Durr kids attended Sunday school at the Church of Christ.

Veda wanted this Easter to shine. It was her senior year, and she was going to make the best of it. They owned an old Singer machine that was more like a piece of furniture. It had drawers on the side for thread, measuring tape, scissors, and thimbles. The device had a lever that started and stopped the machine. Veda hit the lever with her thigh when making a stitch. She was a master at it.

Edna found her a McCall's pattern for the cutest dress, and Veda selected white chiffon material. She woke up early to finish the dresses. Lita wasn't particularly interested in the pattern Veda chose, instead choosing a cute yellow dress she made last spring.

While sewing, Pete came in and distracted Veda. He had found a horned toad outside and brought it in. Edna saw it and screamed at Pete to take it back outside. Amidst the chaos, Veda's stitch went crooked. Her being a perfectionist, the entire seem had to be pulled out and redone. She had the mentality that something worth doing was worth doing right, and by Saturday evening, both dresses were perfect. She called Clare to come by and try hers on.

After church the next day, everyone went to Ross Snyder Park to show off their Sunday best. As the girls arrived, Clare came out and said what Veda was thinking.

"Do you think Romie will be here?"

"Of course, he will."

"I hope so. I don't want this dress to go to waste."

"Hey. I slaved on these dresses. I'm the one who doesn't want them to go to waste. You can thank me later."

Clare felt contrite for what she said because Veda did do all the work on the dresses. She got over-excited and didn't think before she spoke.

"Oh, I'm sorry, Veda. You know what I meant."

It was a perfect spring day with the smell of Eucalyptus trees in the air and everyone dressed to a tee. Young children were running around, and the teens had frilly dresses, gloves, and hats. Clare and Veda strutted around as heads turned and smiled at them. Both longed for the same man yet tried to act normal, not wanting to compete.

"There he is!!!" Clare blurted out.

Immediately, butterflies flocked to Veda's stomach, causing a fluttering deep within. When she looked in the direction Clare was pointing, it intensified. Romie was conversing with this beautiful girl with long hair, a bonnet to die for, and an exquisite dress. Could Romie have a girlfriend she didn't know about? No. She checked with everyone and knew everything about him. Her investigation could not have missed that important detail.

Romie looked terrific in his zoot suit attire and wavy hair. He laughed with the girl as he touched her hat. Looking around, he noticed Veda and Clare, then bided her farewell.

"Look. Here he comes." Clare said excitedly.

Veda calmly fixed her hair and checked her dress for wrinkles, fanning over the blanket to make it look perfect. Seeing Romie talking to that girl left her feeling a tinge of jealousy she didn't understand. Forced to shake it off and get a grip, Veda acted like she did not see him. Then his voice emerged.

"Hey, beautiful ladies."

Veda looked up, pretending to be surprised.

"Romie. Hi. When did you get here?"

"I been here minglin' fo a bit."

Clare was enamored with Romie, saying the first thing that came to her mind.

"Look at you, Mr. Smooth."

Romie laughed, making Clare feel she scored some points.

"Smooth? I don't know bout all dat. Tell you what though, I'm ready for some grub. Where it at?"

Jumping in before Veda could answer and hoping to score more points, Clare quickly pointed to the food area.

"The BBQ is right over there," she said in a slow sexy voice.

Romie gave Clare a second look before turning his head in the direction of the food.

"Let's go get some."

Immediately Clare got up, ready to hang out with Romie. Mesmerized by his smile and his charm, she began to walk by his side. Then suddenly, he stopped and took two steps backward to Veda, whose heart skipped a beat when he reached his hand out to her.

"I know you don't eat but a little bit but come on now... make my day."

Romie had just made her day as they joined hands while he helped her up. She smiled at him as he continued to hold her hand after they started walking. When they arrived at the food area, the three looked at the table with BBQ chicken, ribs, corn on the cob, peach cobbler, beans, and tin plates. Romie grabbed two plates and whispered to Veda.

"What you want?"

"Just some chicken and beans," she said.

Romie put three pieces of chicken and a big scoop of beans on Veda's plate. Veda noticed the amount of food and screamed out.

"That's way too much!"

Romie leaned over to Veda's ear.

"Don't worry, I'll finish what you don't."

He then smiled and winked at her. Veda knew, at that moment, she liked Romie a lot. The butterflies woke back up and started fluttering inside her stomach once again. He fixed his plate, which was more than Veda had ever seen anyone eat, except for her brother Pete. But even Pete put rations on his plate and went back for seconds. The two of them walked away together towards the spot they were sitting.

Clare felt a little left out after initially thinking it would be her. Nevertheless, she fixed her plate and slowly walked to where Romie and Veda were. Veda had just begun asking Romie questions about himself.

"So, where does your family come from?"

"Oklahoma."

"How come you go to Belmont instead of Jefferson, like everyone else?"

"I kinda got kicked out."

"You barely moved here, and you already kinda got kicked out?"

"Well, Well. What can I say? I'm a fightin' country boy."

"You flirt like a city boy," Veda said, laughing.

"It's just some beautiful gals here. Not much to look at in Oklahoma."

"You look like you're having fun with it. I bet you have a trail of broken hearts you left behind."

Clare rolled her eyes as she took a bite of food.

"So, Romie, who's older, you or your sister?" she asked, trying to chime in.

To Clare's dismay, Romie did not answer. Clearly, he had an interest in Veda, who also had a gleam in her eyes. Romie then leaned over and whispered into Vedas' ear, creating a seed of envy that penetrated Clare's mind.

Veda, a real competitor, was thrilled at the attention and what she felt inside was something brand new.

"I am havin' fun wit it. But today is special cause it's wit you," he gently murmured.

His breath caressed the lining of her ear, leaving her head feeling light and woozy. Snapping out of her momentary trance, Veda responded.

"You need to have fun with some books if you're going to make it at Belmont," she said, instantly regretting bringing up school.

"Maybe you could help me," Romie said flirtatiously.

"Maybe I can't," Veda said, posing a challenge to create a cat and mouse game.

Veda knew this was the beginning of something and sensed it might be problematic with Clare. She did not want Romie to affect their friendship, which was so close they even completed each other's sentences at times. It wasn't surprising they fell for the same guy. Veda had confidence their bond could survive turbulent times because they always resolved their issues. Ultimately, she concluded Clare would understand because he was open game.

Clare and Veda, best friends since childhood, often dressed alike

Romie had captured Veda's heart hook, line, and sinker. She had encapsulated him as well. In an instant, her whole world changed. No longer were student council or school plays a priority because her mind never stopped thinking about Romie.

One beautiful warm spring day, they decided to go to the park so she could help him with his reading. Veda chose "*Gone with the Wind*," the most popular book out. She had read it twice, loving Scarlett's spirit and resolve. Veda admired Scarlett's instinct to survive, including marrying her sister's beau after hard times hit the plantation because he was doing well at the wood mill. Veda saw a lot of herself in Scarlett O'Hara, except being a confederate.

Sitting on the grass at MacArthur Park, the two enjoyed spending time together. With graduation quickly approaching, Veda wanted to help him be his best. Lacking reading skills would hold him back, she felt. Veda was an exceptional reader and thought teaching him would be easy. Not to mention, it presented an opportunity to be with Romie up close and personal.

Romie was excited as well. Veda was beautiful and had that spunk that appealed to him. Although thinking Clare prettier, he knew Veda would succeed. However, Romie wasn't sure he could live up to her expectations.

As they sat, Romie watched Veda meticulously fix her dress on the blanket, spread out freshly made sandwiches, and open the book. She thought of everything, which made him determined to win her over.

As they began to read, Romie felt self-conscious, but Veda explained things patiently.

"You kay... kay," Romie began. The word 'know' was a tough one for him.

"The K is silent," Veda clarified.

"You now..."

"No, it's not 'now,' it's no."

Romie raised his right eyebrow and contorted his face.

"You wonder why I don't like to read. This don't make sense."

This was going to be more difficult than she anticipated. How do people teach all the ins and outs of the English language? He continued reading slowly.

"You know... there is...n't go...ing to be any war...said Sss Sss."

"You have to sound it out. 'SC' is tricky ska...ska-ar-let. Then put it together, Scarlett."

Romie grew tired of feeling dumb, and this was not what he expected when he solicited her help. They need to have fun and laugh, Romie thought.

"Scarlett. OK, Veda. This ain't me. Can't I just sit here and look at you? Your hair is so pretty. I just can't concentrate when I'm around you."

"You can never get a good job if you can't read, Romie."

Moving closer to Veda, he reached for her curl.

"How come your hair so thin?"

"Your hair is thin, too," Veda replied in a soft tone. "It's nice and wavy."

"My folks have Muskogee Creek Nation Indian blood. Mama was beautiful, but she died young, though. I was jus bout four. I barely rememba her."

"That's so sad. My mother never knew her mom. She died giving birth. I can't imagine not having Edna."

"What about yo daddy?" Romie asked.

"They divorced when I was four. He's in Detroit alive and well. I think he remarried."

"Your mother is doing a good job. Look at chu."

"I have goals. I know one thing. I don't want to clean houses. What are your goals?"

Romie had to think about it. He didn't have goals and never gave it much thought. Since his father was a mechanic who worked on cars, Romie figured on helping him but had thought no further.

Looking across the grass, Romie noticed a couple of white boys headed their way. Their look was disconcertingly familiar. Anger, maliciousness, and malevolence were all over their face — something he could smell from a mile away.

"Right about now, I'm tryin' to get to tomorrow. We gon have to leave outta here."

Veda looked over and saw the boys. Romie was right. They were talking loudly and pointing at them, looking for trouble and clearly on a mission. Veda watched as they approached. One of the boys with a golf cap, baggy pants, and a button-up shirt was the first to speak.

"You folks in the wrong park."

"I don't see no signs," Romie said.

"We don't do that here in LA. We are the sign, nigger," the other boy said.

With that, Romie stood up. Veda looked at the boys and recognized one of them. Standing there wearing coveralls with his hair combed to the side just like the last time she saw him, was Jimmy Tristan from Grammar school. He was a bit taller, but his slouchy posture never changed.

"Jimmy? The more things change, the more they stay the same. When did you move to LA?" Veda asked.

Everyone was stunned by the words that came out of Veda's mouth. Romie stepped in front of her.

"Let me handle this."

Romie was 6 foot 3, thin but muscular. He had been in these situations before. Suddenly he realized what Veda said.

"Wait, you know him?" Romie asked.

"She knows you, Jimmy?" the boy in the cap asked. "You know her?"

"Hell no, I don't know that darkie."

"But she knows your name!"

Jimmy looked stunned. At first, he did not recognize Veda as he looked her up and down. Her short stature, brown hair, olive skin, and high cheekbones were somewhat familiar. But it was the bow in her hair that took him back to grade school. It couldn't be the colored girl that humiliated him, he thought. His life was never the same after she fought him on the playground that day. He got teased relentlessly after being walloped by not only a girl but a colored girl. His furious parents threatened the school, and he overheard them talking with other adults about "burning the race-mixing nigger's house down." That one fight changed Jimmy's entire school experience.

When his family moved from Eagle Rock to Los Angeles, it was a new beginning for him. Finally, he could shed the embarrassment of that incident. Unfortunately, his cousin, who was with him, knew everything and here he was facing this girl again.

"Jimmy, you don't recognize me? I haven't changed that much since Eagle Rock. And apparently, neither have you," Veda voiced.

Feeling an air of anxiety, Jimmy just stared, reliving that dreadful time of his life. Frozen, he found himself unable to speak.

"Well, if it's gonna go down, let's do this," Romie said, putting his hands up, ready to fight.

Jimmy's cousin sensed this might not be a good fight to pick, especially after seeing the blank look in Jimmy's eyes.

"You all just need to go to Elysian Park. This is our park," he said.

But Romie was not going to back down. They had challenged him in front of his girl and drew first blood. He needed to show his manhood.

"This is a city park, and we can be here too. What it gonna be?" After a few tense moments of silence, the boys backed down.

"Let's go," Jimmy said, walking away. His cousin followed, and Veda could hear him say, "You act like you were scared. That wasn't the nigger gal that beat you up, was it?"

Then he began laughing at Jimmy. "It was!"

"Shut up," Jimmy belted, humiliated once again.

Veda reached down, picked up the book, and started folding the blanket.

"You were gonna take them both on?" Veda asked.

"I ain't no coward. I took on mo' than that before."

"Well, just so you know. I would have helped you," Veda confided with an air of confidence.

"I'm a good fighter. I beat Jimmy up in grammar school, and he was way bigger than me."

Romie looked at Veda with admiration. At that moment, her spirit hit his soul like a stampede of wild Oklahoma stallions. Yes, she definitely was the one for him.

"I neva' met anyone like you. I want you to be my gal."

"What makes you think I'm the girl for you?"

"I just know. And I think you feel the same."

"Really?"

"I can't keep my eyes off your lips. My mind keeps wondering if they feel as good as they look. Can I get some shuga?" he finally asked.

Wanting to kiss her so badly, Romie wiped the sweat from his palm to conceal his nervousness, surprised the thought of a kiss could bring such emotion. After all, he had kissed many women before and never felt this way. Without waiting for an answer, he drew closer, seeing a look of approval in her eyes.

Veda's excitement exploded as she prepared for her first kiss. Romie was tall, handsome, and strong. His lips were full and perfectly tucked under his thin mustache. His right cheek curled up when he smiled, which she thought was so cute. With puckered lips and eyes closed, she anticipated what was coming. When their lips touched, her whole body tingled, and head began to spin. Romie lightly sucked on her bottom lip, giving Veda a chill down her spine. When he slipped his tongue in her mouth, the charge was electric. Pulling her closer, he rubbed her back, and the book fell to the ground, but she didn't care. With her heart pounding and mind racing through a myriad of thoughts, Veda's first real kiss was everything she had ever imagined.

The next day at school, Veda was in a daze hanging onto every detail of her kiss with Romie. She had woken extra early to make lunch for them and sat anxiously at the table awaiting his arrival. Veda hadn't seen Clare that day, which was unusual, but her focus was on Romie Craig. While daydreaming, she felt a rub on her shoulders, then a kiss on her head.

"Hey beautiful," Romie whispered as he sat down next to her.

"Hi," Veda said with a beaming smile. "I brought you lunch."

"Thanks, Shuga. I'm starvin'. My pops ain't much on shopping. We raise some chickens and stuff, but there ain't much for school."

"Well, I don't mind bringing you food," Veda said. "You guys raise chickens? Edna is planning on buying a few acres and having a farm. They are selling the land dirt cheap, only $5 an acre. But it's way out in Saugus, wherever that is. It will be a while before she builds, though. My aunts already own property there."

"What kind of animals she want?"

"I guess some cows and goats. I'm staying in the city, though. No way I'm living in the desert."

As they were eating their lunch, Clare walked up to the table. She was a bit overdressed, wearing an adorable white dress, flared around the knees, and a black polka dot waist-length jacket with puffy short sleeves, matching belt, and bow ties. She stood there for a minute before speaking.

"Hey," Clare finally said.

"Hey, where have you been. Haven't seen you in a while," Veda replied. "A new dress? It's adorable. You must let me borrow that pattern. Is it McCall's or Butterwick?"

"Where have you been? You didn't come to our so-ro meeting?" Clare blasted.

"Oh. I've been helping Romie with something. I'm sorry. I'll make the next one."

"You have never missed a meeting."

"What do you want me to say? I'm sorry."

"You are looking beautiful today Clare," Romie intervened, sensing the tension.

"Thanks, Romie," Clare said. "Well, I hope you make the next one. We were kind of lost without you."

"I'll be there," Veda assured her.

"The pattern is Butterwick," Clare finally answered.

A few days later, Veda and Romie sat on the steps at Veda's house. Six broad stairs led up to the huge porch that had a large wooden window overlooking it. Romie was holding the "*Gone with the Wind*" book as Veda sat to his side. The street was relatively quiet with a gentle cascading breeze when Veda noticed Clare walking past the house. It hurt Veda that Clare was no longer in her daily life since Romie now occupied all her spare time. But she could not let her walk by without speaking.

"Clare!!" She shouted. "Clare!!" She said again.

Clare stopped and turned around, feeling like she did not have her best friend anymore. The secrets they shared, the time they spent together, the sisterhood all seemed to have evaporated in one fell swoop. After many years, it was now gone. Yes, she was bitter, and adding insult to injury, Veda got what Clare wanted, which created a deeper wound.

"What?" Clare asked as she turned around.

Veda got up and headed toward her.

"You're going to walk by and not say hi?"

"Well, you looked busy."

"Don't be that way. Feel happy for me."

"OK. I'm happy for you. I gotta go." Clare snapped and walked off.

Veda just stood there for a minute, watching her best friend leave. She had such mixed emotions and didn't know how to fix the strain Romie was putting on their friendship. She strolled back to him feeling a little sad. He picked up on it right away.

"What's wrong?"

Veda didn't want to get into it because he would feel like it was his fault. But the reality was that this was inevitable. Sooner or later, one of them would get a boyfriend. So, Veda kept it simple when she replied.

"Nothing."

With her and Clare's friendship on the rocks, Veda began spending time with other students. Veda was always friendly at school and enjoyed helping others, whether colored or white. One day, she was socializing with a red-headed girl named Susan in the lunch yard. The white kids liked to tease this girl for some reason, but Veda found her intelligent and sweet. She wore glasses, and her red hair was super curly. Susan reminded Veda of Little Orphan Annie, one of the comics she loved to read.

"I love your hair. I've never seen that color before," Veda said.

"I get teased all the time," Susan confided.

"They're just jealous. I saw you reading *Gone with the Wind*. What do you think of it?"

"It's pretty good. I'm almost done."

"I love that book. I've read it three times."

As she was talking to Susan, Veda looked across the yard, hoping to spot Romie. She saw him near the cafeteria talking with

Clare and wondered what they were saying. Feeling somewhat insecure, she decided to walk over.

"That's a pretty dress ya have on today," Romie said, flirting with Clare.

"Thank you, Romie."

"You know I think you're pretty."

"Oh, you do?" Clare responded with a subtle grin.

"Course I do. Look at dat beautiful smile," he complimented, rubbing her cheek.

Clare couldn't help but beam, after all, who could resist Romie's charm? At that moment, she envied Veda so much. This guy made you feel good when you were around him. His charisma was intoxicating. When he gave you his attention, it was magical.

"You're such a flirt."

"I know. That's what I do."

"You know Veda wouldn't like you touching me like that."

"Well, I guess we'l jus have ta keep dat tween us."

At that very moment, Veda walked up. She saw Romie caress Clare's cheek, which induced a startling sense of jealousy. Knowing Romie was probably just being Romie, she didn't expect to feel this way.

"Hey baby, how's da other world living?" Romie reacted with a smile.

"They have their struggles, just like us. What were you two talking about?"

There was an awkward moment of silence. Veda looked at Clare and gave her a half-smile. Both seemed to ignore the question.

"Don't talk all at once."

"I was jus' tellin' Clare bout those white boys at the park. That's when I knew I loved you."

"Is that right?" she questioned as the watchtower bell rang.

They all headed to class, and Romie wrapped his arm around Veda's waist then kissed her on the cheek. He whispered something in her ear that she couldn't decipher, but that didn't matter. His voice still melted her, and Romie could do no wrong.

After School, Veda was looking forward to her first rehearsal for the *Wizard of Oz* musical. She auditioned and, because of her extraordinary voice, received the role of Glenda, the Good Witch of the North. Knowing Romie was waiting out front, as usual, she went to explain.

"I have play rehearsal today. It's gonna be a while, so you go ahead."

"You really doin' dat Wizard of Oz thang, huh?"

"I wasn't at first, but Max talked me into it. He's been wanting me to sing in his band too, but I decided to do this. They gave me a decent part."

"So, how come you've neva sang for me?"

"Let's just say...I'm saving that for later."

"Alright, I'm gonna miss you by my side for this long journey home," Romie said lovingly.

His disappointment pleased Veda and reassured her about his feelings. Romie watched her walk up the stairs, happy he had landed such a beautiful woman. He couldn't mess this up. Just then, he felt a tap on his shoulder. It was Clare.

"Hey, you."

"Beautiful Clare. We meet again."

"Where's Veda?" she asked, looking around.

"She had rehearsal for that school play."

"She's really doing it?"

"Yeah, she got talked into it."

"So, you're heading home alone?"

"Nope, I'm heading home wit chu."

Clare and Romie began the long trek home from school. First, they caught the 5113 Trolley, which dropped them a few blocks from their side of town. Then, after riding the crowded streetcar, they began their walk home.

Across the street were Pete and one of his friends just goofing around. Pete was particularly interested in the apricot trees that lined the sidewalk. His mother made the best preserves, which he would spread on her delicious fluffy melt-in-your-mouth biscuits.

On the weekends, Pete looked forward to having a full breakfast. Edna would make grits, bacon, eggs, and biscuits on Saturday, then scrapple, pancakes, and hash browns on Sunday. Wanting to bring some apricots home, Pete opened a few he found on the ground, but they were no good, so he tossed them across the field. Finally, he located some on a low-hanging branch and grabbed them, hoping that would be enough. He then noticed Clare and Romie.

"Clare, you are beautiful. How come you don't have no one?" Romie inquired as they began walking home.

"I'm getting over losing my best friend," Clare replied.

"Veda?"

"We've been best friends since grammar school."

"You can still be best friends."

"No. Everything has changed."

"Because of me?"

Clare just looked straight ahead and did not answer. Feeling a sense of responsibility, Romie tried to make her feel better.

"Look, Clare. Don't feel like you losin' your best friend. Now you have two best friends."

"It doesn't feel like that. Me and Veda did everything together. I don't want to feel like a third wheel."

"So dat jus means we gotta get you a man. Then all of us can hang out together."

"Well, there is someone, but I don't know how to tell him I like him. Plus, it's complicated."

"Gurl!! Sometimes you just have to go for it! Trust me."

"Like I said. It's complicated."

"We have a saying in Oklahoma—closed mouths don't get fed."

"Guess I'll starve then," Clare conceded.

"Well, you're great, Clare. Sometimes ya jus never know. Any guy would be lucky to have you."

Clare had never spent this much time with Romie alone and feared it might never happen again. Thinking about their streetcar ride, amongst the people noise, bells, and trolly bumps, left her mind wondering, 'what if she was the one who landed him.'

Romie reminded Clare of her dad, who was a porter for Southern Pacific Railroad. Her father displayed the same charisma, personality, and charm. But working for the railroad left little time for Clare. Despite having one of the best homes in the neighborhood and financial security, she always longed for her dad's attention.

As Clare's mind drifted briefly to Veda, who was always upfront and true, an urge came over her. Perhaps it was teenage hormones or disappointment that Romie chose Veda. Whatever it may have been, she knew this was her only opportunity to do something, although she may regret it.

For reasons she couldn't explain when they reached the corner to part ways, Clare made a choice. She hugged him, pulled back, and planted a sensuous kiss on his tender lips. Then, looking deep into his brown, almond-shaped eyes, Clare whispered, "This is where we part. I'll see you later."

Smirking, Clare proceeded to cross the street with a sexy stride knowing that Romie was watching. She felt empowered despite what this could mean.

Pete, still across the street, was astounded at what he had just seen. Romie had just kissed Clare with no shame. The question was, should he tell Veda?

Saturday was always cleaning and chore day. It consisted of scrubbing the walls, dusting, mopping, and laundry, which included hanging the clothes on the line to dry. In the evening ironing and putting the garments away concluded the day. Edna always wanted the house clean, and the kids all handled their responsibilities.

This week included yard work, which happened once a month. Pete usually push-mowed the lawn and pulled the weeds, Veda trimmed the shrubs, and Lita cleaned the windows. Edna insisted they wear hats. She said it was to protect them from the sun, but they all knew what she meant.

It was close to 1 pm, and Lita, Pete, and Veda were doing their respective jobs when Edna came outside with a tray and three glasses of iced tea.

"I have cold drinks for you kids."

They all dropped what they were doing and went to the porch. Pete was quick to remind Edna that they weren't kids anymore.

"You're my kids," Edna replied.

Pete took a long sip of his drink and began to make his usual sounds of pleasure.

"Um, um, um!! This is just what I needed."

"You act like you've done some work," Veda clowned.

"I have. Look at that lawn."

"Well, my hedges are perfection."

"Yeah, yeah, yeah. Well, Miss Perfect, everything ain't what it seems."

"They look good to me," Lita chimed in, sipping on her drink.

"That's not what I'm talking about."

"What on earth are you talking about, Pete?"

"I saw something."

"Do tell. What did you see?"

"I saw Romie and Clare kiss," he blurted out.

Shocked at what Pete just said, Veda looked up. She had just taken a sip of her drink, and some dribbled down her chin. She slowly wiped her face seeking clarification.

"What do you mean, Pete?" she asked.

"I said what I mean. I saw them kiss."

"When was this?"

"Yesterday."

"Well, what kind of kiss?"

"The kind of kiss where two lips meet," Pete chuckled sarcastically.

"Where was this?"

"Walking home from school."

Veda finished her drink and went back to the hedges. She didn't speak to anyone for the rest of the afternoon. Her mind flashed back to seeing Romie touching Clare on the cheek and the awkward moment when she walked up to them. Was Romie playing her for a fool? Was Clare? Veda's mind ran wild. She couldn't even eat dinner that night. She stayed in her room, just looking at the ceiling. Lita came and told her Romie was at the door, but she wasn't ready to see him.

"Lita, tell him I'm not feeling good. I'll call him later."

"OK."

Sunday was the usual routine, church and family dinner. This week, everyone gathered for supper at Esma's house with their families. Veda usually looked forward to seeing her cousins because laughter always filled the air. However, enjoying Sunday dinner was difficult because of a dull piercing ache in the pit of her stomach. Her mind could not escape lingering questions about Romie and Clare.

After strategic calculation, Veda decided to confront Clare first. Romie would come later, and she wasn't going to make his damn lunch anymore. She was glad to be away from the house in case he stopped by again.

The next day at school, Veda waited for Clare out front. Upon seeing her, she called out, "Clare!"

"Hi Veda," she said, smiling.

"How was your weekend?" Veda inquisitively asked. "Anything new?"

"No. Same ole thing."

"Really?"

"Yeah," Clare said.

"I hear you left school with Romie on Friday?"

"Yeah, we walked to the trolley."

"What did the two of you talk about?" Veda asked.

"You always ask that, Veda. I don't remember," Clare snickered.

"Were you gonna tell me you two kissed? You're supposed to be my friend."

Floored, Clare tried to remain cool. How did Veda know? Did Romie tell her? He must have. What a betrayal, she thought. He ran back, and gosh darn told Veda. Well, she wasn't going to let him get away with that. It was his word against hers.

"It's not what it looks like, Veda," Clare explained.

"Well, what is it, Clare?"

"Romie kissed me, okay."

"He kissed you out of the blue?"

"Veda, Romie's a cheater. He's going to cheat on you regardless. For the record, I don't want him."

"If that was the case, why didn't you tell me? You wait until I confront you to say this? I don't believe you, Clare."

"I don't want your man."

"I think you do. My best friend would not kiss my man. She would have told him where to go. She would have told him to jump off a bridge, and then she would have told me. You are not my friend, and now I question if you ever were. In case you are unclear on what I'm saying, we are no longer friends, Clare."

Veda walked up the stairs into the school. Clare stood with her jaw open as she watched Veda walk away.

At lunch, Veda was mulling over how to approach Romie. His charm always managed to win her over, but the dagger now piercing Veda's heart was in the way. Could Clare have been right? Did Romie initiate the kiss? Were emotions skewing her judgment? Regardless, she had to confront him, and the time had arrived, as she waited apprehensively.

"What's up shuga?" he asked. "You're looking good today, as always. I missed you this morning. You left without me."

Veda took a bite of her sandwich, then took her napkin and slowly wiped her mouth.

"What's wrong with you?"

"Nothing."

"I sho likes that dress you got on. Where's that pretty smile?"

Romie rubbed the side of her lips gently with his finger.

"Come on. You can do it."

Veda gave a half-smile while quietly fuming inside. She was mad at two aspects — one, how he could always soften her, and two, what happened with Clare. Then Romie said something that totally caught Veda off guard.

"You know I'm gon marry you."

Marriage was something every girl, especially her, dreamed about — but how dare he bring that up now.

"You sure it's not Clare you want to marry?" Veda unleashed.

"Why you say that? It's you I want."

Veda started putting her remaining lunch in the bag. This conversation was not going to work at school. It had to happen when they were alone on her turf, and she needed to stay strong.

"We have to talk. Come by tonight," she said and walked away.

Romie stood there trying to figure out what had happened. Why was she acting this way, he thought? He knew it had something to do with Clare, but what? Could she possibly know that Clare kissed him?

After dinner, Veda picked up the newspaper and sat uneasily on the armchair with her legs folded. She tried to concentrate on an article but couldn't focus. Lita was sewing on the machine and paused it for a second.

"It's gonna be fine. You should just talk to him and iron it all out."

"Lita, I don't know if he's the right guy for me. He's a flirt, he can't read, he... he..."

"He's gorgeous," Lita added.

"He's gorgeous. But I don't know. For some reason, I can't resist him. At the same time, I know he's wrong for me."

"Just admit it. You love him, Veda."

"But he kissed Clare!"

"Veda, consider the source. Pete? Find out what really happened. Ask him," Lita pleaded.

Just then, there was a knock at the door. Veda looked at Lita as she stood up and slowly opened it. Romie was standing there with his usual button-down short-sleeved shirt and pants with suspenders.

"Romie, come on in," Lita said.

Veda sat up straight and buried her face in the newspaper. Romie walked over, and her heart began pounding erratically as she looked up at him. He was so tall and irresistible, yet she was still hurt and angry.

"Hello, Veda," Romie said in a sweet voice. "Can we talk?"

Veda looked down at the ground, unable to find her voice at first.

"Do I even get a hello?"

"Hello."

"Can I talk to you? Please?"

Veda stood up and walked to the front door. Turning the knob, she looked back at Romie, who hadn't moved.

"Are you coming?"

Taking a seat on the patio chair, she had entered unchartered territory. Organizing a discussion, or mapping out a plan to solve a problem, was never confusing before. She hated the feeling of not having complete emotional control. Romie sat next to her and broke the ice with the fresh smell of Lifebuoy soap radiating from his body.

"Shuga, why you mad at me?"

"I'm not mad. I just don't think… I don't think we are going to work out."

"What do you mean?"

"I mean... I'm just not sure about you."

"What you mean? Not sure?

"I don't know. I see you flirting with all the girls. It makes me uncomfortable. I don't know if you're the one I should give my heart to."

"I'm the only one you should ever give yo heart to."

Romie's sweet words were hard to hear. She could feel her heart thawing. Dammit! He always said the right things, but she had to know what happened.

"Did you kiss Clare?" she blurted out.

"Clare's your best friend. Why I'm-ma do that?"

"I don't know. She's pretty."

"No one is as pretty as you. Didn't I tell ya, I'm gon marry you? But so you know, Clare kissed me."

"Did you kiss her back?"

"It was just a peck. It was nothing. She was saying goodbye."

Romie was convincing, but Veda didn't want to let her guard down. She couldn't, despite feeling his sincerity and love for her.

"Romie, I really care about you, but I can't do this. You're a gigolo."

"I ain't no … no... what chu call it. I'm just me. And I want you. I always have."

"Yeah, well, I need you to want only me. Not me and everyone else."

"Girl... They ain't no one else I want."

"Yea. Well, my brain tells me otherwise. I don't want to be hurt."

"You the last person I'd ever hurt, Veda. I want to take care of ya. You my girl, and we belong togetha. Don't you feel it?"

"Feelings get people in trouble, Romie."

"But you know you feel it cause I feels it too. That don't come round every day."

"But I have to trust you, and I don't."

"What I gotta do? I'll do it. Just name it. Cause you gonna marry me." Romie said with confidence.

"You sound so sure. Am I?"

"Yes, you are. And you can trust me."

Romie clutched her face and passionately turned it towards him. He gazed deep into her eyes and softly kissed her top lip, then her bottom, before putting his whole mouth on hers. When the kiss was over, he gently whispered, "I've never kissed anyone the way I kiss you."

Veda knew he had her.

Married right out of high school, Romie and Veda took their vows on November 9, 1937. It was a beautiful wedding, with Lita catching the white carnation bridal bouquet. The whole family was there, and everything was perfect.

Romie, who dropped out of school before graduating, began working as a mechanic. His father, Tommy, worked for a wealthy white man who had numerous cars on his property that frequently needed repairs or painting. Car paint was not durable in those days and often required touch-ups. Romie liked working with his father because he could set his schedule.

They lived on 35th street in the house around the corner from where Veda grew up. Lita stayed with them; however, Edna moved to Saugus just north of Santa Clarita. It was a rural place they called "the country" because of all the jack rabbits and rattlesnakes.

Because Veda got pregnant right away, Edna quietly counted the months to confirm she was "fresh" before marriage. It was important that both her girls retained their virtue until matrimony. Although her situation with Rufus violated Christian morals, Edna maintained those values and believed in preserving one's chastity. She prayed regularly for God's forgiveness because of not achieving that herself. Proud of Veda and happy to be a grandmother, Edna got them a Taylor Tot stroller, the best available.

Veda gave birth to a bouncing baby boy named Romie Jr. He was 8 ½ pounds and cute as a button. B. S. Maternity Home on North Hoover Street was where the delivery took place, with help from a midwife named Goldie Marion. The Christian Science religion believed that sickness was an illusion curable by prayer, and doctors were deemed unnecessary for the most part. However, Veda regretted having her baby this way. It seemed primitive, and she felt childbirth should be in a hospital with doctors and nurses. Although Edna would disapprove, Veda decided she would use western medicine from here on out. Her next delivery would not be like this.

While she sat in the living room with baby and husband by her side, Veda thought about her family's future. Since before they were married, Romie was content just working for his father. Veda wanted him to have a regular job and income, so she picked up an employment application while out one day.

"Hey sweetie, what do you plan on doing today?" Veda asked.

"Uhhh, Imma helps my pops later," Romie said, taking a drink of his beer.

"You know it's time we start making real money. Working with your father is good, but it's not stable."

Romie, trying to avoid the conversation, reached for the baby and picked him up. He was so happy about having a son. August 22, 1938, would be a day he would never forget. His boy had beautiful bright eyes, a perfect nose, and hair like his father. His forehead was a little large, but that was to accommodate his exceptional brain, Romie thought.

"Did you hear me, sweetie? I picked up an application for you."

"Yeah, I don't know, babe. We doin' okay."

"Well, you know I can get a job. I would love to work. And you could watch the baby," Veda said.

Romie continued playing with Jr, thinking for a moment, maybe that's not a bad idea. Then, suddenly, Jr. began to cry. His crying became more demanding as Romie tried to soothe him. He looked at Veda, who offered him no immediate support. He felt panicked, thinking about having no one to pass off a fussy baby to, and quickly realized a steady job might be better. He then held out Jr. for Veda to take.

"Where's that application at?" he half-heartedly asked.

"It's on the table."

Veda took the sleepy infant to the room. As Romie looked at the application, Lita came in from the kitchen and sat down with her magazine. Wearing a plain housedress and hair pinned up, he wondered why Lita never let down her long, black silky hair. With deep-set eyes and high cheekbones, she had an exotic look, Romie thought.

Veda came out of the room and grabbed her purse.

"Okay, the baby is asleep. I must run to the market."

She kissed Romie on the cheek and turned to Lita.

"Do you need anything?"

"No, thank you."

"Okay, I'll be right back."

Romie took a sip of his beer and looked over at Lita.

"Lita, you ever think bout wearin' yo hair down? You know, you would look good in one of those sleeveless dresses."

Feeling uncomfortable, Lita didn't know how to interpret what Romie had just said.

"Thanks. I'll keep that in mind."

"You ever been with a man?" Romie asked, slurring his words.

Just then, the baby started crying. Lita was so relieved. What on earth made him think he could ask a personal question like that?

"I'll go check on Him," she said.

Romie felt the inebriated effect of several beers and wanted to get some air. Since Lita was there to care for the baby, he decided to visit a friend.

When Lita returned to the living room, Romie was gone. She had no idea where that odd conversation was going, but it was extremely awkward. Unlike her sister who dealt with things head-on, Lita never liked confrontation. Moreover, she did not want to cause any friction so decided to remain silent.

Lita was quietly reading her favorite comic strip, "Blondie," when Veda returned home with a few brown grocery bags. The blonde housewife and her husband, Dagwood, always made her laugh. The first thing Veda asked after she put down the bags was, "Where's Romie?" The only thing Lita could say was she didn't know. They discussed dinner, but clearly, Veda was feeling concerned about his whereabouts.

Veda always wanted to attend college. She believed everything Edna instilled in her about the importance of education. Yet, she also knew the racial challenges she would have to endure. So, her strategy was to gain as much knowledge as possible and use her memory skills. She was not going to let being a mother stop her; instead, it served as motivation.

Romie got the janitorial job, which made her very happy. With Lita living there, and Romie's new schedule, Veda sought to attend school part-time. She applied for Los Angeles City College and was ready to get her classes.

Located on Vermont Ave, Los Angeles City College opened in 1929. It was formerly the UCLA campus before the university relocated to Westwood. The uniquely designed building, built-in 1913, featured three distinct arched entries to the main structure.

After being assigned a date and time to register, Veda meticulously memorized the catalog and decided which courses to take. However, it required visiting each classroom to see if spots were still available. Administrators posted index cards on the bulletin boards, and once they were gone, the class was full.

Upon arriving, she entered through the center arch after walking up a circular walkway. In awe of the school once being a university, Veda wished she could have attended that instead. There were plenty of students looking a little lost, just like her. She noticed no coloreds anywhere. Luckily, she was comfortable with Caucasians — never feeling out of place or inferior. On the contrary, she wanted them to know her ability to match wits and knowledge with the best of them.

The college placed first-year students in the last group of registrants, so many of her preferences were already gone. However, the administration office had a consolidated bulletin board with the remaining available classes. After picking up her registration packet, she began filling out the forms. Looking at the depleted board, thinking her choices were limited, two stood out; "Typing I" and "Intro to Criminal Justice." Typing had quite a few cards, but Criminal Justice only had two. She took those cards off the board and went back to the registration table. There was a plain-looking woman at the desk in her late 30's handling the paperwork to whom Veda presented her forms. She looked at them then looked up at Veda.

"You can't take this class," the woman stated with a frown on her face.

"Which one, Typing?" Veda replied, knowing that's not the class she meant.

"No. Criminal Justice."

"There are two spots left."

"That's for men," she said as she pushed her glasses up on her nose.

"That's not in the prerequisites," Veda firmly told the worker as she whipped out the school catalog, went right to the page, and showed it to her.

The woman looked at it reluctantly.

"But you're colored too," she said with attitude.

"It doesn't say that's a prerequisite either."

There was no viable defense for Veda's position, which shook the woman. She took the paperwork over to her supervisor, who was a middle-aged dark hair, pale-faced man with thin lips and a big nose. He looked over at Veda through his square, thick-framed glasses when the clerk handed him the papers.

"She doesn't have a chance at passing, but give it to her," he whispered smugly.

Veda always wondered how Caucasians felt denying equal opportunities to women and people of color. It always baffled her. The lady returned and noticed Veda's smug smile and wanted to knock her down a notch.

"Well," she said. "You can try it, but to warn you, you probably won't pass."

"I appreciate the warning," Veda smirked as she left.

While still perturbed at being assigned to the last group, she felt a sense of accomplishment about being enrolled in college. The first of her lineage to attend an institution of higher learning, she knew her grandfather Wesley, born a slave, would be proud.

Veda still had a host of required classes to take, but this was a start. With a newborn and attending college, keeping Romie happy would be difficult, but she was determined to get her degree.

Whizzing through her first semester earning an "A" in both classes, Veda's passion for criminal justice exploded. She waited anxiously for the advanced course to begin. Fortunately, everything was going according to plan, and the future felt great.

However, that feeling was short-lived when Veda shockingly discovered she was pregnant again. It threw a wrench into her plans, turning her whole world upside down. What would she do now?

Ironically, Veda had an epiphany when she realized babies came from having sex. For as bright as she was, and for all her reading, she was completely naive about sex and babies. Edna never shared "the how" of making babies, and nobody discussed it at school. The bible talked about a man and woman but not the exact details of conception. She wished conversations were not so hushed in her family. Somebody could have told her, she thought.

Fortunately, Veda's morning sickness was not bad, and despite the pregnancy, her focus was still on graduating. Romie was working steadily, so finances were much better. Veda prided herself on budgeting their money well. However, they faced numerous day-to-day challenges. It was a tight schedule. She needed to make it home from class on time so Romie could use the car to get to work. It was not easy, but together, they made it.

Criminal Justice was Veda's intellectual release, and she always participated in discussions. The professor was an older blue-eyed man, and the entire class was full of young Caucasian men. Veda was the only female, which was nothing new to her. This class had some of the same students as the "intro" class, and Veda had already established she was someone who knew her stuff. She never hesitated to factually challenge Professor Smith and could tell he liked it. He couldn't figure out how this five-foot-tall-colored woman knew so much and always raised her hand to answer his questions.

"Evidence is sub-divided into three major classifications—direct, real, and circumstantial." Professor Smith began. "Who can tell me which one of the following applies to 'direct evidence?' A — evidence based on expert opinion; B — testimony of an eyewitness describing something observed; or C — a weapon introduced into evidence."

Veda knew the answer, as usual, so she raised her hand. Professor Smith called on her.

"Eyewitness testimony is deemed direct evidence, and courts accept it as such," Veda answered.

"And why is that, Veda?"

"Juries tend to find it reliable. However, people can also misinterpret what they see. They can lie too. So, whereas it's viewed as the most reliable, I think there are holes in that logic."

"Class. Eyewitness testimony is considered very reliable and can and will influence the decision of a jury. It is uncommon for witnesses to lie under the penalty of perjury," Professor Smith lectured.

Ready to cite a case she read about where the witness lied and a man was convicted, Veda prepared for her argument.

"Well in Oklahoma 1921...."

Just then, Professor Smith cut her off.

"Thank you, class. That concludes our lessons for today. Finals are next week."

And with that, the class was dismissed. Feeling cheated, Veda looked at the clock and realized the time. She hated being late for anything, and this class went over. Grabbing her stuff, Veda headed out.

Now seven months pregnant, she was glad the semester was ending. One thing held true; law enforcement was her calling. However, she would have to perfect her typing and stenography skills to get in the door. Being a female and colored, she felt lucky not to have any classroom problems. 1939 was not a friendly time, but that didn't matter because nothing was going to stop her.

When Veda got home, Lita was playing with Romie Jr. He walked around the house saying "boppin boppin boppin," which made them start calling him Boppie. Veda was okay with that because she didn't want people calling him Junior. It was too common.

Praying for a daughter, she hoped this would be her last child. She began thinking of girls' names, wanting something different and unusual. Nothing struck her while looking through books, so she played around with unique names. To Romie, it didn't matter. However, Edna wanted Glodine, and there was no way Veda was naming her daughter that. Aiming for something more exotic, she came up with Alithra Denise. If it was a boy, she had no idea, so it had to be a girl.

Veda apologized to Romie for being late as soon as she walked in the door. She handed him the keys and could see in his face he was irritated.

"I'm gonna be late," Romie said as he grabbed his jacket.

"Hold on, sweetie, let me get your lunch. I am so sorry."

Veda hurried into the kitchen, grabbed his lunch bag from the fridge that she made before going to school, and dutifully handed it to him.

"I put a surprise in there for you."

"Thanks," he replied, kissing her goodbye.

Veda was exhausted and sat down on the couch to calmly meditate. She looked at Lita playing joyfully with Boppie and was so grateful for her at that moment.

"How was your day?" Lita inquired.

"It was okay."

"You seem quiet lately. Everything fine?"

"Yeah, everything is good," Veda responded, rubbing her stomach, trying to get comfortable. "I've been thinking. This is my last baby."

"Does Romie know that?"

"I'm gonna tell him once I figure out how."

"Is that all that's bothering you. You seem a little different."

"I just want to live comfortably and be happy. I know it's not the norm, but I don't want to be a housewife. I have too much to offer. My mind will go nuts if I don't use it and stay productive. I feel alive when I'm in class."

Veda then looked at Boppie playing with his toy gun and cowboy hat. She loved her son, but too many kids could mean not fulfilling her dreams. Hopefully, Romie would understand.

"I'm just gonna have to tell him two kids is enough."

"How are you gonna keep from getting pregnant?" Lita asked.

"Abstinence, something I should have known about before. Sex and babies, who knew? Thanks, Edna."

They both laughed. Veda then casually looked at the end table and saw an empty beer bottle.

"Was Romie drinking before he left?"

"Yes," Lita replied.

"I wonder if he'll make it home after work. He gets off at midnight and seems to work a lot of overtime. But it's not on his check."

"That's strange. Have you asked him about it?"

Veda blankly looked at Lita but did not respond. Things were going well with the marriage, and she did not want to start questioning him now. She honestly loved being a family. Nurturing her husband and child came naturally. Every day she made the beds, cooked, and kept the house immaculate. Clothes were always washed and put away.

After proudly acing her finals, Veda was finally able to relax and prepare for their new child. Luckily, she could reuse most of Boppie's stuff. The crib and baby items were ready. She made a pink blanket hoping she had a girl, and on January 10, 1940, her dream of having a beautiful daughter came true. Alithra Denise Craig was born, and her family was now complete.

Veda's wedding day, November 9, 1937

In 1938, Romie shares a playful moment with Boppie in their front yard

In 1939, one-year-old Boppie has his Taylor Tot stroller parked next to Uncle Bubs' new car — Edna purchased the stroller, one of the finest of its kind, as a gift for Romie and Veda

Los Angeles, 1940, the Craig family sits in front of their home — Veda, Romie, Boppie, and the youngest new member, Alithra

Having two children was an adjustment for Veda. She kept Alithra on a strict schedule, and Boppie was usually content playing with his cowboy and Indian toys. Although in the midst of his terrible two's, he had a good temperament. That afforded Veda time to read and learn all she could about criminal law.

While reading one day, the doorbell rang. Alithra was quietly lying on a blanket that Edna knitted with beautiful multicolored yarn she found at a five-and-dime store. When Veda opened the door, a short man wearing a wool suit and fedora hat was standing there, with a pen and paper.

"Hello. How can I help you?"

"Yes, Hi mam. I am taking the 1940 United States Census, and I need some information from you."

Veda was quite familiar with the Census, but this was her first time participating. She felt grown at 20, with two kids, a husband, and a home. Most young couples stayed with family but not her.

"Oh, of course. Come on in. Watch out for the baby," she said. "We can sit over here at the table. Can I get you something to drink?"

"No, thank you, I have a lot of houses to cover. So, let's get started. Your name?"

"Veda Delois Craig."

"Do you own or rent?"

"Rent."

"What's the highest grade you completed? Did you graduate high school?"

"Yes, I graduated high school, and I have a year and a half of college."

"You must be pretty smart being a colored gal in college. Times sho is changing," he said, rubbing his head.

"I've been told that," Veda said, smiling.

"Your marital status?" he continued.

"Married."

"Age?"

"20"

"Do you work?"

"Taking care of a house and kids is work," Veda said, laughing.

"That's woman's work. You know that don't count. Let me rephrase that. Are you employed?" he said.

"If you mean do I get paid. The answer is no."

"And your husband's name?"

"Romie Craig"

"Highest grade completed?"

"3rd-year high school."

Just then, Romie came in the front door. Boppie ran right up to him, excited at seeing his dad. He lifted his arms to be picked up and gave him a big hug.

"Hey, buddy," he said as he kissed him.

Veda loved seeing the closeness they shared. Romie put Boppie down and looked at the stranger.

"This is my husband, Romie," Veda quickly said. "Honey, this is the Census taker."

The two men nodded to acknowledge each other. Romie walked to the refrigerator, grabbed a beer, then curiously stopped at the table to see what was going on. He looked at the document, boldly headlined "*Sixteenth Census of the United States 1940*." Then he noticed the words "head" and "Veda Craig," which infuriated him. Romie struggled daily, dealing with her superior knowledge over his. Although wise, he lacked formal education and was acutely aware of it when Veda was around. It was beginning to take its toll, and before he knew it, he lashed out.

"So, this says you're head of the house? I thought the man was?"

Before Veda could discover what Romie was talking about he stormed to the bedroom in a huff. Completely baffled and embarrassed, Veda inquisitively looked at the man.

"Can I see what you wrote?"

Veda noticed Romie had misread it instantly. The line with her name said "wife," and his name underneath said "head." He must have confused the two lines. There was no error. After finishing up his questions, the Census taker left. Veda now had to smooth things over with Romie.

Walking into the room, Romie was sitting on the chair next to the dresser. Veda wanted to comfort him.

"Don't be upset. That was an honest error. He fixed it," Veda explained, covering up his mistake, not wanting Romie to feel stupid or dumb.

As a matter of fact, she often downplayed situations just to appease his ego. She had never done that for anyone.

"Yeah. But me not finishing high school and you goin' to that college makes me look bad. I want you proud of me, not ashamed."

"Romie, you are a good provider, and I am proud of you. You tried with reading, but it was tough. You read that report pretty good, though."

Romie and Veda both snickered over that.

"Yeah, I did," Romie said. "I just saw your name and head. That's all. You know I love you."

"Baby, I love you too. You are working hard for this family with all the overtime you're putting in."

"We gonna fill this house with lots of kids. You can't deny how good I am with them," Romie boasted.

Veda's heart sank. She had to tell him that two kids were enough. He had to know.

"Romie. I only want two."

Romie instinctively started laughing.

"Now you jokin' round. We havin' six or seven at least. I can't wait for the next one."

That was definitely not what Veda wanted to hear. There was no way, absolutely no way she was having six or seven kids. Perhaps there was a book on how to avoid getting pregnant, or maybe a doctor could help. Regardless, it was going to be challenging. She stood up and reluctantly smiled.

"Dinner is almost ready."

Despite Veda's feelings about having more children, they remained a happy family. Christmas had come, and Alithra's second birthday was just around the corner. Romie was like a big kid when it came to holidays. He loved being Santa and spent the entire night putting together a pedal car station wagon and trainset while Veda wrapped the presents.

"You do that so well," she said, watching Romie screw the tires on meticulously and place the bell so Boppie could see it.

"What?"

"Fix things and put them together."

"It's you who taught me if I'm gonna do something, do it right."

"I taught you that?" Veda laughed.

"Yes, you did. Think we got enough stuff?" Romie asked, concerned.

"We don't have room for anything else."

"Sure, we do. Nothing is too good for my kids."

"What about me?"

"Nothing is too good for you either. I still pinch myself that I have such a beautiful wife and kids."

"You're not so bad yourself," Veda smiled and winked. "What was your Christmas like as a child, Romie? Ours were always fun. I think Edna enjoyed it as much as we did. One year I remember her getting me, Pete, and Lita skates to share, and we were thrilled."

"Our Christmases weren't that great. After mom died, pops wasn't much for holidays."

"You never told me what happened to her."

Romie's face changed as his mind drifted solemnly to a place far away. He never talked about his mother and didn't want to. It was too painful. His father never mentioned her either.

"At least tell me her name," Veda said gently.

"Her name was Tenolia. She died May 31, 1921, when I was four. You see, my pops had his own car shop in Greenwood, Oklahoma, that was doing well. We moved there from Muskogee shortly after I was born. I don't rememba much about it, but the whole town got blown to dust by a white mob."

Romie paused and put his hand on his head, rubbing his temple. He slowly looked at Veda.

"Oh my Gosh, Romie!"

"He grabbed me and my brotha and put us in da car. Then daddy went back into the house to find my mama and little sista. He looked everywhere, trying to get us out of there. When he found my sista, she was looking out the window at mamas' body on the ground. We left and went back to Muskogee until we moved to California. That's it."

"That's terrible, honey. I can only imagine how difficult that was for you and your family. I understand why you don't talk about it."

Seeing the pain in Romie's face, Veda hugged him and rubbed his back.

"Let's turn in. I can't wait 'til morning," she said.

Romie glanced one last time at the tree as he took Veda's hand and headed to their bedroom.

At daybreak, Romie was excitedly the first one up, waking Veda, a change from his norm. In the living room, the Craigs just stared at their perfect Christmas ambiance. Tree tinsel electrified the festive, joyous morning. Romie turned around, and Boppie was standing there with bright-wide eyes.

"Whoa… Santa came! Look at this!" he screamed, running to the pedal car.

"Hold on, Boppie, let me get your sister," Veda said, loving his excitement.

After getting Alithra from her crib, Veda cleaned her up and changed her cloth diaper. She loved the smell of baby lotion and was glad her kids woke up happy.

Alithra smiled when she saw all the presents. Both excited kids jumped in the toy car and began playing. Boppie quickly got out and ran to the train set.

"You have some presents to open, Boppie," Romie exclaimed as he handed one to him.

Boppie enthusiastically ripped the paper to discover a cowboy outfit, a hat, and a cap gun.

"This is neato!" he yelled. "Can I put it on?"

"Of course, buddy... Alithra, you have something too," Romie said, handing her a doll.

Excited about the gift, Alithra hugged her new doll.

"I have something for you too, Mrs. Craig," he said. "And here's one for you, Lita."

Romie got Veda a necklace and Lita a scarf. Both ladies were surprised at his Christmas spirit.

"Yours is under the tree, sweetie," Veda said.

The morning was picture perfect. Lita and Veda began cooking the turkey, trimming the green beans, and peeling the potatoes. Pete was bringing Edna over for the family dinner. It was a beautiful Christmas, something both Romie and Veda cherished.

Christmas day, 1942, the Craig family enjoys a blissful morning with toys and gifts

Unfortunately, their joy was short-lived when the army drafted Romie to serve during World War II. He was gone two and a half years before being discharged. Boppie was now six, and Alithra, who they had all begun calling Tipy, was four.

When Romie returned, his old job was waiting, and things seemingly went back to normal. One day, while doing the laundry, Veda emptied his pockets as usual and pulled out a crumpled piece of paper that read, ' Romie, mi amour. Laura misses her daddy, and I do too. Please come as soon as you can. Love Alicia."

Veda just stared at the note in a daze. She flashed back to school, seeing Romie flirt with her best friend, then relived the moment she heard they kissed and Clare's chilling words, "Romie will cheat on you." The note also connected the dots as to why there was no overtime money on his paychecks. What a fool she was. Not only did he cheat, but he had another baby.

This shocking revelation was too much for Veda. She somberly went to her room, closed the door, and cried like never before. The stabbing pain felt like a heart attack penetrating the depths of her soul. Hyperventilating, she tried catching her breath as tears drenched her pillow. What was she going to do?

Tipy crept into the room and saw Veda, who had never shed tears in front of her children, crying.

"What's wrong, Veda?" Tipy said, really concerned.

Veda had followed Edna's lead, having the kids call her by her first name.

"Nothing, sweetie," Veda sorrowfully said, sniffing her nose.

"It's gonna be okay. Don't worry," Tipy said. "I take care of you. Does your tummy hurt?"

"Yes, baby. Thank you. I'll be out in a minute."

"Okay," Tipy said sadly.

Laying lethargically down on her bed, she stared at the ceiling. Veda couldn't have a pity party, not now! Figuring out her next step was imperative. After a few moments, she got up and went into the living room. Lita had fixed dinner, and Tipy was engrossed playing with her doll. Lita had never seen Veda looking so defeated and sad. With puffy eyes and hair a mess, Veda lit up a cigarette.

"What is going on with you? You seem upset," Lita asked.

"She was crying," Tipy said.

"Tipy. Go to your room so I can talk to Veda. You go too, Boppie."

Both the kids left the living room. Lita looked at Veda and sensed this was serious. Veda just came out with it.

"Romie is cheating."

"Oh, no, Veda! What makes you think that?" Lita asked.

"He has another child too," Veda added.

"What on earth?"

Lita was somewhat surprised but had never forgotten Romie's inappropriate comments and how he stared at her. She had written it off, but this was a game-changer.

"I found a note. I suspected something was going on before he went away. Like a dummy, I just ignored it," Veda explained, blowing her nose. "I tried to be the perfect wife — the perfect mother. I tried Lita. I tried."

Veda pulled out the crumpled note from her pocket and handed it to Lita.

"I feel like I got punched in the gut. But I knew who Romie was. I knew it when Pete said he kissed Clare. But, oh, Lita, this hurts so much," Veda said as she pulled her knees to her chest.

"But that was nothing. Remember?" Lita said.

"Has he ever tried anything with you?" Veda asked.

Lita was not sure what to say. Technically he had not tried anything.

"No. No Veda," she said softly.

"I knew who he was but married him anyway!!! I married him anyway. How dumb could I be? I thought love conquered all. I really did. All those books I read. They were just fantasy. Not the real world, and now I'm humiliated. I'm a fool. I am a damned fool. This will never happen to me again. Never!!!"

Lita was unsure of what to say. Relationships were something foreign to her. She had never even kissed a man. So, she just let Veda get it all out.

"He always flirted. He always looked at other women, but I thought that's all it was. What was I thinking?"

"What are you gonna do?"

"Nothing right now. I must figure this out. Don't say anything, Lita. Not a word," Veda pleaded.

"Don't worry, I won't say anything."

"I'm going to pretend like everything is okay. I have to. I can't kick him out right now. We need his paycheck for a few more months."

"Then what?"

"I have my college degree. As soon as Tipy starts school next month, I'm getting a job, and he's out of here."

"You're going to divorce him?" Lita asked.

"He's got another family, Lita. I guess I'll end up like Edna, alone, raising kids by myself. But that's okay. I'm a survivor. If she could do it, so can I."

"You can forgive him, Veda."

"There's no forgiveness. Romie made his choices, and now I'm making mine. I just need a few more of his paychecks, and then he's out. I'm getting the forms tomorrow. It's a done deal!"

"Where do you think you're gonna work?"

"That's easy. I'm going to work for the LAPD, just what I always wanted to do. He's not gonna break me. Now excuse me, Lita, I just need one more good cry."

Veda carefully put out her cigarette and headed back to her room. She knew Romie would be home in a while and had to pull herself together.

"This womanizer won't be the end of me. He's going to make me stronger," she thought to herself.

A few months passed and Veda had secretly filed the divorce papers. She packed Romie's bags and was patiently sitting in the room smoking, anticipating what was about to happen. Romie had been coming home intoxicated lately, and Veda had no reason to believe tonight would be any different. She heard the front door close and knew it was showtime. Like clockwork, he came straight to the room while everyone was asleep, and the house was quiet. He clumsily opened the door and stumbled in. Veda looked at their family pictures on the dresser and felt a sense of loss but knew she was about to enter a new stage of her life. A chapter that did not include Romie Craig, her first love.

"Hey, baby," he said slurring.

Even though he was drunk, he could see she was upset.

"What wrong wit you?"

He asked as he took off his jacket.

Veda had thoroughly played this scene out in her mind for the last two months. When he gave her his check yesterday, it was such a relief. She had enough to make it.

"Who are Alicia and Laura?" she demanded.

"What?" he asked, surprised.

"Alicia and Laura, who are they, Romie?" she repeated slowly and clearly.

"Who? What, what you talkin' bout?" he stammered.

Veda pulled out the note and dramatically threw it on the bed right in front of him. Her evidence spoke loud and clear for itself. He stood there, stunned, knowing he messed up. Romie loved Veda and did not want to lose her.

"Romie, you need to leave now. I have filed for divorce and want you out of here."

Those words stung like a bee to Romie's ears. "What are you talking about, Veda? I ain't goin' nowhere."

"Do you have another kid Romie?"

Rubbing his head, Romie contemplated how he could charm her, but something was different. The look on her face was cold. It wasn't like high school this time. But this was his family, and he wasn't going to let her go that easy.

"Alright. Come on, baby. Come on. Let's talk this out," he said.

"There's nothing left to talk about," Veda snapped back. "I could ask you why, but what difference does it make? You made a fool of me."

"But I love you, Veda. It was a mistake, but I don't wanna live without you."

"Well, you should have thought of that earlier."

Veda puffed on her cigarette and got an odd sense of pleasure, seeing Romie like this. He was feeling stabbing pain like she did. "Good," she thought, tapping her cigarette on the ashtray, calm, cool, and collected.

"I packed your clothes. They're by the front door," Veda said in a monotone voice.

"Just like that? Veda, you're impossible! I was never good enough for you. You had to have the Taylor Tot stroller, Model A car, things I can't give you. What do you want me to do? You don't even want more children. What do I have to do, Veda?" Romie pleaded.

"You chose another woman. You made your choices, and I'm making mine. This marriage is over. The only thing you can do is leave."

At that moment, Romie became insanely angry. He swiped his hand across the dresser, knocking down all the pictures. Veda hoped this didn't wake the kids up, but they were sound sleepers. Romie was visibly upset and seemed even madder that Veda was so calm.

"What about my kids?" he yelled.

"That's up to the court to decide. They will send the papers to your fathers' house. I filed them yesterday. Now go!!"

"Can I at least say bye to them?"

"They are sleep, Romie. You will not wake them up... and be quiet on your way out."

"You haven't heard the last from me," Romie screamed.

"I know. You have child support to pay. I'm not my mother. I will collect," Veda said coldly.

With that, Romie left and slammed the door. Exhaustedly, she let out a sigh of relief then slowly began picking up photos from the floor. Some she placed back on the dresser, others inside a drawer.

Veda was starting fresh and putting him in her past. Tipy was now in kindergarten, and there was an LAPD test to take. Her life would be moving rapidly forward without Romie Craig, her first love.

1945 photo of Veda, Boppie, and Tipy

Chapter 8:
Stronger

As Veda woke, she felt a sense of independence and freedom. Life seemed renewed, while an air of excitement filled her day's agenda. The Los Angeles Police Department scheduled her interview at Newton Street Division for 10 am with Commander Robert Coppage. She had passed the clerical test for civil service, LAPD entrance exam and performed well on her oral assessments. Skillfully prepared and mentally ready for the challenge, the final step to achieving her goal had arrived.

Veda came dressed in her favorite white cotton blouse with puffy sleeves, a wool skirt, and a matching jacket. She usually topped off her brown hair with a headband and bow but decided to go with just curls today. She had slept with rollers, as usual, and fluffed it out exactly right with a hint of bangs covering her forehead.

Entering the building, a sense of belonging came over her. She saw officers in uniform, men in suits, and another woman who also happened to be colored. That woman, dressed in a white blouse with a tan skirt, stood in a room with two large phones on her desk with thick black wires running down the side.

She then approached another room with six tables, used as desks, spread out each with typewriters. Metal file cabinets lined the wall next to bookshelves made with mahogany wood. The men were all engaged in work, but one noticed Veda and asked if she needed help. Veda inquired where to find Commander

Coppage and was directed to an office down the hall labeled "*10 Division Commander*." Knocking on the door, Veda could feel her heart begin to race and took a deep breath. Her moment was here; she had to be strong and confident.

"Come in," a voice bellowed from the room.

Entering the office through a brown wooden door having billowed tempered glass with writing on it, she saw a desk containing stacks of papers. The typewriter on the side appeared to be broken, with the return arm hanging dormant. The bookshelves were in disarray, and cigarette smoke filled the room.

Sitting at his desk was Commander Coppage, who appeared to be in his fifties, with a noticeably receding hairline. He wore his hair parted to the side, with strands across his scalp, attempting to hide this unpopular flaw. Thin oval glasses covered his eyes, and a trimmed mustache was above his lips.

"Please take a seat," Coppage said. "You must be Veda Craig."

"Yes, I am."

"How are you today? You're right on time. I like that."

"I'm fine, thank you, and I'm never late. I'm usually early for everything," Veda replied as she sat down, noticing he did not stand when she entered the room, like most men.

Coppage picked up her file and slowly flipped through it. Veda looked around carefully, observing only one plaque citation from the City of Los Angeles in a frame. There were no family pictures or degrees. The ceiling light hung lower than most, with a large white bulb protruding from a fan with large blades. Coppage pulled out her application then looked at Veda.

"Mrs. Craig, you didn't check the box on your nationality."

"Oh, sorry, I'm American."

"No, I mean your color."

"I'm a caramel color," she said, holding up her arm.

Putting the application down, Coppage looked at her over the top of his glasses.

"Mrs. Craig. What race are you?" he said in a slightly irritated tone.

"Oh, that. I'm human race, same as you, but my birth certificate says I'm Negro."

Coppage shook his head, wondering why this woman was testing him. He then pulled out another document from her file.

"It says here you scored high on your written tests."

Veda smiled, pleased at the acknowledgment. She had known every answer on both exams and scored 80 words per minute on the typing test. Veda felt a higher score would have been possible with a better typewriter, but for 1945 that was considered excellent.

"Yes, I did," she humbly said.

"So why do you want to work for LAPD?"

"Commander Coppage, I've always wanted to be a detective, but my understanding is you're not hiring women for that position… yet. I excelled in criminal justice in college as well as typing and stenography. So, I would like to work in this unit and utilize all my skills."

"Being a detective is the most difficult police assignment," Coppage expressed. "We don't think a woman can handle it. Besides, I'm having a hard time believing how well you performed on our tests. How could you possibly get every question right? Did you have the answers in advance?"

Veda was insulted at the insinuation but remained calm.

"How on earth could I get the answers? Are you accusing me of cheating? If you are questioning my knowledge, I suggest you give me an oral exam."

"Hold your horses, Mrs. Craig. I'm not accusing you of anything. It's just highly unusual."

Taking a moment to think, Coppage pondered how he could vet this woman more thoroughly.

"Give me a second," he said. Standing up, he walked over to a file cabinet and pulled out a picture from one of his current cases. Veda feared she might have blown it by saying too much, but he returned with the photo and handed it to her.

"I'm going to test your observation skills. Study this for thirty seconds, and then I'm going to ask you some questions."

Veda looked at the photo for a few moments then placed it face down on his messy desk.

"Are you sure you don't want to look a little longer?"

Not answering, Veda just stared at him.

"Alright. Here you go. How many men are in the picture?"

"Five," she said without hesitation.

"How many women?"

"Six."

"How many men were in suits?"

"Four," Veda said, beginning to sound bored. "Let me make this easy for you. I will give you a detailed account of the photo, and you tell me if I missed something."

"Okay. Let's do it your way."

"There are eleven people in a bar-type establishment—four men in suits and one with just a black and white shirt, all wearing ties. One was smoking a cigarette with his arm around a silver-haired woman holding a drink. Two women had light-colored dresses, and the others had dark clothing. There are five bottles of beer and a couple of cans on a table with two candles and a floral covering. An RC Cola sign is on the wall next to a clock that reads 9:55."

Taking off his glasses, Coppage reclined in his chair.

"Not bad, but there's no clock in that picture."

"I believe there is. If you look above the dark man in the brown suit, you can see the shape of an obscured clock behind him. You can see the tiny hand pointing at the ten and the big hand on the eleven if you look closer."

Coppage picked up the photo, put his glasses back on, and stared at it.

"Oh my," he said as he pulled it closer to his face. With a puzzled look, he stared for a moment. "That changes every..."

Veda, puzzled by his response, asks, "Changes what?"

Not responding, Coppage continued to look carefully at the picture, amazed at the detail she gave. Never in his long law enforcement career had he encountered someone with that type of memory.

"How did you do that?" he asked.

"I just remember everything. I take a picture of it in my mind. You can ask me in a month, and it will still be there. The images are engraved," Veda said.

"That's very impressive, Mrs. Craig. Tell me this, how are your organizational skills?"

Veda looked at his desk, the bookshelves, and all the papers.

"Let's just say I think I can help you out with that."

Coppage offered a momentary slight smile before getting serious again.

"Let me warn you that you are the first female to work in this unit," Coppage added. "You will be around men that use graphic language not suited for women."

"I was a tomboy, so that won't phase me. I fought with boys in grammar school."

"Well, I'm hoping we can avoid the fighting, but it will be a little rough. Can you handle racial language?" Coppage asked.

"Directed at me?"

"No. No. Just police officer talk."

"I'm sure I can handle it. But one thing I do require is respect."

She didn't talk like a typical colored, nor did she look like one. Coppage thought this woman could be of great use with a memory like hers and may have just unknowingly solved a nightclub murder. He made his decision.

"Okay, Mrs. Craig, you're hired. Welcome to Newton Division."

Veda was delighted. She walked out of the building with her head high and a feeling of accomplishment. Although Romie had broken her heart, he did not break her. Now embarking on a new life, she could make a difference and knew it.

Arriving for her first day at work, Veda's preliminary duty was taking notes at morning roll call. She wore a white skirt with a unique print of Indian headdress and tomahawks blended with abstract symbols, a black cardigan sweater, and a scarf around her neck. Veda entered the room with her notepad and pencil in hand. There were six rows of tables that seated two people each. She quickly noticed the colored officers on the far side in the back. Not sure where to sit, she went to their section and sat in the last row. All the men looked at her with shock, not used to seeing a woman in roll call, and an uncomfortable murmur filled the room.

"I don't think you are supposed to be in here," the officer sitting next to her whispered.

"I think I am," Veda confidently whispered back.

Coppage stood up-front with a chalkboard behind him. Like the other room, some lights hung from the ceiling with bulbs shaped like candle fires. Three fixtures ran above the aisle in the room's center. Making eye contact with Veda, Coppage motioned her to come sit at the front table. She confidently stood up, winked at the officer next to her, and proceeded.

"Gentlemen. I would like to introduce you to Veda Craig, our new stenographer. Will everyone please welcome her?"

"Welcome, Veda," most said at the same time.

"Hi, fellas," Veda said, waving to them.

"Veda will be working in the detective unit. She will be at our daily roll call and morning brief taking notes, a long-overdue necessity. So please be respectful and try to watch your language. She will be processing the paperwork and reports for you fine gentlemen," Coppage explained.

Veda didn't look at their faces but felt a bit of tension in the room.

"Will she be doing it for everyone or just the coloreds?" a white officer with a raspy voice asked.

"She will be responsible for everyone, colored and white," Coppage replied.

"Okay. On to our morning brief. A trucking company had seventy-nine thousand dollars of cigarettes stolen on Santa Fe Avenue. They were in a big rig truck, so be on the lookout. There may also be two trailers involved with the theft. We think it's part of a local crime ring."

Veda felt invigorated hearing and writing down what was going on in the department. The room itself was a little dark for her liking, but the information was exciting. When the meeting was over, she went to her desk. She was a bit disappointed at the size and location of her workspace. It was like they took the walk-in closet, shoved in a desk, and added a chair. Fortunately, there was an opening on both sides, so she wasn't completely isolated despite being segregated from the whites.

Right outside her door was the detective area. There was a bunch of men in suits shuffling papers or on the phone. She looked around to find the colored lady, but her room was empty. She noticed a Caucasian man with bloodstains on his pants getting booked and fingerprinted at the counter. She couldn't help but wonder about the circumstances of his case. After typing up all her notes, Veda finished her day feeling optimistic about working at Newton Police Station.

The next day after the morning roll call, Veda reorganized her desk. There was a stack of handwritten reports to process that she placed in the top tray. Blank typing paper was put on the middle shelf and completed work on the bottom. She picked up a report with chicken scratch writing that was illegible. The name on it said, Pinkerton. Needing to find him, Veda stepped outside the door and saw a familiar-looking officer.

"Hi, I believe we met yesterday," Veda said.

"Yes, we did, and I guess you do belong here Mrs. Craig," he replied, slightly embarrassed for having questioned her at roll call.

"My name is William Broady. Welcome to Newton Division."

"Thank you."

Broady was a nice-looking, fair-skinned man with a clean-shaven face.

"I have some reports. Where do you want me to put them?"

"My top tray is fine. I'm curious, where do the colored officers do their paperwork?"

"We have a corner in the other office down the hall," he said, pointing. "They like keeping us separate."

"I figured that out. Coppage wants me close to him, I guess. But this closet, I mean office, needs some work. Anyway, can you show me who Pinkerton is?"

"Right there," he pointed. "Hey, Pinkerton. You're needed."

Veda smiled and thanked Broady. Pinkerton, a clean-shaven white male in his thirties with short brown hair, walked over.

"What's up?" he said.

"Hi, I'm trying to type your report, and I'm having a problem."

"What's the problem?"

"I can't read your writing."

"That's not my problem."

"How do you plan to solve a murder case with these half-done notes?" Veda asked.

"Excuse me?"

"Who can read this? It looks like chicken scratch?"

With attitude, Pinkerton took the report and studied it.

"Anyone can read this," he snidely said, holding it out to her.

"Read it to me then."

Pinkerton studied it, squinted, and then frowned. He said nothing.

"You need to be thorough if you want to solve a murder case. Also, where are the crime scene photos? I need them for the file."

"The film is still in the camera. It's not developed yet. We've been short-staffed."

"Can you please get me the camera so I can get it handled?"

Pinkerton was stewing inside at a colored woman giving him orders and even madder at the prospect of following them. But, since her connection to Coppage seemed strong, he opted to abide by the request just in case. He wanted to put her in her place but needed to see what he was up against first.

As Pinkerton left, a tall, soft-spoken colored officer came to Veda's area. He had a presence about him as he spoke her name.

"Mrs. Craig. It looks like you're settling in nicely, although you don't have much room. I'm Officer Bradley, Tom Bradley."

Bradley was a tall, handsome, brown-skinned man wearing a black uniform and police hat with a large LAPD emblem in the center. The insignia featured large eagle wings that stood out, making him an impressive figure.

Veda noticed his kind smile and held out her hand, "Nice to meet you."

Remembering his face from roll call, she found him very attractive.

"I hear you scored high on the exam, actually both exams. That's remarkable," Bradley said.

"Yeah, I guess I did. No one believes it though."

"They didn't believe mine either."

"No one thinks coloreds can score the highest."

"Well, I guess we're not colored," Bradley said, as they both chuckled.

"The truth is, I'm just honored to be here," Veda confessed.

"Congratulations. If you ever need any help, I'm always here for you."

"I appreciate that Tom, but I'm sure I'll be fine."

Bradley smiled at her response, enamored with this spirited young woman.

"I also hear you're assigning squad cars?"

"Yes. I'm surprised that you can't mix colored and white officers when allocating them. I thought segregation was mostly in the south, not so much in LAPD."

"Well, you still have a lot to learn. My folks were sharecroppers from Texas, so this is a step up for me."

"My mother is from Sherman, Texas," Veda added.

"I'm from Calvert. Sherman is a good 3 hours from my hometown. But I love California, and the beaches here are great."

Veda flashed back to the memories of Edna taking her, Lita, and Pete to the ocean. They mostly went to Inkwell or Bruce's Beach. Edna made them matching swimsuits and caps each year. She loved the family bonding, but more than anything, the wonderful smell of the sea.

"Growing up, my mother always took us to the beach," Veda reminisced. "I take my kids too."

"You have kids. How many?"

"Two, a boy and a girl."

"You really are quite a woman. Coppage said you helped solve a murder case without even knowing. You're the talk of the station."

"You mean that clock in the picture? I'm not sure that qualifies as solving a case."

"Well, you know in law enforcement, it's the little things. I'll tell you a secret. I think you'll do great here, Mrs. Craig."

"Thank you, officer Bradley. I'll tell you a little secret, I think so too."

Laughing, Bradley took one last look at her and the tiny space she was forced to occupy.

"Oh, and we gotta work on getting you out of this closet." They both laughed as Bradley walked away.

This was going to be fascinating, Veda thought. She instantly liked Bradley and Broady, finding herself attracted to their police uniforms. It made them seem so handsome and distinctive. Also, she admired the comradery amongst the Negro cops with how they looked out for one another.

On the other hand, white officers were different, and Veda knew she would have to win them over like the criminal justice students. However, she was confident her skills and personality would prevail once they got to know her. It would just take time.

When Veda got home that night, she was tired but optimistic. Her mother was visiting to lend support by helping with the kids. Everything was peaceful and dinner was ready when Veda arrived. After eating, Edna expressed she had something to discuss.

"I raised the three of you without your father. I never brought any men around you. I want you to be mindful of bringing men around your kids when you start dating."

"Well, fortunately, I don't have to worry about that right now. I'm not thinking about dating with my new career. However, I seem to remember officer Williams coming around the house once or twice."

"Tom and I were just friends," Edna responded with a slight blush.

"Did he know that?" Veda said, giggling.

"My point is, don't bring men around the kids unless it's serious."

"What makes you so suspicious of men?"

"Just trust me, they can be deceiving. Be careful with your babies."

"I'm sure I can handle it, Edna," Veda assured her.

"I'm sure you can too, but it's easy to let loneliness cloud your judgment."

"Everything I'm doing is for Boppie and Tipy."

"You know I'm here for you, and I will help any way I can."

Grateful for Edna, Veda wondered if she could ever measure up to her as a mother.

The next day at work, Veda mulled over the best way to be comfortable with such a limited space. Staring at the back of a closet wall would get old fast. Something like a bulletin board or photos on the wall would be nice. While reading some documents, Pinkerton came in and dropped a camera on her desk.

"Good morning, Pinkerton," Veda said in a cheerful voice.

She waited patiently for a response but heard nothing. Veda looked at him and thought, what a jerk.

"Good morning Mrs. Craig," he finally answered.

"You can call me Veda," she replied. "I deciphered your notes the best I could, but still have a few questions."

"Like what?"

"Do you know the estimated time of the incident? And were there any witnesses?" she asked.

Still irritated from yesterday's conversation, Pinkerton snapped at Veda.

"Look, I've been doing this a long time, and I don't need some... you, coming in here telling me how to do my job. This station was running long before you got here. So, I suggest you stop telling other people what to do and just do your job."

Pinkerton arrogantly slammed down an envelope on her desk.

"Here! I had the photos you wanted developed."

She picked up the envelope and pulled out the prints. Veda was horrified at how gruesome they were. They showed a young colored female and her 8-month-old baby with their heads bashed. The female's hair was in braids, covered in blood. You could not tell what she looked like because her face was so swollen. Veda looked at the young mother's name on the report, Jeannie Wright Woods. She was only 16 years old. Seeing photos like this was something Veda hadn't anticipated. It left her feeling a little nauseous, but she continued to flip through them. That poor baby. Who could kill a child like that? She wanted to make sure this crime got solved.

"Have you seen these?" she asked after composing herself.

"I took them," he callously replied.

"This is a serial murder case."

"A what? It looks like domestic violence to me. She was bashed in the head with a crowbar and her baby too? It was probably the husband or boyfriend. You're still new to this. You need to stick to typing."

Ignoring the jibe, Veda responded.

"That's where you're mistaken. There was another comparable murder a few weeks ago. I read about it in the newspaper. It was remarkably similar to this one."

"You don't know what you're talking about."

"We need to look at all the traffic stops, arrests, and incident cards for that night."

"That's why we don't have women detectives. You don't know nothin' about crime," Pinkerton said in a demeaning tone.

Ignoring Pinkerton, Veda continued. "You take the traffic stops, and I'll handle the arrests."

"I'm not doing nothing. You don't tell me what to do," Pinkerton belted.

"Even if it's not a serial killer, the husband or boyfriend may have been stopped. You still need to cover all your bases," Veda explained. "It's a long shot, but it's a start. You don't have any other leads, do you?"

Pinkerton walked away irritated but reluctantly decided to give Veda's idea a try. What did he have to lose? She was right. They had no other suspects or leads, and the sooner they got this killer, the better, he thought.

Veda got the arrest reports and flipped through them. Nothing stood out, but then she remembered a few days earlier seeing that guy getting fingerprinted who had blood on his pants. That report was not in the file, so she flipped through the arrests to be typed, and there it was. He was apprehended for disorderly conduct but released that night.

"Pinkerton," Veda called out. "This guy was arrested the morning after the murder for disorderly conduct. I remember seeing him, and he had blood on his pants."

Pinkerton looked at the file. "Hum. That was hours after the murder. But this is a white man," he said.

"They kill too," Veda replied.

"No, I just mean I thought it was a colored since she was."

"There's your case. You take it from here. Check the records for the nights of the other murders. Do yourself a favor, just use names and not color, and you'll be a hero."

Pinkerton thought about that. He knew he hated darkies and would be thrilled to pin this on one. But he had the fingerprints on the crowbar and the ones from the arrest Veda was talking about. It would be a slam dunk if they matched, and the department would recognize him for solving a double homicide. As it turned out, the prints were a direct match, and Pinkerton made the arrest.

In the roll call meeting a few days later, Veda was taking notes. She liked knowing everything that was going on. Between typing reports, memos for the captain, and answering phones, there wasn't much that didn't go through her desk first. This roll call meeting was of particular interest to Veda.

"We staked out an address at 2032 E. 111th Street, after a woman, Mayever Milliner was found stabbed to death in her home on Ascot Blvd. The suspect was her boyfriend, William

Chambers. Officers Jenkins and Salseda were waiting for him at the Chamber's home when they heard what sounded like rats in the ceiling. The landlord denied any rodents were in the building. Upon investigating, the officers found Chambers hiding with a bottle of gin and arrested him on murder charges."

"On another note, we had a serial killer on the loose, and no one realized it until Pinkerton solved the case, with his exceptional detective work. Joseph Burke was apprehended and arrested on multiple counts of murder thanks to him."

The officers all clapped for Pinkerton. Veda looked up from her notetaking to see him wallowing in his glory. Obviously, this was the first time he received any recognition. As the meeting concluded, pats on the back were in abundance, so Veda decided to take her turn.

"You owe me for this one," she said as she patted him solidly.

"I'm sure you will try to collect."

"Yes, I will. Do I at least get a thank you?"

With that, Pinkerton left with a half-smile, not saying one word to Veda.

Turning to walk back to her desk, Veda saw Tom Bradley walking towards her. "What a man," she thought as he approached.

"I see you and Pinkerton have become buddies."

"He's a work in progress. I gave him a little help solving his case," Veda said, smiling.

"So, how did YOU figure that one out? I know it was you because Pinkerton is the laziest detective on the force. He seldom solves a crime, and when he does, it's a colored. He would have pinned this on one."

"It was just basic police work, but this was an eye-opening case for me. She was so young, and he killed her baby too. I've never seen that type of violence and cruelty. I never imagined what it would look like."

"I know this sounds like a cliché, but you'll get used to it. It's a part of the job. How did you ever connect these murders?"

"I'm a newspaper junkie that reads about all murder cases," Veda explained. "By the way, I heard some of the officers talking about you switching up and becoming a lawyer. They said you were trying to be an eggplant."

"Eggplant, huh? The truth is, I feel like my opportunities in LAPD are limited, so I started going to law school at night," Bradley said.

"Oh wow! Which one?"

"Southwestern Law School."

"That's impressive, Tom. Good for you."

"I may need your help on something else."

"What's that?"

"I want to start an LAPD Community Relations Department. You have good organizational skills. Can you help me out?"

"I would love to," Veda said.

Veda wrote her phone number on her notepad, ripped it off, and gave it to Tom with a big smile. She knew he would be someone special and was proud to be working with him.

Veda's closet desk at LAPD's Newton Street Division in 1945

Veda loved working at Newton Division despite facing many obstacles. She became friends with Norma, the woman in the front office who answered phones and did filing. Norma knew all the gossip and was careful not to say anything disparaging about the officers or detectives. Often wording her comments so you could read between the lines, Veda took a mental note to be tactful in the same way. Norma gave her the low-down on everyone.

While developing unique relationships with both white and colored co-workers, none were more intriguing than Tom Bradley. Veda admired him tremendously because he was well-read and displayed strong command of the English language. She was disappointed to find out he was married but respected it as well.

Bradley, a patrol officer, tended not to focus on petty things while seeing the bigger picture. Veda discovered this during a unique experience they shared.

One routine day, Bradley and his partner Hutchinson were patrolling the streets. Hutchinson, a darker-skinned man, had been on the force for about a year. He was disturbed at how white officers treated colored policemen. Hutchinson had a chip on his shoulder because a fellow white officer had lied about him, and he couldn't shake that experience. But he liked the pay. No other civil service job could top his salary, so he stayed despite his constant complaints.

"Did you hear how Adams talked to Moore?" Hutchinson asked.

"I try not to focus on that unless I have to," Bradley replied.

"It was savage. I'm tired of how they treat us."

"You have to learn to play their game, Hutch."

"Not me," Hutchison said adamantly.

As they drove down Jefferson Blvd, the streets had surprisingly little activity. While checking alleys and behind businesses, they passed a cul-de-sac in an industrial area, where they spotted a big rig truck. Bradley backed up then turned down the street.

"Didn't we hear something about a truck a while back? Did anything come of that?" Bradley questioned.

"Let's check it out."

Bradley drove around the truck, stopped, got out, and walked up to the driver's side door. He leveraged up on the step to look inside the window. There was a big stack of cigarette packages in the passenger seat. Thinking this was significant, Bradley returned to the squad car and picked up the radio.

"This is 13 Adam 21. I have a possible code 37. Commercial plate 1 Lincoln 9286."

"Copy," the dispatch said. "Vehicle was reported stolen by a trucking company on Santa Fe Avenue. Proceed with caution."

"13 Adam 21 requesting back up," Bradley replied. "Let's check this out."

"Shouldn't we wait for backup?" Hutchinson asked.

"We need to look around. Let's go."

Bradley and Hutchinson went to the rear of the truck.

"Cover me, Hutch."

Hutchinson drew his weapon as Bradley opened the door, and they saw thousands of packages of cigarette boxes stacked inside. Bradley looked at the other trailer parked about 100 yards away and told Hutchinson to check it out. As Hutchinson approached, a black 1946 Pontiac Streamliner pulled up, almost running him down. The white male driver appeared to have a gun, so Hutchinson fired, shattering the window. The suspect was struck in the head, instantly killing him. The passenger immediately got out and began running, so Bradley took chase. Finally, he caught up to the suspect, who reached a dead end and stopped.

"I would suggest you be smart about this. Put your hands up." Bradley ordered.

With nowhere to run, the suspect held his hands in the air. Bradley put his gun in the holster and cuffed him. After checking the driver's neck pulse, Hutchinson went to the squad car and got on the radio.

"Shots fired at 4701 Ramona Avenue suspect down."

Just then, a squad car pulled up with two white officers, Stevens and Wilcox. Stevens, known for being mean to colored cops, was a thin man with beady eyes and a nose that resembled a beak. His racist attitude entered an area long before his physical body did.

"Are there any more suspects, boy?" Stevens asked.

"No, both pulled up together," Hutchinson said.

"Why did you shoot him?" Wilcox asked, looking at the body.

"He pulled a gun on me."

Stevens strutted over to the car and looked around for a weapon. He opened the driver's door but found nothing.

"Where's the gun?"

"I'm not sure. I just saw one pointing at me."

"A colored shooting an unarmed white man. This don't look good, Hutchinson."

"Bradley," Stevens yelled. "Did you see the gun?"

"I was over by the truck with the cigarettes," Bradley replied.

Stevens and Wilcox walked to the rear of the squad car and began talking softly.

"This is going to be a problem. The man he shot didn't have a weapon," said Stevens.

"That's the problem with giving a nigger a gun, even if he is a cop. They start thinking too much of themselves."

Bradley walked over to the two officers.

"Hey, fellas I know how this looks but let me just say that things happened really fast. They pulled up at high speed. Hutch thought he saw a gun. What was he supposed to do? We know Hutch is colored, but there's no need to highlight that anywhere. It's just a cop shooting, period."

"That's not how I see it," Stevens sneered.

Two additional units pulled up with Commander Coppage, who arrived to survey the crime scene.

"So, what's the story here?"

"Looks like my boy Hutch over here shot before looking," Stevens blurted out.

"That's not exactly true. It was a quick judgment decision with little time. He had no choice," Bradley explained.

"No choice? That's a greenhorn move. You people don't need no guns."

"Hold on here," Coppage said. "Start at the beginning."

"Sir, I was heading towards the trailer, and this car pulled up at a fast speed. I moved out of the way, and it looked to me like he had a gun. I fired in self-defense. That's the nuts and bolts of what happened. I thought he had a weapon pointed at me. Bradley took chase to the other suspect and caught him."

"I'm surprised he didn't shoot this guy too," Wilcox chimed in.

"That's enough. Do we know the deceased name?" Coppage asked.

"No, sir. But the suspect in custody is Wallace Baldwin. Someone should question him." Bradley said.

"Wilcox, radio PD, and have Veda bring the camera to get some pictures. Stevens, get a statement from the perp."

Bradley saw Hutch staring at the ground and walked over to him.

"Are you okay?"

"This is my first time killing someone. I don't know how to feel," Hutchinson said.

"A lot of bad stuff happens on these streets, Hutch. We take a lot of heat. Remember this, they need us out here."

"I know."

Coppage walked up to Bradley and Hutchinson, seeing the turmoil they were facing.

"Bradley, you and Hutchinson head back to the station and write your reports. We'll finish up here."

"Yes, sir," Bradley replied.

Veda pulled up in a squad car. Not used to seeing women driving police vehicles, the white officers raised their eyebrows and shrugged their heads. It was a man's privilege, they believed. Exiting the car, she approached Coppage.

"Where do you want me to start, Commander?"

"Start with the car, then get both trucks and the cigarettes."

She walked over to the car, wondering why the commander wanted her to take pictures when plenty of officers were available.

Both Wilcox and Stevens seemed like they had an attitude about something, but Veda just ignored them. She felt a rush. It was her first time photographing a crime scene.

When she approached the window, there was blood splattered everywhere. The driver was slouched back with his eyes still open.

Veda took a deep breath as she snapped pictures of the body, bloody red windshield, and steering wheel. She also noticed something peculiar on the floor behind the passenger seat. It was a wrench splattered with blood. As she took the picture, it seemed odd there was no other blood surrounding it.

While wrapping up shots of the car, Veda could overhear Coppage talking to Wilcox and Stevens.

"Wilcox, we got coloreds on the force now. There's not much we can do about it," Coppage said.

"Niggers can't fuckin' shoot white men. I don't care if he's a cop or not," Wilcox lamented.

"It's too late. It's over. I'm going to talk with those officers. You and Stevens need to calm down about this and let me handle it. Do you understand?"

With that, Veda walked to the trailer to snap some more shots. She had never seen so many packages of cigarettes. Veda had begun smoking after marrying Romie because it looked so elegant. A few packs for herself wouldn't be wrong, Veda thought, since fifteen cents a pack was highway robbery, but she refrained from taking any.

"Is that it?" Veda asked Coppage after finishing.

"Yes, you can head back. Bradley and Hutchinson should have their reports ready when you get there."

Riding back to the office, Veda felt she handled the crime scene well and concluded Coppage was testing her. This had nothing to do with stenography or typing. Nonetheless, despite experiencing a dead body for the first time, she contained her emotions. Success in law enforcement required mental toughness, and this proved her ready for action. However, after seeing the Los Angeles County Coroner's black Chevrolet van going the opposite direction, she felt conflicted. Another life was gone, Veda thought.

After returning to the station, Bradley and Hutchinson engaged in conversation about the day's events.

"These muthafuckas have a problem with me defending myself," Hutchinson said. "It's okay for them to shoot our people, but we can't shoot theirs."

"It was bound to happen at some point. They never wanted colored officers at Newton to have firearms anyways, and now they may decide to take them away."

"I know, and it will be my fault."

"Don't worry about that. LAPD is going to do what they do."

"I can't let these fools do something crazy. My life and family are at risk. Maybe I should just quit the department," Hutchinson said with emotion.

"You don't want to do that. Why don't you request an administrative leave? They might put you on one anyway."

Hutchinson thought for a moment and concluded he could be overreacting a little.

"Maybe that wouldn't be a bad idea. It would give me time to get my head together. Maybe they'll give it to me paid."

"It is for white officers, so it should be."

"Let me ask you something," Hutchinson said. "What made you become a police officer?"

"I was attending UCLA and tagged along with a couple of my friends who were taking the examination. So, I took it too. They called me and said I was a top candidate."

"You gave up college for this?"

"I needed to make money and was tired of being broke. Plus, I still attended classes. It just took me longer."

"You know, I never told anyone, but my mother was the first policewoman for LAPD in 1916. I've wanted to be a police officer since being a kid. But I never thought it would be like this—never thought about being colored," Hutchinson confessed.

'Listen, Hutch. Changing the culture will take time, and officers like us will pave the way. We can't quit now. The best way to deal with them is to play their game and not fall into the trap."

"What do you mean by that?"

"Play it smart and learn to talk their language. That's why I'm going to law school. They can't feel smarter or superior as long as you have diction and knowledge. That's how we change things."

"You're always calm and cool-headed, Mr. peace man. Would you have fired that shot?"

Bradley paused to think for a moment.

"I can't say. But I know in this line of work, there's no second-guessing yourself."

"How do you keep going, man? How do you keep doing this?" Hutchinson said with a look of defeat.

"I keep my eye on the prize, and this is a stepping stone for all of us. We must keep making strides and not get caught up. White folks will always be white folks."

"I feel like I'm marked now."

"You don't know what's going to happen. Just keep stepping, Hutch. As I said, don't fall into the trap."

Although they had been partners for nearly a year, Hutchinson never got to know this side of Bradley. He now saw him as a natural-born leader and felt inspired to persevere.

When Veda entered the station, she went to the area where colored officers worked. Both Bradley and Hutchinson were sitting at a table writing, and she walked up to them.

"How are you guys doing?"

"We're alright," Tom said.

"I'm going to the lab to drop off the film. Just put your reports in my inbox when you're done," Veda said as she walked away.

"How come she gets treated like one of them? What makes her so unique? Is it because she's pretty?

"As I told you, she talks their language," Bradley replied. "You can't disguise your color, but you can control the way you communicate. She has confidence, knowledge and knows how to use it."

"No matter what I do, I'm still just a nigga to them," Hutchinson muttered.

"Hutch, the trick is to help them overlook the obvious. Some people name it Uncle Tom and have called me that, but there's an art to making them see past color. Veda is a master. I've watched how she commands respect. You do that with knowledge and temperament."

"But what if you're not a great communicator but an average guy like me?"

"It's all about education. I'm a reader. I always have been. I believe you can achieve anything if you educate yourself."

Hutchinson pondered what Bradley just said. But the weight of his current situation was still hard to get past.

Veda returned and asked for their reports. That way, they would not have to walk to the detective room. Coppage thought it would be better if Bradley and Hutch stayed away. Racial tensions were very high following the shooting. Most of the white officers and detectives were questioning coloreds having guns. Coppage found himself in an awkward situation and decided Veda would be a good liaison in the matter.

"So, how are you guys holding up? I know things are crazy right now," Veda said.

"I've been better," Hutchinson replied.

"The commander asked me to pass a message to you both. He didn't want to make a big scene by calling you into his office with things being a bit strained. Hutch, you're going to be placed on administrative leave. Tom, you are being reassigned. They want you in the Juvenile Division. Coppage indicated they have been working on this for a while and are just pushing it up."

"What does that entail?" Bradley asked.

"Investigating juvenile activities, supervising juveniles on probation and counseling them."

"The man can't even come over here and look me in the eye. Do I still get paid?" Hutchinson asked.

"I don't know Hutch, but I'll do everything I can," Veda replied. "One thing, there was a bloody wrench in the car that could account for what you saw."

"For a white officer, that would be enough, but for me, I'm not so sure."

Veda headed back to her desk to begin typing the reports, hoping things would work out for Hutch. When she arrived, there was a waist-length mink fur coat on her chair. She looked back into the detective room and saw Pinkerton sitting there sifting through jewelry. He was holding up what appeared to be an expensive watch, most likely recovered stolen property, Veda thought. Pinkerton looked up, and they stared at each other from across the room. He gave a subtle smile then continued sorting the jewelry.

As much as she hated the closet, it allowed her to observe people's character, and some detectives were as criminal as those they arrested. It was clear from where the fur came, and Veda struggled with whether to accept it. Smart enough to know she had to play by their rules to stay safe in the game, Veda folded the coat, placed it in her bag, and considered Pinkerton's debt paid in full.

Arriving home that night, she felt a little unsettled by the day's events. Everyone was at the dinner table as Edna and Lita had cooked their usual good meal. As she entered the house, Veda had the mink coat hanging on her arm, which Tipy noticed immediately.

"Veda!! Where did you get that? Can I try it on?" she said as she got up from the table and ran over to her.

"Can I get a hello first?"

Tipy gave Veda a big hug, then rubbed the mink feeling the silky texture.

"Hi, Veda. It's so soft!"

Tipy removed the coat from Vedas' arm and put it on. Although too big, that did not stop her from posing like a model.

"See. Hard work pays off," Veda said.

"Where on earth did that come from. You didn't buy it did you?" Edna asked.

"Of course not. It was a gift."

"You don't have a boyfriend. Who gave it to you?" Lolita said.

"One of the detectives. He owed me for a favor."

"No one gives that type of gift for a favor. What did you have to do for that?" Edna asked.

"Well, I didn't have to sleep with anyone. I can tell you that," Veda replied with a bit of attitude.

"The kids, Veda!" Lolita muttered out loud.

"Oh, Lita. Don't be so, so, you. I worked hard for this."

"I want one," Tipy shouted.

"For heaven's sake, take that off Tipy and come finish your dinner before it gets cold," Edna lashed out.

The conversation about the coat did not go exactly the way Veda expected, but she shrugged it off. After putting her things in the room, she washed her face and hands and went to the dinner table. Looking at how much the kids had grown made her feel proud. Boppie smiled when she rubbed his forehead.

"Dad came by today," he said.

"He did?" Veda replied.

"Laura was with him," Tipy added.

"Oh, really, it was just the two of them?"

"Uh-huh," Tipy said.

Everyone finished eating and grabbed their plates to take in the kitchen, except Boppie. He left his on the table and headed towards his room. Annoyed that her brother never had to help in the kitchen, Tipy spoke out.

"Veda, Boppie, didn't put his plate in the kitchen."

There was nothing Veda hated more than a tattletale. Edna raised her, Lolita, and Pete not to do that.

"You're being a tattletale Tipy. You know how I feel about that. Now go help Aunty with the dishes."

"How come Boppie never has to help?"

"Tipy! Hush now. Do what you're told," Edna interjected.

"He never has to do anything just because he's a boy."

After cleaning the kitchen, Edna and Veda went to sit in the living room. Veda could see in Edna's face she was about to be lectured. Edna always played by the rules and was critical of those that didn't. Prayer and faith in God led her to a strict ethical consciousness.

"I hope you didn't do anything dishonest for that coat," Edna said.

"Of course not. Like I told you, one of the detectives owed me a favor."

"Hum. Don't get tainted at the police department Veda. Stay honest and truthful. I'm asking you."

"So, you let Romie in the house?" Veda asked, changing the subject.

"He has a right to see his children."

"You never let Rufus see us."

"That was his choice. He never came to California to see you guys. I don't think he ever left Detroit."

"Well, Romie doesn't deserve to see them unless he pays child support, and I haven't seen a dime."

"Oh, Veda. You're something else," Edna said in an irritated fashion.

"Just wait until he gets picked up for it," Veda mumbled under her breath.

"Don't be so vengeful. That's not nice."

"I'm tired. Can you put the kids to bed for me?"

As Veda laid down exhausted and closed her eyes, something unexpected happened. The bloody face of the crime scene victim suddenly appeared clear as if standing there. His open eyes and blood-soaked body were unnerving. Eventually, she drifted off to sleep.

Two years had passed, Veda's desk was still in the closet, but her duties and workload had grown. She was always up and down because the file cabinets and bookshelves were in another room. Despite this routine getting old, she loved working for the Los Angeles Police Department and Newton Division in particular.

Morning roll call was something Veda always looked forward to because of the excitement and adrenaline it generated. Today was no exception when Coppage brought up the most prominent case in the country.

"We have a high-profile situation with a few clues that need our attention. The Elizabeth Short murder is flooding the papers. Someone claiming to be the killer called the Herald-Examiner, saying he was turning himself in. He also suggested that they should expect some souvenirs of Ms. Shorts in the mail. We need to be on the lookout for that. The press has named this case 'Black Dahlia.' We need our best on this," Coppage announced.

On the morning of January 15, 1947, 22-year-old Elizabeth Short's naked body was discovered on undeveloped land about 8 miles from the Newton station. It was severed at the waist and drained of blood, leaving it a pasty white and colorless sight. The medical examiners determined she had been dead for about 10 hours before her body was found. The case gained national attention almost immediately, which is why LAPD reduced Newton Division's role. Instead, downtown homicide detectives and the FBI became the primary investigators.

Veda became fixated with the case, following it in the newspapers and daily teletype bulletins. She looked forward to reading the current developments regarding the investigation. The latest teletype revealed they were searching for a cream or light tan 1940 Studebaker coupe with California license plates. The suspect was a white male named "Red" or "Bob," approximately 25 years of age, 6 feet tall, with red hair, blue eyes, and a light complexion.

As Veda followed the case, she noticed the killer was toying with the police by sending notes made with magazine letters. He also mailed the victim's wallet to the station to taunt them. With a unique interest in profiling, Veda's instincts told her they would never catch this killer. Having access to the crime scene pictures, she studied the details of what the killer did to the victim's body. He had slashed her face from the mouth's corners to the ears. There were several cuts on her thigh and breasts, and he positioned the lower half of her body a foot away from the upper half. Her intestines had been tucked carefully beneath her buttocks. The corpses' hands over her head, her elbows bent at a right angle, and her legs spread apart. He appeared to have washed the body before dumping it.

Veda was dismayed by the mind of this killer. She knew he was sicker than anyone on the force could imagine and had a high IQ. They would not catch him, she concluded.

A month after the Short murder, Veda was in Coppage's office taking notes regarding an unrelated case.

"Burbank executive Eugene White may not have been murdered as previously thought," Coppage dictated. "The alleged victim took two suitcases from his home with considerable clothing before vanishing last Friday. We found his car with smashed eyeglasses and a blood-stained iron pipe, but a lengthy search has failed to produce his body."

"Do you want this for immediate release to City News Service as usual?"

"Yes."

"No problem," Veda replied. "Captain, it's been a month since Elizabeth Short's murder—what are your thoughts on it? I hear the detectives talking, and our guys seem baffled."

"Well, they pulled the case from us because they didn't think we could handle it. I'm a little sensitive about that. But what kind of stuff do you hear?"

"They think the FBI is blowing the case."

"I think they are feeling the pressure like everyone else," Coppage said. Knowing Veda's unique ability to analyze, he began to wonder what she thought.

"Tell me, Veda. What is your take on Black Dahlia?"

"I don't think that my take would help."

"Tell me anyway. You're a part of this unit. What do you think about the case of the century?" he prodded.

Veda thought about it for a moment, not sure how straightforward she should be. She didn't want her opinion taken the wrong way.

"I read everything that comes across the teletype, and I've read every article in the LA Times and the Herald. It's like he knows law enforcement better than we do. He knows how we think, and he plays on it. When he said he was going to surrender and did not, that spoke volumes."

Veda reached over to a file on Coppage's desk and pulled out a photo.

"Look at the torso's clean cut. That takes medical training, but I don't think he's a doctor, maybe more like a military veteran or field medic. I believe he's right under our nose. He's smart and might even be a cop."

"That's quite an analysis of the case. Do you believe we can catch him?"

Veda hesitated before she answered, not knowing how he would take her directness.

"Look at how many we have arrested already and nothing. One hundred fifty persons of interest, and none have panned out. Only time will tell, but I honestly don't think he will get caught."

A month later, there were more people of interest but no clear, solid suspects. Despite multiple confessions, logistics or lie detector tests ruled them all out.

Coppage echoed Veda's sentiment about the Short case in a meeting with the Chief of Police CB Horrall, as if they were his thoughts. He was surprised when Horrall agreed it might never get solved. Moreover, her instincts proved to be correct.

It was at that moment he realized Veda's value. As he made it back to the office, he stopped and looked at her work area and knew he had something to do. He ordered a new desk and placed it in the front of the detective room. Now, Veda would be the first contact for anyone entering and more accessible for everyone. After 2 ½ short years, she had become a fixture and asset at Newton Division Police Station.

Veda taking notes with Commander and LAPD officer

Norma and Veda collaborate at Newton

By 1950, Veda reached her fifth anniversary at Newton Division. These five years were a learning experience both socially and emotionally. Coping with the ugly side of humanity, in real life, proved to be her biggest challenge. The first two years were the hardest because while Veda prepared herself to solve crimes, her mind was unprepared to see death. She tried disassociating from the images by focusing on the facts. Who, what, when, where, and why became her baseline formula, particularly when handling murder cases. However, unexpected was the lingering pictures in her mind at night, when she often found herself waking up terrorized in a cold sweat. Veda's photographic memory began to work against her, and she was forced to deal with it.

Staying focused while trying to ignore plaguing nightmares was not easy. Veda's role at Newton was essential. Many detectives were poor note-takers, and she became good at reading their minds and asking the right questions. She handled all major reports now, along with Coppage's letters, memos, and press releases, which all went through her. He relied on her for everything and showed his appreciation with occasional gifts.

The Negro officers seemed to appreciate her too. Good relationships with everyone made her job enjoyable. Still, she saw racial disparity and a playing field tilted in favor of white officers, which was bothersome.

Veda's duties also included walk-in crime reports from the public. While sitting at her desk, a tall, extremely fair-skinned Negro man came into the station. He wore a tan army uniform, long-sleeved shirt, neatly tucked, with patches on both arms, and a Garrison hat that fit his head perfectly. Veda was only slightly familiar with military ranks, but he looked like more than just a private.

"Hello. Can I help you?"

"Yes. I need to report a stolen car."

"Okay. Come take a seat."

He sat at the desk and smiled. His light-colored eyes were somewhat unusual for Negro men and complexion so fair you had to study him carefully to tell his race. His diction, although good, gave him away as Negro.

"So, what is your name?" Veda asked.

"George James."

"Where was your vehicle when it was stolen, Mr. James?"

"Well, I parked it by the army base before I left for Germany."

"Germany? How exciting."

"It's work. I wouldn't exactly call it exciting."

"I would," she said enthusiastically. "Germany?"

"Well, It's a living."

"What is the year, make, and model?" Veda asked.

"47 Chevy Bel Air."

"What color?"

"Tan."

Something familiar about this car emerged in Veda's mind.

"Hum, how long was it parked there?"

"I was gone for 18 months."

That was it. Veda remembered typing a report on a car they towed from the base. Everyone loved that vehicle and wondered what they should do with it. It had been sitting in the tow yard all this time, covered in dust.

"Well. We don't need a report."

"What do you mean?"

"The car got towed to our yard a while ago. I remember when they did it. How come you parked it on the street instead of inside the base?"

"I'm embarrassed to say, but I ran out of gas. I thought I had enough to get inside the gate, but no. Then I thought no one could steal it without gas, so I just left it. Can I file a stolen car report against LAPD?" George asked, laughing.

"Nice try. You're lucky the car is still here. I checked it out when it came in. Good-looking ride."

"You like it, huh?" George gleamingly responded.

"Yes. You're going to have to take me for a drive."

George smiled as he looked at Veda's name plaque.

"I thought this was a bad day, but it's actually my lucky day, Miss Veda Craig."

"Well, it's Mrs., but I'm divorced."

"That explains no ring... Like I said, my lucky day. What are you are doing Saturday?"

Veda was thrilled to have a date with George. In every respect, he was different from Romie, being established and reputable, plus he looked great in his uniform. Georges' authoritative demeanor was alluring as well.

Getting ready, she chose a cute striped summer dress, white cardigan sweater, and white sandals, topped off with hair-down and bangs fluffed up. Lita would watch the kids, even though they were old enough to care for themselves. Rusty, their Golden Labrador retriever, would help protect the house.

While waiting, Veda's anticipation and anxiety grew. She found herself a little nervous, having never been on an actual date despite being 32 years old. Sure, she flirted with men at Newton but never dated one.

When George arrived, Veda was impressed at how handsome he looked in civilian clothes. After introducing him to Lita and the kids, they hopped in his Bel-Air and were off. She noticed a cigar in the ashtray, which was another sign of class to her.

"How can you afford this car?"

"Well, being in the military, I have no bills and no rent to pay. I've been stationed in both Germany and Korea. When I come home, it's only for a few weeks a year, and I stay with my folks. So, I save all my money."

"That's pretty smart," Veda said. "My ex-husband made a small income and spent like crazy. I had to control the finances, and he didn't like that."

"When I get married, my wife can handle everything. I have no problem with that. Less for me to worry about."

"You must like strong women."

"Absolutely."

"What made you stay in the Army after the war was over?"

"To be honest, it was the respect. Although I saw many Negros treated badly, they kept promoting me, probably because I am light-skinned and assertive. They've put me in charge of Negro units."

"Do the white army officers forget you're a Negro and say things they shouldn't?" Veda asked.

"All the time," he said, laughing. "Once, they were talking about this dark-skinned private and called him a monkey who needed a banana. When they remembered I was Negro, the look on their face was priceless. One thing about me, I don't play that."

"What did you say?" Veda queried, thinking about her similar experiences.

"Since I outranked them, they could have been written up. But I just told them don't let me hear that again. Negros outranking white soldiers is something they don't like. I love that feeling of power and respect. That's my reason for becoming a career military man."

George was a senior Sargent in the Army who had traveled overseas, something Veda admired. His conversation intrigued her because of the many books she read about foreign places. After driving for a while, he stopped the car off Highway 1, where nothing was around for miles. The sky was blue and clear, with ocean sounds echoing in the background.

"You're so beautiful," he said. "Can I shoot some pictures of you that I can take back with me to Korea?"

"Sure," Veda said. "Want me to pose for you?"

"I would love that. Sit on the car and give me a sexy smile?"

Veda was happy to oblige George's request. With the wind blowing her hair and cigarette to the side, he snapped the pictures and smiled with a look of approval.

Afterward, they walked down a hiking trail. George took a few more photos with the beach in the background and by an old platform stage. It was like a dream for Veda as they laughed and seemed to connect with instant chemistry. The day was perfect. After arriving back at her house, they sat there for an awkward moment of silence. Veda did not want the date to end, and neither did George.

"When can I see you again?" George asked.

"That depends. When do you leave for Korea?"

"I depart in about two weeks."

"Well, how about coming over for dinner next Saturday? I'll cook you something special."

"What time?"

"How does five sound?"

"I'll be there."

He then reached over and kissed her, something she had not experienced in years. Feeling warm and tingly inside, she entered the house thinking this man was perfect for her.

During the week, Veda and George spoke on the phone just about every day. She loved how easy it was to talk to him. Relating to Negro men had become a problem, especially those who blamed everything on the "white man" and let it hold them back. She knew there were barriers because of how the detectives spoke. But not finding a way to combat that obstacle and overcoming the challenge, as she did, was a problem.

Her brother Pete would tell her she was out of touch with the plight of the Negro man and never would understand. He was right because she always dealt with challenges head-on and no longer had the patience for those who did not. She heard Negro officers talk all the time and knew their complaints were valid, but they seemed to roll over and accept it and not stand up. The only exception, she thought, was Tom Bradley, who maneuvered just like her. George was the first potential suitor who carried himself like that, and their connection was growing stronger. He even offered to let her keep his car while away on duty.

The following Saturday, Veda spent cleaning and figuring out what to cook for dinner. She loved enchiladas and made them reasonably good. She also liked making liver and onions, although not a favorite of the kids. They would complain about the texture and make faces when forced to eat them. Veda had a strict rule about eating everything on their plates, making that dish problematic. She could always go with good old fried chicken, which she was not fond of cooking, but always seemed to be a hit. The chicken, mashed potatoes with gravy, green beans, and homemade biscuits were her final choice. Baking a chocolate cake would top off the meal.

George showed up right on time. Lita and the kids were excited to have a guest for dinner while Edna had her doubts. They had not seen a man around the house except Uncle Pete and Bubs. Romie would come around now and then but not often. Edna was quick to question George at the dinner table, mainly because she saw the determination to move forward with this man in Veda's eyes. After saying prayers, Edna began the conversation.

"So, George. When do you go back to service?"

"I leave for Korea in little over a week," he replied.

"Oh wow. How long will your tour be? That's what they call it, right? Tour?"

"They call it a tour when we are in hostile combat. We're close to that, but we're just making sure South Korea doesn't turn communist right now. I'm stationed there for eight months. But you never know with the Army."

"George is leaving his car with me. He says I can drive it," Veda said with a grin.

"You sure about that, George?" Lita joked as everybody laughed.

"He knows I will take good care of it," Veda smirked.

George looked over and noticed Boppie playing with his green beans.

"So, Boppie, what grade are you in?"

"I'm in A7," Boppie replied, putting one in his mouth.

"Do you play any sports?"

"He plays the clarinet," Tipy blurted out.

"Tipy!!!" Boppie protested.

"Well you do," she chided. "You don't play any sports."

"Tipy, he can answer for himself," Veda scolded.

"That's good, Boppie—a musician. Nothing wrong with that," George said.

Just then, there was a knock on the door. Veda had no idea who it could be but got up from the table to answer it. To her surprise, Romie stood there, looking a bit shabby, with 8-year-old Laura.

"Romie. What are you doing here without calling first? You know I disapprove of that," Veda said.

"I just came to see my children," he said, slurring his words.

"You're drunk."

"Common Veda. Let me see my kids."

"You leave now, or I will call the cops."

Unphased by Veda's threat, Romie persisted by ignoring her request, which infuriated her.

"Look how big Laura is getting. She looks just like Tipy. Come here, Tipy and see your sister," he persisted.

Veda gave Tipy a look she knew all too well, so she did not move. Veda's first concern was Laura, who rode in a car with an intoxicated man. She could not, in good conscience, let him drive her home.

"Laura, come on in," Veda said.

Dressed cute, Laura was adorable and did look just like Tipy. As soon as she was inside the door, Veda slammed it and turned the lock. Romie instantly started banging. Veda prayed this would not scare off George. Of all times for Romie to come over and act like an ass, Veda thought. She walked straight to the phone, picked it up, and started dialing.

"Hi, Norma. This is Veda. Can you send a car to my house right away? I have a disturbance here."

George got up from the table and walked over to Veda, concerned with the events taking place.

"Do you want me to handle this?" he asked.

"No. I got it. He needs to go sleep it off."

She then dialed another number.

"Hi, Shalana. Romie is over here about to go to jail, and he brought Laura. Can you come and pick her up?"

The kids seemed a little uneasy with their father banging at the door but instinctively knew Veda would handle it. They had seen her in action all their lives, and she always stayed calm when she resolved situations. Then, a patrol car pulled up quickly, with its lights flashing through the sheer white curtains. Veda opened the door and recognized the patrolman immediately.

"Hi Adams," she said. "He is disturbing the peace, endangering a minor, public intoxication, shall I continue?"

"Come on, buddy," Officer Adams said as he handcuffed Romie. "I'll take it from here."

"Veda, you bitch!!!" Romie yelled out. "I just wanna see my kids."

"Next time, call first," Veda responded as she closed the door and looked at George.

"I am sorry about this, George. I'm so embarrassed."

"Remind me that I never want to get on your bad side," George said, laughing.

"Trust me, no one does. I can use a drink after that. How about you?"

"Just one. Then I'll have to take off. Who's coming to get the little girl?"

"Romie's sister. I still keep in touch with her."

"Did you get to finish your dinner?"

"Yes, I did, and it was delicious."

"Well, you can't leave without having some chocolate cake.

"Cake sounds good too."

"Have a seat," Veda said. "Laura, are you hungry?"

"I'd like some chocolate cake, please."

"Okay, sweetie. Go sit at the table."

Veda was numb because of what had just transpired. Her main thought was hoping it didn't discourage George. He seemed to be alright, but she was not sure. Veda went into the kitchen and got Laura's cake. She thought Tipy and Boppie would take issue with that, but they did not.

"You two can have cake after you finish eating."

She got a slice for George then proceeded to make them both a drink. Although Edna would disapprove of the alcohol, it was Veda's house, and her mother technically had no say. The kids all finished eating, then Romie's sister, Shalana, picked Laura up. While Edna and Lita cleaned up, Veda walked George to his car. She couldn't help but wonder what he was thinking.

"This was certainly an exciting evening, Veda."

"Believe it or not, it's usually pretty dull around here."

"Your life may be many things, but I don't think dull is one of them."

"I hope you mean that in a good way."

"Thanks for the great meal. I'll talk to you later," George said, kissing her on the forehead.

Over the next two days, George didn't call, prompting concern. On Tuesday night the phone rang, and she was thrilled to hear his voice. With things busy at work, the week passed quickly. She and George talked, but they never saw each other. Veda hoped to have a date on Friday, but nothing. So, Saturday, cleaning day, she decided to ask George over but needed a reason. It had to be something she could not do by herself. Then it came to her. The bathroom light bulb needed to be changed, well, not really, but she could get the step ladder and loosen it, so it appeared to be out. Then Veda went straight to the phone.

"Hi, George."

"Hey, pretty lady, what are you up to?"

"I have a little problem and was wondering if you could come over and help me really quick."

"Right now?"

"If it's not too much trouble."

"You're never too much trouble. I'm on my way."

Veda had planned this perfectly. The kids had finished their chores earlier and were outside playing while Edna and Lita were preoccupied. She put on some short shorts and a tube top to add a little spice. Tube tops were new and sometimes frowned upon, but Veda did not care, thinking it was sexy with her shoulders uncovered. Turning up the radio, Ella Fitzgerald's "A-Tisket A-Tasket" played, setting the mood. She was excited to see George.

When he pulled up, Boppie was riding his bike, and Tipy was roller skating. They both greeted him before he got to the door. When Veda answered it, George's mouth opened wide, just the reaction she wanted.

"Well, well. I'm speechless. You look so sexy," George said.

"Oh. This is just my cleaning wardrobe."

"You look like this every Saturday? All I can say is...wow."

"Come on in," Veda said, smiling.

As George entered the house, Edna was walking to the kitchen. She noticed how Veda was dressed and knew it was pre-planning on Veda's part. She never looked like that on cleaning day.

"Oh, George. What brings you here?" Edna said.

"I came to help out. How are you, Mrs. Durr?"

"I'm doing well, thank you."

"He's here to help me change that lightbulb in the bathroom," Veda added.

"Is something wrong with the step ladder?" Edna asked.

"This way, George," Veda motioned, ignoring Edna's comment. She had to stay on George's mind, and this was one way to do it. Edna could not mess this up. She led him to the bathroom, where their bodies would be in tight quarters.

"That's it," she said as she pointed to the ceiling.

"I'm happy to help. Do you have a new one for me to replace it with?"

"Oh yes. Hold on, let me get it," Veda said, provocatively maneuvering by him.

George could not help but look at her rear as she walked away and wondered about her feelings on pre-marital sex. He had a previous relationship with a Korean woman near the base but let her go when she got pregnant. Not sure the baby was his, that possibility did not escape him. However, what he wanted was an American wife.

Veda returned with the bulb in hand. Looking into his eyes, she held it out to tease him.

"Here you go," she said in a sexy voice.

George took the lightbulb, all the while keeping his eyes on hers. He reached up, took out the old one, and carefully twisted the new bulb into the socket. Veda looked at his muscular arms while standing next to him. He wore a cotton ribbed white tank top and casual tan pants with his wavy hair pulled back.

"You have such strong arms."

George smiled when he saw her looking at them.

"You like 'em, huh?"

"Uh-huh," Veda whispered.

George looked down at Veda. The height discrepancy was nothing new to him. Most of the women he dated were short, especially in Korea. The same was true for Veda because Romie was tall, and all the men in her family were too. She found it odd that Pete came out tall, and she was only 5 feet 1. But she loved strong, tall men. George then bent over and kissed Veda passionately. While kissing her, he rubbed her behind, something he had wanted to do for a while. To both their surprise, Edna saw them as she walked down the hall, past the bathroom.

"What on earth?"

George and Veda looked at each other and laughed. They both felt like they were in high school at that moment and not adults in their 30's. They went back to the living room, feeling a bit awkward.

"Can I get you something to eat?" Veda asked. "I can make you a sandwich."

"That would be nice," George said, completely mesmerized.

Veda walked into the kitchen on cloud nine. Knowing Boppie and Tipy would be hungry soon, she made them sandwiches as well, after making George's. His was topped off with her homemade butter cookies on the side.

"Thank you so much for helping me."

"My pleasure," George replied. "You know I leave on Thursday?"

"I know. We didn't get much time together."

"Well, let's make up for that. I made reservations at the Dunbar for Tuesday. Count Basie and T Bone Walker will be there. I was hoping you would join me."

"That sounds wonderful."

"I'll pick you up at seven."

After George left, Veda felt like mission accomplished, but Edna rained on her parade rather quickly.

"Veda. Why are you rushing him?"

"He's leaving soon."

Edna knew her daughter well. She was never compulsive and was acting out of character. Maybe she felt lonely right now, but Edna couldn't help but think there was something more.

"Veda, what's with the outfit and getting him to change the lightbulb," Edna said.

"I like George, Edna. He makes me feel good. We have fun together, and he takes care of me, something Romie never did. Plus, he's active military, with a steady income, job security, and benefits. That's important for me and the kids. What's wrong with looking out for us? I need someone like him."

"Oh, Veda. I don't know. He seems nice enough, but just don't rush it."

"I appreciate your concern, but this is right for me. I don't see anything wrong."

The following morning Veda was reading the newspaper, which she did faithfully every day. Then, low and behold, one article caught her eye.

"Los Angeles Calif (AP) Joe Louis Homes, Inc is the firm name under which the former heavyweight world champion seeks to build several hundred nonrestricted homes on a 53-acre tract in the San Fernando Valley."

Bingo, this would be perfect on so many fronts. If she married George, his GI Bill would allow them to purchase a home in the suburbs. The kids would be out of the city and closer to Edna's house. The only drawback would be her drive to Newton PD, about 30 miles, but Boppie and Tipy could pretty much care for themselves now since they were older. A new hope was on the horizon.

George James (center) poses with fellow soldiers off the coast of Korea, shortly before the United States declares war in 1950

Veda poses for George on their first date

Arriving to work on Monday, Veda was in a great mood. Figuring out what she would wear to Dunbar Hotel was foremost on her mind. A social hub for Negro elites, since 1928, the Dunbar was known for its art deco lobby, regal Spanish theme, and spectacular chandelier. The hotel housed many NAACP delegates, Black dignitaries, celebrities, and politicians. Numerous jazz legends performed there, including Duke Ellington, Billie Holiday, and Louie Armstrong. Focusing on work would be difficult.

The weekend had numerous arrests, so her workload was full. Veda no longer took notes at roll call; a new office clerk did that now. Coppage summoned her to his office mid-morning, so she grabbed her notepad, expecting a request to type up a memo or press release.

"Veda, how long have you been here now?" Coppage asked.

"Five years."

"You have a pretty good idea of the pecking order, right?"

"I understand the chain of command," she stated, wondering where this line of questioning was going.

"That's not what I'm talking about. I mean men, women, white, Negro, you know?"

"I see how things are if that's what you mean."

"I have never treated you like an inferior."

"What exactly are you getting at?"

"You know you're the first Negro female to work in the detective unit for LAPD, right?"

"Correction. I'm the first woman period to work in this unit."

"Yes, well, you're still Negro, and they want to put a story in the newspaper about it."

"Still Negro, really?"

"Yes. But some of our staff don't take kindly to sharing the spotlight. Especially, you know."

"No, I don't know," Veda said. "When you say I am the first Negro woman to work in this unit, it's a slap in the face to all women. I don't understand why everything is always race. Just have the story say, woman."

"They want your picture."

"Then put my picture, and they will figure it out."

"This is something you should be proud of—why are you being so difficult?"

"Captain, I don't wake up in the morning saying I'm a Negro woman. I don't drive to work thinking that, nor do I fall asleep thinking that. I think about organizing my day, feeding my kids, and doing my job. The only time I think about race is when whites remind me. You guys have the problem, not me. I can't change my color, nor can I change being thought of as inferior. But what I can be is a woman doing the best job possible."

"You do an excellent job, Veda," Coppage back-peddled.

"I'm surprised you don't add for a Negro woman."

"I don't want to anger you, Veda. You're different."

"Why, because I'm educated and articulate, and I can spell better than all the men on the force."

"Veda, this isn't coming out right."

"I understand what you're trying to say commander, and you've always treated me with respect. But I work as hard as anybody here. I'm tired of people viewing my success through the lens of color or sex."

"You're right. It shouldn't be that way. And this department couldn't run without you."

"And that's why I'm still here," Veda said with a sarcastic grin. "Now, where do I go take my damn picture?"

Bothered at the conversation but flattered the newspaper wanted to do her story, Veda got up with her notepad.

"By the way, I'm helping Officer Bradley with organizing the Community Relations Department. I don't want to hear one word from you about it," Veda said with attitude as she left his office and headed back to her desk.

Walking into the detective's room, she noticed a familiar-looking man conversing with some colleagues. Watching him for a moment, he casually looked towards her, and the raisin-shaped mole under his chin was a dead giveaway.

The man continued talking then abruptly took a second look, suddenly realizing who she was. Bronze skin, curly hair, and small stature—it had to be Veda, the little girl who captured his heart all those years ago. He eagerly walked over to her.

"It can't be."

"Mr. Williams," Veda said with a big smile, giving him a warm hug.

"Veda Durr. I'll be damned."

"It's Craig now."

"You're married?"

"Well, I was married. I'm divorced now, but I have two beautiful children."

"You're a mother! And you're working in the detective unit. This girl was profiling me at four years old," Tom said as he turned to the other detectives and laughed. "Why am I not surprised?"

"It's true. This man was my inspiration. He told me I could break any barrier I wanted if I just believed in myself."

"Well, it looks like you shattered those barriers," Tom said, beaming with pride. "I heard about a Negro woman at Newton who was a force to be reckoned with. I should have known it was you."

"So, you're the reason we have to put up with her every day?" one of the detectives joked as they all broke out in laughter.

"Let's get some coffee," Tom suggested.

He gently grabbed Veda's hand and they headed to the break room. Tom was glad to see nobody there as they sat at the lunch table.

Still beaming, his look nostalgically changed as his mind drifted to a woman whose love he never forgot.

"How's your mother?" he asked with a warm smile.

"She's doing well. I know she would love to see you."

"Your mom's an incredible woman. She took great care of you guys and raised you well. It has been years since I talked to her. Where does she live these days?"

"She purchased some property near Saugus and built a house."

"In the desert?"

"Yep, she loves it there. It's on a hill all to itself on two acres of land. Sometimes she comes down and stays with me."

Noticing how well he had aged, Veda looked at his hand.

"I see there's still no ring on your finger."

"Things haven't changed much since the last time you asked," he said, tickled by her displaying the same traits as when she was younger.

They spoke for a while, and Veda found out he worked out of the central precinct in downtown LA. She was surprised to learn he was still a detective and not a commander or Captain. After all, he had been in law enforcement for over forty years.

"I'm proud of you, kid. I gotta get going." Tom said as he winked and stood up to leave. "Please tell Edna I said hello."

"I will. It was great seeing you again, Mr. Williams."

Veda watched him walk away, wondering if she would have joined law enforcement if not for him. She also pondered whether he and Edna could have had a future if race was not an issue— remembering their passionate kiss in the car and how they looked at each other. They seemed so right together and knowing neither of them ever remarried—it was a very sad story, she thought.

After an exciting morning, the rest of her workday was uneventful. When it ended, Veda's mind returned to the Dunbar and her date with George.

As Tuesday night arrived, Veda's excitement grew. She picked out a tan long-sleeved tailored dress to wear, thinking it classy but not over the top. Badly wanting to wear her mink, Veda reluctantly decided against it, afraid of giving him the wrong impression.

George arrived looking handsome, wearing a shirt and tie with his hair combed back. Veda could not get over how attractive and classy he looked. Upon entering the hotel, the ambiance was indescribable. Men were all dressed in suits with top hats, and the women in furs. An aura of success filled the air. Guests were dancing and socializing, with music vibrating off the walls. The atmosphere was electric.

"Damn, I should have worn my mink," Veda thought, instantly regretting her decision.

After being seated at a table, they ordered their food and drinks. Veda went for prime rib, broccoli, and wild rice, while George decided on grilled salmon, baked potato, and salad. A blues band played on the stage while couples stylishly danced, with twists and turns, to the beat.

"You look stunning tonight."

"Thank you. You look dapper yourself," Veda replied with a sexy smile.

"Veda, I have never met anyone like you before."

"That's because there is no one else like me."

"Yeah, I kind of figured that out already. So, what happened with you and Romie?"

"We married right out of high school, and before I knew it, I had two kids. Then I discovered he was cheating on me and worse yet fathered another child."

"Oh my?"

"Yeah, it was the most painful time of my life. But it made me stronger. A part of me took some blame because I only wanted two kids, and he wanted more."

"That's no excuse for what he did. His feelings for you are still evident. That's why he showed up at your house without calling."

"Once you cross me, I'm done. He's someone else's problem now."

"So, how can I get your heart?"

"What makes you think you don't already have it?" Veda replied, tilting her head to the side as she took a bite of prime rib.

"I was hoping you would say that."

"Oh really. Why is that?"

"I haven't married for a reason."

"What is that reason?"

"It's simple. I never found the right woman."

"But you have had relationships, right?"

"I have had a lot of dates, many encounters, but no, there was never anyone I was serious about."

"So, you're like a playboy?"

"No. No. Nothing like that. I guess I'm just picky. But I knew I would find her one day," George said winking. "And know she was that woman right away."

Veda wasn't quite sure what to think. Was he referring to her? Then, as they enjoyed their meal, the Master of Ceremonies came on stage.

"Welcome, everyone! Our headliners tonight are teaming up for the first time. One is a regular here at the Dunbar. He has recently formed his own jazz orchestra and will undoubtedly become a jazz legend—pianist extraordinaire Count Basie!!!"

The audience applauded the introduction.

"Joining Count Basie tonight is an innovator in his own right. He has changed the sound of blues with his electric sound. So please, give it up for Master T-Bone Walker!!"

Everyone stood up, clapping as the band began to play. Veda loved the music and excitement. The saxophone, trumpet, and clarinet players, all dressed in suits, were seated behind a wooden rail in what resembled a jury box. Count Basie sat at the piano to the band's left with a cello player standing behind him. Front and center were T-Bone Walker with his big guitar and a mike stand. Full of energy, they put the entire crowd in a frenzy.

As Veda watched and bopped her head to the music, she recognized Max Armstrong from Belmont High School playing the trumpet. He was the one who encouraged her to try out for *The Wizard of Oz* musical, which was a huge hit. She hadn't seen him since graduation. "What a small world," Veda thought.

She and George got up and danced to a few songs. George was a good dancer and had some sexy moves. They laughed when Veda tried to dance a little provocative. As they walked back to their table, Veda noticed Max whispering in T-Bone's ear and pointing in her direction. She wondered what he was saying as the music stopped for a minute. Then T-Bone looked at Veda and smiled.

"You know, sometimes we like to bring talented people up on stage to perform with us," T-Bone said, still looking at Veda. "Particularly when they're beautiful women. I'd like to ask Miss Veda Durr to please come up here and help me with my next song."

Veda was completely shocked and a little embarrassed. Since high school, she had not sung in public, but when the audience applauded, she could not resist. Performing was something not thought about in years.

"You never mentioned you were a singer," George said with surprise.

"I haven't sung in forever."

"Well, it looks like your about to. Knock em dead!" he beamed, assisting her up from the chair.

She went up to the stage with confidence and smiled at T-Bone, "It's Veda Craig now," she whispered. T-Bone laughed and made her feel at ease.

"Do you know 'Call it Stormy Monday?'

"Of course," Veda replied.

"Please welcome Veda Craig," T-Bone announced.

The piano started playing first, followed by the guitar with a long intro that included horns and saxophone. Then T-Bone started singing and encouragingly smiled at Veda when it was her turn.

"They call it stormy Monday, but Tuesday's just as bad," T-Bone sang, then motioned her.

"They call it stormy Monday, but Tuesday's just as bad," Veda followed.

"Lord, and Wednesday's worse," T-Bone crooned.

"And Thursday's all so bad," Veda sang with gritty sass.

"The eagle flies on Friday and Saturday. I go out to play," T-Bone belted out.

"The eagle flies on Friday and Saturday, Saturday I go out to play," Veda sang out in deep baritone, improvising her line.

T-Bone then motioned for Veda to join him on the next line.

"Sunday, I go to church…Then I kneel down and pray," they both sang, looking into each other's eyes.

As he watched Veda on stage, George knew she was the one and had to make her permanent. Waiting eight months would be too long, and somebody might snatch her up. She sang like a bird with her alto voice and crisp notes. Her mannerisms, beauty, charm, and now her voice sealed the deal. He decided at that very moment, he would ask this extraordinary woman to be his wife!

The audience gave them a standing ovation. Despite the passage of time, Veda still had it! When she left the stage, there were numerous nods from the crowd, making her feel like a celebrity for that moment. When she approached George, he stood up and gave her a big hug.

"Wow, that was amazing!"

"Thank you," Veda replied, still adrenalized from the experience.

A few people came up and congratulated Veda on her performance. The band continued playing, but the mood changed to soft jazz, and George determined this was the right moment.

"You know I only have a limited amount of time before I leave. When I come home, I want something to look forward to. Maybe someone to share my life."

Veda was trying not to tilt her hand, but she was ecstatic. This just might happen.

"What are you asking me, George? Don't beat around the bush," Veda said with anticipation.

"I want you to be my wife. Will you marry me?"

"If you insist," Veda said, trying to be coy.

"Is that a yes?"

"Yes," Veda said. "Yes!"

"You just made me so happy," George exalted, thrilled with her answer. "I've dreamed about having a woman like you my whole life. Whatever you want, whatever you need, I'll make sure you have it. As soon as I get back from Korea, our fairy tale begins."

"That sounds wonderful and guess what?" Veda said. "I read about a new housing tract being built in the San Fernando Valley in a town called Pacoima. We could buy a house and leave the city behind us. It would be like a new beginning for our family."

"Nothing would make me happier. I'm getting the most beautiful woman I have ever seen, two amazing children, and a new home. Man, I'm lucky!"

He rubbed Veda's hand, then reached over and kissed her. It was magical. Best of all, this perfect man would be her new husband.

On Thursday, Veda dropped George off at the Army base.

"I'm really gonna miss you. I've never felt this way about anyone before," George admitted, dreading the thought of leaving her.

"I'm going to miss you too. But me and the car will be waiting when you get back."

George loved hearing that because it made everything real. He also had some great news for Veda.

"Oh, and about those houses they're building in Pacoima. I looked into it, and my GI Bill can get us in."

"Really? You looked into it?"

"Yes, I did, but you'll have to do the rest."

"I'm just the soldier for the job," she said, saluting him.

George laughed, thinking how cute Veda looked while giving a salute.

"So, what about our wedding? Do you want a big ceremony?" George asked.

"Let's keep it simple. Las Vegas would be fun."

"Sounds good. I'll leave everything up to you."

"I got this. You better get going."

They lovingly kissed goodbye finding it difficult to leave each other, but knew, for now, they had to part ways. Veda's mind was racing a mile a minute, organizing the details of what she needed to do. Moreover, the family needed to be told she was getting married.

Veda performs at the Dunbar with blues legend T-Bone Walker and jazz legend Count Basie

Joe Louis Becomes Builder of Homes

Los Angeles, Calif.-(P)-Joe Louis Homes, Inc., is the firm name under which the former world heavyweight champion seeks to build several hundred nonrestricted homes on a 53 acre tract in the San Fernando valley. Louis petitioned the Los Angeles planning commission Monday for a zoning change to permit construction of the low cost housing project at Pacoima. The former champion said the houses, containing 700 to 900 square feet, would sell for $7,000.

1949 Associated Press news release reporting about plans to build the Joe Louis Housing Tract in Pacoima

More than a week passed since George's proposal and Veda had not said a word. The family gathered at her house for Sunday dinner. Pete was there with his six-year-old son Rufus III entertaining Tipy and Boppie, while the women cooked. The house smelled of beef stroganoff, one of Edna's specialties, and fresh biscuits. Music from the radio played in the background until they finished preparing the food.

After everyone was seated at the table, they prayed, then began to eat. Veda looked around, noticing everyone in good spirits.

"Umm, umm, umm Edna. I sure miss your stroganoff. You outdid yourself this time," Pete said.

"I'm glad you two could make it," Edna responded.

Laughter filled the table as mealtime went on. Veda dreaded dropping her bombshell news but knew it had to be done.

While looking at the family she loved so much, Veda hesitated nervously then excitedly announced, "I'm getting married!"

The room was so silent you could hear a pin drop. Boppie and Tipy looked shocked and confused at what seemed to come out of the blue. Even Lita and Pete were stunned, not knowing what to say. However, Edna was livid. In her opinion, whirlwind romances mostly failed, which could result in Veda and the kids getting hurt again. Edna was extremely proud of how Pete married and got a great job with Los Angeles County doing masonry and Lolita working for the Social Security Administration. But Veda, who excelled above both, was being extremely irresponsible, she thought.

"Getting married?" Edna gasped.

"Yes, George and I are getting married when he comes back from Korea."

"Congratulations!" Lita said.

"Who's George?" Pete blurted out.

"Exactly," Edna replied. "Who is George, Veda? You barely know him and don't know his family."

Veda looked at Edna for a moment, then turned to Pete.

"He's a military man who's traveled around the world. That's his car out there I'm driving."

"Do you know him, Lita?" Pete asked.

"Yes, he was over for dinner. He seemed nice enough."

"Is he going to live with us?" Tipy asked.

"Sort of. Right now, George is stationed overseas, but when he's on leave, we'll all be together."

"Hah!" Pete said, laughing. "Maybe this one will last."

"Pete!" Lita said. "That's not nice."

"Well, she's going on number two. When are you going to marry, Lita?"

"Pete. Knock it off," Edna scolded. "This is not funny. Lita is playing it smart and waiting for the right one. Marriage is nothing to rush. Bad marriages lead to bad divorces."

"George and I will be fine."

"Veda, you said 'when he's on leave.' What does 'on leave' mean?" Boppie asked.

"When you serve in the military, your time off is called leave. That's when you can go home.

"So, is he gonna be our new dad when he comes home?"

Veda looked directly at her two children.

"Kids, when George comes home, we will all be a family. Not only that but we're also going to have a new house and you can each have your own bedroom."

After Pete and Rufus III left, Veda sent the kids to get ready for bed. A lingering sense of tension still filled the air as the women washed dishes.

"Veda, just tell me why. Why are you rushing this?" Edna asked.

"It's not like I'm marrying him tomorrow. He won't return for eight months."

"Real courtships take longer than that."

"It's almost 1950, Edna," Veda said mockingly.

"I think Veda should follow her heart. Besides, he is gorgeous," Lita chimed in, sharing a sisterly chuckle with Veda.

"I remember you both saying Romie was gorgeous too. You know what happened with that," Edna clapped back. "Veda, I will support you, but you know I have my doubts. I realize you're going to do what you want anyway."

"Don't worry, Edna. I know exactly what I'm doing," Veda declared confidently.

After informing the family, Veda moved towards what tasks she needed to accomplish in the remaining eight months. She was pleased with the prospect of homeownership. The first thing on her list was driving to the San Fernando Valley and seeing precisely where Pacoima was.

While shinning up the Bel Air, a feeling of hope and anticipation overcame Veda. She grabbed the kids and drove down San Fernando Road alongside the railroad tracks, observing the open plain, fruit trees, and scattered stands along the way. The air in the valley somehow seemed fresher and the sky bluer with miles of land surrounded by beautiful, majestic mountains. It was a stark contrast to the city.

After about an hour's drive, she turned right onto Van Nuys Blvd, then left on a newly paved Herrick Ave. To Veda's surprise, there wasn't much there. Most of the streets were still dirt roads lined with citrus trees that led to nearby mountains. The houses were primarily shacks, except for a few Victorian-style homes built in the late 1800s.

"This is it?" Boppie said disappointedly.

"They still have to clear the land and build the houses," Veda explained.

"But where is everything? I don't want to move here."

Veda pulled into a tiny real estate office operating out of a house. While the air smelled clean, the area had a dusty feel.

"Wait here. I'll be right back."

Inside the office was a blonde middle-aged man wearing a gray hat, mustache, and smoking a cigar.

"Can I help you? I'm Mr. Berg," he said.

"Hi, I'm Mrs. James. I'm interested in the Joe Louis homes."

"Alright. Come on in and take a seat," his grainy voice said. "These homes are for veterans."

"My husband is currently serving. I want to get on the waiting list."

"Where's he stationed?"

"Korea."

"Dam. We got serious problems over there right now. Those commies are trying to take the south. Chinese troops are moving in, I hear."

"Did that just happen? I haven't read about that yet."

"Today's paper," Berg said, pushing the Times across the desk. "It's right there."

Veda paused to glance at the article, concerned about the ramifications of war in Korea.

"Wow! This looks serious. Let's hope things don't escalate further for the sake of our troops."

"Yeah, let's hope for the best. Well, the good news is that you qualify to be placed on the waiting list. We just need a $5 deposit, and this formed filled out."

Filling out the form, Veda began feeling nervous for the first time. When the Army drafted Romie, it was tough, but he wasn't on the front line. He was just doing maintenance-type work. George oversaw combat troops, which was a lot different.

"When will the homes be ready?"

"This tract is scheduled to be finished in February of 51. We'll call you to meet with the lender for financing when the time comes. They'll need your husband's GI certificate. Here's a map of where the homes will be and the layout. They're 900 square feet, three bedrooms, one bath."

"Okay, thank you. That sounds wonderful," Veda said excitedly.

That time frame would work fine for them. The house would be ready in February, and George would be home by then to sign everything. She knew purchasing property required lots of paperwork, so her next step was getting documents together.

The kids were getting antsy by this time, but Veda read about Hansen Dam and wanted them to see it. Constructed as the largest earth-filled reservoir in the world, the LA Times featured a front-page story in 1940, when it was completed. She hoped going there would make them excited about moving to Pacoima.

They pulled up to a sign that read "Holiday Lake" and could see boats speeding across sparkling water, with swimmers, sunbathers, and lifeguard stations around the shoreline. In the distance, folks were fishing, hiking, and relishing this striking water oasis. Across the lake was a massive dam with six concrete pillars. The entire recreational area was unlike anything in Los Angeles.

"Wow! Look at this!" Boppie said. "Are we going here?"

"We're just looking today, but we'll come back," Veda said, happy at the enthusiasm.

"I should have brought my swimsuit," Tipy elatedly expressed.

"Next time, sweetie."

There was an area with pony rides and a choo-choo train for children. This place is wonderful, Veda thought.

"When we move here, we can come all the time."

"Yay!!!" Boppie and Tipy hailed.

Hansen Dam was a big hit and distracted the kid's attention from the isolated town of Pacoima. The idea of getting away and moving to a new place captivated Veda. She couldn't wait to return to work on Monday and share the news.

"Guess what, Norma!"

"What?"

"I'm getting married."

"Don't tell me that soldier?" Norma asked, surprised.

"Yep."

"Congratulations!"

"Yes, I'm excited."

"How about the kids? Are they happy?"

"It's hard to tell how they really feel. But so far, so good. We're looking at getting a house in the San Fernando Valley."

"The valley? They don't let Negros in the valley, do they?"

"Pacoima does. At least for veterans."

"Never heard of Pacoima."

"It's on the far side."

"So is your soldier actively serving or is he discharged?"

"He's active duty."

"Are you sure you're ready for that? They can be gone for long periods of time. My best friend married a military guy. She was always alone, and then unfortunately he was killed in combat."

"How awful."

"I'm not saying this to jinx you, but luckily he adopted her kids, and they were all well cared for by the government. Just something to think about."

As Veda sat at her desk, Norma's words permeated her thoughts. Is that something worth considering, and is it even possible? Truth be told, she didn't know George well enough to ascertain his feelings about adoption. But first, she would have to learn the laws. However, knowing Romie wasn't paying child support or contributing to the kids made this a viable option.

Checking her phone book, Veda looked up an attorney to ask what adoption entailed. She needed more information before she could present it to George. He was friendly and playful with the kids and said he wanted a family. It couldn't hurt to check it out. If you don't ask, you don't get, she concluded.

She learned that Romie needed to sign off all his parental rights. But, knowing how much he adored his kids, Veda wanted to see his reaction before mentioning it to George. Romie was especially fond of Boppie, his first-born son, and might need some extra incentive to give him up. Veda decided relief from child support might help. He had already been arrested for nonpayment, but his father and stepmother bailed him out.

After having legal papers drawn up, Veda decided to make her move. Arriving at his house, she rang the doorbell. Veda knew he was still with Alicia but had never seen her and was curious about her looks. Romie opened the door and standing behind him was a beautiful Mexican woman about eight months pregnant. She had a full face and short dark curly hair with penciled-in curved eyebrows. Veda was surprised she wasn't Negro.

"Well, well. Look what the wind blew in. Where are my kids?" Romie said, looking around as if he was expecting them.

"I came here with a proposition."

"You know, we don't use big words like that 'round here."

"I have a deal for you. Sign this document. If you do, I will drop all child support. No more jail for nonpayment."

"I know you. What's the catch?"

"No catch. You just have to give up your parental rights."

"What does that mean?"

"You sign this paper giving up your parental rights for Boppie and Tipy, and everything is dropped."

"I don't know what that means," Romie repeated.

Alicia walked up to Romie with her eyes big. She knew money would be even tighter with a new baby.

"Romie, it means you're giving up any say about your kids," Alicia said, with a slight Spanish accent. "Do it. Then you can take care of your other ones."

Romie wasn't sure what to think. Child support was a thorn in his side, but he loved his children. It was inconceivable not seeing them again. But he had two kids with Alicia and one on the way. He rubbed his chin, very confused.

"I don't know," he mumbled under his breath.

"From the looks of it, you need to get rid of a few kids," Veda said callously. "How many do you have now? I see one more is in the oven."

"Wait a minute. You don't come to our house talking like that." Alicia said before turning to Romie. "What do you want to do, honey?"

"Look. I am getting married, and my new husband is willing to adopt Boppie and Tipy. He can take care of them, and Romie can't," Veda said.

"You're getting married?" Romie said, changing his tone.

He took the document from Veda and looked at it. There were a lot of big words that looked like Greek to him.

"This is a lot of legal stuff I don't understand."

"I'm telling you what it means. It means you won't get picked up for failing to pay child support anymore."

"Romie, this might be better for everyone," Alicia suggested.

"This ain't better for me. I might stay out of jail, but I cain't see my kids. I'm damned if I do, damned if I don't."

He saw the look on Alicia's face and knew if he didn't sign, they would have problems. He loved Alicia and their kids, but he loved Boppie and Tipy too. After the split with Veda, Romie had many regrets, and losing her was one of them. However, the most significant was leaving his kids. Afterward, he began to drink heavily to hide the pain, and this poured salt into those wounds. Now the kids would no longer be his. But they were. He could not deny money was an issue and getting arrested was too much drama. Alicia did not work, and couldn't help financially, so he reluctantly took the pen and signed.

Easier than she thought, Veda, smiled and took the document. However, it did not elude her that Alicia's problem would have been hers had she and Romie stayed married. His drinking, no money, and having lots of kids were never what she envisioned for herself.

Veda had mixed feelings about this. On the one hand, she wanted to hurt Romie as he did her, but on the other, she had to forgive him so her soul could be free from the pain. Knowing what she was about to say would sting a bit; there was one last thing he needed to know.

"By the way, their new last name will be James," Veda said as she turned and walked away.

"Damn you, Veda!!!" Romie yelled at her.

Veda never looked back as she walked to her car. Owning a house along with trips to Korea and Germany were on the horizon. But, best of all, Romie Craig was entirely out of her life forever. Now she could heal for good.

Over the phone, Veda discussed the adoption with George, and he was thrilled. The thought of marrying Veda, with Boppie and Tipy as their kids, was more than he ever dreamed. Suddenly, having a new family became real to him.

Everything was arranged and looked good. That was until Veda read the morning paper. ***"War Erupts as Reds Invade Korea!"***

This is bad, Veda thought. It was now June, and he was supposed to be home in August. George's calls lately were brief, and his letters had slowed down. He told her things were getting tense since China arrived, and now everything was coming to a head. She could feel things beginning to crumble.

While waiting patiently to hear from George, Veda received a call from Mr. Berg, the realtor, who said the frames were going up along with water pipes. Everything was coming along. They were still on track to complete paperwork in two months, but a bank approval by Home Savings and Loan would help expedite things.

"They won't be ready until February, right?" Is there any way we could delay the paperwork a few months? My husband may be detained overseas."

"I suppose you could get us documents such as his GI info, your marriage certificate, and both your birth records, but his signature will still be needed," Berg explained.

Marriage certificate, Veda thought, that would be a problem. There was still time. Maybe he would arrive home as planned after all.

"Alright. I will work on it and keep you posted about August. Thank you for calling."

The entire month of July passed, and Veda heard nothing from George. Only a postcard clued her that he was alive. Of course, she followed the newspaper stories on the Korean war, but that wasn't the same as hearing from him. Was everything falling apart?

August arrived, and finally, his voice was on the line.

"Hello, love," George said.

"George, I was beginning to worry."

"All is well. I'm sorry I haven't been able to get to a phone."

"No worries. As long as you're okay, that's all that matters."

"Baby, I don't have long, but I have to tell you they extended my tour."

"I was concerned that might happen. Any idea how long?"

"Looks like six months, maybe longer. You'll still wait for me, right?"

"Of course, I will."

"How are the kids, and what's going on with our new home?"

"The kids are fine, but the realtor needs your signature and our marriage certificate. Don't be mad, but I presented myself as your wife."

"Mad? No, that's the soldier in you. Just do what you can. Everything will work out."

"Well, this soldier has some orders for you," Veda spoke in her sexiest voice.

"And what orders do you have for me, ma'am?"

"Make it back home safely—I love you, George."

"I am so in love with you, Veda. It feels incredible having you love me. I must go now, but I will call again as soon as I can."

"Alright. Bye, sweetie."

When Veda hung up, she felt a sense of concern. They would not be moving in February, that was certain. But George was safe, and that is what mattered. Waiting six more months or so was not the end of the world.

Veda called Mr. Berg to see if she could buy the home without George present, and he reiterated not without his signature. However, he mentioned a second housing tract in development called San Fern Manor, which would be ready the following year. So, she transferred their paperwork and down payment to the new waiting list and prayed George would be home by the deadline.

After being gone over a year, the military finally placed George on leave. Veda picked him up and greeted him with an extra-long hug then planted a big juicy kiss on his lips. She studied his face, which almost seemed unfamiliar.

"You are a sight for sore eyes. I thought about you every day," George said.

"I thought about you too."

"You're still beautiful."

"Well. I have been busy. You gave me a scare. We got the second tract of homes instead of the original. But we have lots to do. First, we head to Vegas and tie the knot. Then, we have a court date for the kid's adoption, and lastly, we sign the papers for the house."

"Wow. You're right. You have been busy. Just the kind of wife I need when I'm serving the country. Have you always been this coordinated?"

"Ever since I can remember."

"All I can say is I can't wait 'til our wedding night."

"I have special lingerie for that," Veda whispered.

"Now you're teasing me."

"Trust me. This won't be a tease."

The wedding in Las Vegas was quick and simple. However, when it came time for the honeymoon, Veda got a little nervous. Sex with Romie was initially painful. She loved the closeness but felt like it was a chore. Her aim was to please him, but rarely did she get any pleasure. So, she planned to lay it on George, hoping to fulfill his every fantasy.

As they got to the room, Veda set her luggage on the bed and opened it. She pulled out her black see-through nighty then looked at George.

"Would you like to see me in this?"

Aroused by the thought, he knew she wouldn't be in it long. He wanted her flesh against his. George put the suitcase on the floor, grabbed Veda as they both fell to the bed. They kissed passionately then he ripped her clothes off, kissing her breasts and rubbing between her legs.

Feeling his mouth on her body, Veda experienced unexpected sensations. She found herself getting wet and ready for him to enter. When he finally did, it was like nothing she ever felt before.

Veda relaxes on a summer day at Elysian Park, joyful about her new marriage

The family moved to Louvre Street in Pacoima on August 12, 1952. Despite a few delays with construction, the house was finally theirs. George and Pete unloaded furniture while Veda and Lita unpacked boxes.

"Are you sure you'll be okay staying alone at the old house in Los Angeles?" Veda asked.

"I'll be fine. What about you? Now that you're married, still gonna work?"

"Of course, I will never be dependent on anyone. I'm doing good at my job. There is never a dull moment. Plus, I'm the highest-ranking woman in the department."

"What about the kids? You have a long drive from here to Newton."

"Boppie and Tipy will have to step up. All it will take is organization and planning to make this work."

"Doesn't George go back to Korea?"

"He's going to Germany. He'll be gone for a year, but it will be fine."

"You don't seem bothered that he'll be gone that long. You're taking on a lot with this."

"I have a brand-new house and security for my children. What more can I ask for? I will also get to visit him. Imagine that? Me in Germany!"

Pacoima had changed significantly since their first visit two years ago. Families now occupied all houses in the Joe Louis tract as well as San Fern Manor, with the majority Negro and a few Mexican Americans. Most of the homes were two-parent households with a military veteran as the patriarch. Across the street were Mr. and Mrs. Brown, who had children, as did most families. Next door was the Robinsons, who had a daughter Betty, Tipy's age, which was a big plus. All the neighbors were friendly, making the town a pleasant place to live.

Landscaping the property, which consisted mostly of rocks and dirt, became George's major project before returning to duty. He completed both the front and back yard to make it the most excellent-looking place on the block. Boppie eagerly helped, and George gave him tips on keeping the yard nice while he was away.

"Boppie, you're a young man now and part of every man's responsibility is taking care of their home. That includes the lawn. While I'm gone, I'm counting on you to keep it cut and keep it green."

"When do you leave, George? I like it when you're here."

"Soon, but I'll be back before you know it. In the meantime, what do you say we convert the garage into a spiffy kid's hangout where you guys can play music?"

"Cool!"

"We can get a record player and I have an old couch to put in there."

George wasn't happy about leaving. He waited a long time to have a family and enjoyed being a dad. More than that, he loved his beautiful new wife. However, before he knew it, Uncle Sam was calling.

"I'm gonna miss you more than words can say. This past month has been the best time of my life and that's all because of you," George confessed.

"For me too sweety and we still have so much exploring to do with each other."

"I'm looking forward to continuing our exploration, but I'll tell you this, our honeymoon night will be forever engraved in my mind."

The two embraced and George tenderly kiss her neck and rubbed her breast.

"George, you're starting something you can't finish."

Suddenly a honking horn broke up the moment.

"Damn the taxi's here. Never enough time. Call you as soon as I can. Love you!"

"Love you too, George."

The honeymoon was officially over as she bid him farewell, disappointed he would miss Labor Day dinner. Now Veda would be back on her own, something of which she was very familiar.

With the family coming over for the holiday and school starting Tuesday, many details had to be aligned. Tipy was beginning junior high, and Boppie, ninth grade, both would now have added responsibility. Veda needed to plan meals for the week and depend on Tipy to put dinner in the oven. Boppie had to water the grass every day. Both would be responsible for doing their homework before Veda got home.

When Labor Day arrived, the entire family came over to see the new house, eat barbeque, and have a good time. Esma and Uncle Bubs were proud to see how well things were going, but disappointed George was not there. The cousins Veda grew up with, Don and Junior, also came, which thrilled her. The family laughed and played their usual board games, so the day was complete. After everyone left, she turned off all the lights, checked on the kids then went to bed.

It was around 1 am Veda awoke in a sweat. The nightmare images were getting worse. She saw that 16-year-old girl and her baby with their heads bashed in, the colorless torso of Elizabeth Short with the intestines laying under the buttocks, and the dead man's open eyes from the cigarette truck heist. There was blood everywhere, and those pictures permeated her mind. After abruptly awakening, her heart was frantically beating. She looked for George then remembered he was gone. Only his extra uniform, hanging from a hook, reassured her of his existence. She wanted to cry but could not because she was Veda and could handle it, or so she thought.

Needing something to take away the edge, she walked to the kitchen, poured herself a glass of grapefruit juice, and added some Vodka. Sitting at the dining room table, the visions from her nightmare still lingered to the smallest detail. It was the only time Veda wished her memory would fail. After taking another sip, she lit up a cigarette while staring at the darkness outside the window. Suddenly she was startled, feeling a presence behind her. Her heart raced once again with fear. She quickly turned and looked to find Tipy standing there, then exhaled.

"What are you doing up?" Veda asked, snapping out of the nightmarish trance that consumed her.

"I couldn't sleep. What are you doing?"

"I just had to get your lunches made for school," Veda lied.

"I wish you could drive us."

"Me too, but I can't. Betty from next door said she'll walk with you. She's new to the school too, so you won't be alone. I already talked to her mother. I put notes on the fridge, and you're responsible for putting dinner in the oven."

"I know. You told me already," Tipy said. "Veda, can we call George dad?"

"No. You call him George just like you call me Veda."

"Okay. When I have kids, they are gonna call me Mommy."

Veda froze for a moment, not knowing what to think. Looking into Tipy's eyes, she questioned what the norm for her always was. It never crossed her mind to be called anything but Veda.

"That's your choice, sweetie. Now, go back to bed."

"Goodnight," Tipy said and headed back to her room.

Sitting at the table, finishing her drink and cigarette, Veda hoped for a few hours of sleep before work. She felt a good buzz, and her eyes were getting heavy, so she headed back to bed and dozed off.

With no freeways, the commute to Newton, on South Central Ave., was an hour and a half. Veda left at 5 am for the drive.

When she arrived at the station, her tray overflowed with work, and Coppage was hustling around the room.

"Veda, I need the Gilmore file. It's not in the cabinet," Coppage said in an unsettling tone.

"Broady has it. What do you need in it?" Veda asked.

"I need the mother's address."

"382 31st Street."

"What's the mother's name?"

"Charmain Gilmore."

Coppage looked at Veda and calmed down from his anxiety. Veda wrote it down for him, knowing he would forget before getting back to his office. He took the note and smiled at her.

"Thank you, Veda," he said, still amazed at her memory. "You're a life-saver. We got major problems with this case."

"Yes, I know. I'm hearing there may also be a Miranda rights issue."

"What? Not that too? Dammit Pinkerton!" he said walking off.

Veda shuffled through her papers, trying to organize her workload, and noticed an arrest report with the name Jimmy Tristan. Curious, she walked to the jail area, wondering if it could be the same Jimmy from grammar school. She began looking in the tall enclosure, which contained dark spooky cells with only cots and urinals, then proceeded walking cell to cell.

The first one had a Negro man sitting on the bed, looking depressed. A dark-haired scraggly man occupied the next one. She almost walked on but stopped when she saw his unique hairline direction, which had one small section growing opposite of the rest. It was Jimmy.

The arrest report said the charge was for assault. Veda just glared at him. He looked up and noticed her standing there, then stood up and walked to the door.

"What are you doing here?" he said.

"Jimmy Tristan," she replied, not surprised to see him behind bars. "I work here."

"Can you help me out? I didn't do nothing."

"If you didn't do anything, you have nothing to worry about. You don't need my help."

Tom Bradley came up behind her as she was walking away. "You know him?"

"We went to grammar school together. I whooped his butt for bullying my brother. Guess he never learned his lesson," Veda said. "I just had to see this."

"Wait. What? You whooped his butt?"

"Almost twice," Veda said casually.

"Impressive. Anyway, I was looking for you. The Gilmore case has caused a public outcry. So, we're having a special community relations meeting tomorrow. I need to know if you're available—Pinkerton completely messed up."

"I know. Coppage is pretty upset. Of course, I'll be there."

"Thanks, Veda. You're the heart and soul of our department."

"Yeah, yeah."

As Veda walked back towards her desk, she noticed a tall officer waiting at the door. This man was bronzed-skinned with a mustache and perfect teeth. He smiled as Veda walked past him to her desk.

"Good morning Mrs. Craig. I'm James Herndon," he said.

"Good morning, Officer Herndon. It's Mrs. James now."

Realizing she needed to check on her new nameplate, Veda picked up the old plaque and placed it in her drawer.

"Trying to bury that forever, huh?" he said jokingly.

"Life has to go on."

As Veda sat down at her desk and looked up at him.

"My Officer Herndon. Do you mind if I ask how tall you are?"

"6'5"

"Hmmm," Veda said softly with a smile. "How can I help you? Oh, wait. Don't tell me. You're new and need a patrol partner?"

"Yes, I do."

"Well, welcome to Newton. Let me see who's working on your shift."

Veda looked through her binder to see where to assign him. The system LAPD used still frustrated her.

"That's pathetic. I have a single-car white officer and now a single Negro and can't put them together."

"Is it still like that at all LA precincts?"

"This is the only station that even hires Negros. Things have been like this since I got here."

"You seem like you're doing rather good. You're in the office with white detectives, which is impressive. I saw your story in the newspaper," he added.

"Oh, you did?" Veda said, surprised.

"Yes, ma'am."

"Ma'am? I'm not that old now."

"Oh, I didn't mean any disrespect. You're beautiful."

"In that case, you can call me ma'am," Veda said with a slight laugh. "I'll figure this out afterward. You still have some paperwork to fill out anyway. First, you need to get to roll call. Come on, I'll show you the way."

James watched as Veda walked away, thinking her gorgeous as they headed down the hall.

"It's right through those doors," Veda said, pointing towards the room.

"Thank you...ma'am," he said, smiling as he departed.

After arriving back at her desk, Veda looked at the mounds of paperwork in her tray. It was going to be a long day; actually, it already was.

She began making progress when the phone rang with a call for Coppage, which she always screened. The detective's unit only had three phone lines, so she placed it on hold and dialed his extension. Veda waited for Coppage to answer, continuing to type, and putting the reports in her completed tray. She looked up, and Coppage was standing at her desk.

"Veda, I need you to take some crime scene photos," he said.

Doing this would further back up her workload, something she did not need today, making her instantly regret wasting time on Jimmy.

"Okay. Can I take the new officer with me? He doesn't have a partner yet," Veda replied.

"Yes, that's fine. Have him drive you in a patrol car."

"What's the crime?"

"Some boys found a skull buried when they were digging a hole. It's at 757 East 21st Street."

"You have a call on line one, Charmaine Gilmore," Veda said.

Grateful it was a skull and not a bloody scene, Veda felt she could better handle that after her night of bad dreams. As she stood up, the phone rang, and it was San Fernando Junior High saying Tipy forgot her lunch. Veda asked them to give her money, and she would pay it back, thinking Tipy needed a lecture about responsibility.

"I'm sorry, Mrs. James, we don't do that," the school clerk said. "It's the parent's responsibility to make sure their children have lunch or money each and every day. Can you bring her lunch?"

Veda thought to herself, this can't be happening.

"I work for the Los Angeles Police Department all the way in the city."

"Well, can she have your permission to walk home for lunch?"

"It's a thirty-minute walk. Can you just give her the money, and I'll pay it back tomorrow, PLEASE?"

"I guess we'll make this a one-time exception, but you must not let this happen again," the clerk scolded.

"Thank you so much," Veda said, thinking how chaotic the day had started.

Veda got up to look for officer Herndon so they could leave. After finding him, they grabbed a squad car from the yard and began to pull out when Pinkerton suddenly approached them. Herndon, unfamiliar with his reputation, was in the driver's seat.

"This is a white squad car," Pinkerton said.

"We promise to bring it back without a scratch," Herndon replied, smiling.

"Oh, you think you're funny, rookie."

"Coppage is looking for you, Pinkerton," Veda said. "The Gilmore case has blown up, so I suggest you get to his office. Let's go, officer Herndon."

After pulling out of the station, Herndon turned right on Central Ave.

"What's up with that guy?"

"He's someone to watch out for if you know what I mean. There are a few whites here that are not 'color friendly,' as I call them. Just try to steer clear," Veda explained.

It was a scorching September day with no clouds in the sky as they drove towards 21st St.

"So, tell me, are you married or have any children?" Veda probed.

"No, neither."

"A handsome man like you?"

"A handsome man like me? I like the sound of that," he said, laughing. "What does your husband do?"

"He's in the military."

"Army or Navy?"

"Army."

"I served in the Navy. Where is your husband stationed?"

"He's in Germany right now."

"Do you have any children?"

"I have two from my first marriage. My husband adopted them," she said. "We just got married recently."

"And he's already in Germany?"

"Yes."

"Do you have girls or boys?"

"One of each."

"Ah, that works out good. Do you live in Watts or Central?"

"Neither, we just moved to the San Fernando Valley."

"I thought the Valley was all white."

"No. There's a little corner in the northeast area called Pacoima. They built houses just for us and even named the tracts after boxer Joe Louis. Go figure that."

"Pacoima? Never heard of it."

"You have now, Officer Herndon," Veda said, laughing.

"Please, call me James," his deep voice vibrated.

Veda found it funny that her last name was now James and his first name James. As they pulled up to the address, a blonde, curly-haired lady in a checkered dress stood in the front yard. The house sat by a vast empty field with scattered fruit trees in the distance. Veda saw a few boys on the porch looking on as she approached the lady.

"Hi, are you Mrs. Keith?" Veda asked as she reached out to shake hands. The lady did not extend hers, so Veda pulled back.

"Where's the skull?" Veda asked sternly.

She pointed to a hole in the field with freshly dug-up dirt surrounded by two shovels. Veda took hold of the camera around her neck, smiled at the lady, and headed towards it. Herndon pulled out his notepad just as two additional squad cars arrived.

"Can you tell me what happened?"

The lady watched the white officers get out of their car.

"I'll talk to them," she said rudely.

Pinkerton and another detective walked up. Herndon could see where this was heading and put his notepad back in his pocket.

"What's the story here?" Pinkerton asked.

"My boy and his friends were playing treasure hunt and burying stuff when they found what looks like a skull and some bones," the lady said.

When Veda got to the hole, she could see the skull, which had a long crack on the front side about a quarter-inch deep. There was also a rusted horseshoe. She snapped shots of them. There was another digging area containing thigh bones, so Veda walked around it and got several angles. Pinkerton walked over after taking the statement.

"This has been here quite a while," he said.

"What are you doing here? Coppage was waiting for you."

"This is my case. Anything in your memory files come to mind?"

"Why? You need me to solve this case for you too?" Veda retorted as she walked away.

Herndon followed her as Pinkerton stood there with an irritated look on his face.

Veda was quiet on the ride back to the station.

"Are you okay?" James asked. "You seem a little shaken."

"Naw, I'm a tough cookie."

"Everyone has their breaking point. I know I'm new, but I sense something. Do you take pictures often?"

"You sense something? What do you sense?" Veda said, feeling agitated. "Would you say that if I was a man?"

"No, I didn't mean, I mean, I'm just saying..."

"Stop, Officer Herndon, quit while you're ahead."

"I just meant you were getting all the good angles on your photos," he said, trying to disguise his comments.

"How about we both keep our thoughts to ourselves?"

Veda got back to the station and finished all her work. She called home to check on Tipy, who said the school gave her fifteen cents for lunch. It was one of those days, and Veda looked forward to a good night's sleep. On the way home, she stopped at the store to replenish her Vodka. That skull was creepier than she thought. It was a person who never received a funeral, whose family never got closure, and whose name may never be known. Maybe James Herndon was right, and the skull had shaken her, but that secret Veda would keep to herself. Yes, she needed a drink.

Lita sits on the porch at Veda's old home on 35th St in 1952

Boppie takes one last spin on his bike in Los Angeles, before moving to Pacoima, California in 1952

In 1952, Tipy poses in the driveway of their new home on Louvre St. in Pacoima.

Veda commuted from Pacoima to Newton for the next six years, driving down San Fernando Road, rarely asking for time off. An integral part of the station's operation, she handled the paperwork for every major case, earning the division and Commander Coppage numerous accolades. In the detectives' station photo, she was at the top of the chart, right under the commander, and the only woman.

However, her personal life was another story. Except for holidays, George was seldom home. He sent her gifts all the time, but she longed for his presence more than anything. Furthermore, her trips overseas never materialized, which was a tremendous disappointment. Worse yet, her nightmares intensified, as did her method of coping.

Despite the internal trauma, she relished her children. Excited that Tipy was graduating this year from San Fernando High, Class of 58, she gave her a credit card with a $50.00 monthly limit. Her goal was to teach Tipy responsibility with money. Veda was able to get her kids nice things, including their prom attire and senior pictures. She could afford most items and spared no expense.

Boppie had graduated in 1956 but was slowly figuring out what he wanted to do. He enrolled in city college but dropped out, of which Veda disapproved. She gave him a choice of working or attending college to continue living at home. However, he spent a lot of time playing cards and hanging out with his best friend, Frenchy, who was going steady with Tipy.

Pacoima had grown immensely during their short time living there. Negros had migrated in large numbers from Los Angeles and southern states, creating a unique American demographic, with Mexicans, Japanese, and Caucasians also residing in the town.

Arriving home from work one day, Veda pulled into the driveway. While getting out, she heard a familiar voice from the sidewalk. It was Ritchie from around the corner. He was a charismatic 16-year-old Mexican boy that seemed to have a crush on Tipy. His family lived in the predominately Negro section of Pacoima.

"Hi, Ritchie. How are you?" Veda asked.

"Hi, Mrs. James. I was wondering if Tipy was home. I have a song I want her to hear," he said.

A little on the chubby side, with full cheeks and an infectious smile, Ritchie carried his guitar everywhere. He loved singing and playing the blues for his neighborhood friends. However, when he wanted feedback on something new, he came to Tipy.

"She should be," Veda said. "I'll check for you. You can wait in the garage if you want."

Veda went inside and found Tipy reading a book.

"Hi, sweetie. How was your day?"

"It was alright."

"Ritchie's outside. He wants you to hear a song."

Tipy jumped up excitedly and picked up the phone. "Betty, hi. Come over, Ritchie's here. Hurry."

Tipy hung up and headed outside to meet Betty, her best friend. When they got to the garage, she was surprised to see Boppie, Frenchy, and their friend Ron Love huddled around Ritchie as he rhythmically strummed his guitar. He was jamming some Little Richard music, and they were loving it. Tipy felt a little put-out that he was entertaining the guys instead of her because she loved Ritchie's attention when he sang. But his guitar was so powerful and voice riveting, it stopped her dead in her tracks.

Ritchie looked over at Tipy and Betty then transitioned to another song about a girl, asking where she could be. The heartfelt emotions of Ritchie's words mesmerized them, but they believed his affections were misguided.

"Betty, why is he singing about snooty-ass Donna?" Tipy whispered.

"I don't know. That stuck-up white girl from San Fernando ain't never gonna give a Pacoima boy no action," Betty whispered back.

"But I love this song."

"Me too."

Inching over to Frenchy, Tipy gently took his hand. She felt lucky to have the cutest guy in the neighborhood with medium-brown skin, stunning hazel eyes, and a cool, hip personality. Lots of girls liked Frenchy but Tipy landed him and was proud.

As Ritchie finished the song, a young dark-skinned girl appeared at the garage motioning for Boppie, who left to join her.

"Hey Ritchie, drop some more blues," Ron Love shouted out.

With a big smile, Ritchie began enthusiastically strumming a guitar solo. Then, he broke into his own version of Little Richard's song "Lucille."

"Hey, Betty, what chu know bout that dance floor."

"I ain't scared. Let's hit it!"

Tipy and Frenchy joined in, and they all joyfully danced with spins, twists, and an air of teenage bliss never to be duplicated.

After becoming a big star, Ritchie was killed with Buddy Holly and the Big Bopper in a plane crash on February 3, 1959. All the neighborhood kids were devastated, especially Tipy. He was her only friend to become famous, and the whole town of Pacoima mourned. Newspapers called it *'The Day Music Died.'*

Glad things quieted down from the garage, Veda sat on the couch relaxing after dinner, smoking a cigarette, while drinking her usual Vodka and grapefruit juice. She began flipping through the *Valley Green Sheet* and saw something that caught her eye. The city planned to build a new police station in Pacoima, which they expected to open in 1961. How great would that be, working closer to home? It was still a couple of years off, but she needed to put a plan in motion to make that happen.

With her mind focused on the possibilities, Boppie solemnly walked into the living room.

"Veda, I have something to tell you."

"What is it, sweetie?"

"Joyce Sorrell is pregnant."

"What does that have to do with you?"

"She said it's mine."

"The Sorrell girls are young. How old is she?"

"Fifteen."

Troubled by the magnitude of what he said, Veda took a long deep breath.

"Boppie. You're twenty years old."

"I know, I messed up. But I love her."

"Boppie! Do you understand the Sorrells could prosecute you? I need to speak with them. Do they know?"

"Joyce is telling them tonight."

Unsympathetically, Veda asserted, "You will have to man up and deal with it, Boppie. You made this choice."

Howard and Marilyn Sorrell were upset to learn their daughter was pregnant. But like Veda, they realized there was not much anyone could do. The Sorrells lived around the corner on Weidner St and owned the first house with a built-in pool, which attracted all the neighborhood kids. Marilyn was a socialite kappa community activist, and Howard was in construction. With no sons and three daughters, Howard often mentored the young men in the area, which somewhat enabled this situation.

That night Howard called Veda and set up a weekend meeting, which went cordial. Abortions were illegal, so the best option was marriage, and the Sorrells would give their permission since Joyce was under 18. However, she would not graduate High School or go to a prom, which made them sad.

―――――――

Boppie got hired at General Motors, and the two married in November. The plan was to stay with Veda until getting on their feet. Tipy enjoyed Joyce being around, and they got along surprisingly well. She loved feeling the baby kick and even bought Joyce a book on childbirth, charging it to her credit card. On December 18, Joyce walked into Tipy's room, holding her stomach.

"Tipy, I'm feeling something, kinda like cramps."

"Let's get the book," Tipy excitedly replied.

"That's right, can you grab it from my room?" Joyce said as she sat down.

Tipy brought back the book and intensely flipped through the pages. Although eighteen, she had never been around a pregnant person before.

"The book says contractions are when the muscles of your uterus contract. If your contraction feels like this, you are in labor. One, contractions are 5 to 10 minutes apart and get stronger while coming in shorter intervals. Two, they are so strong you can't walk."

"Does it say anything else? How do we time it?"

"I'll get Veda's watch. Hold on."

Tipy went to Veda's room and grabbed one of her old ones.

"Let me know when you feel it again."

"It's hurting right now!"

Tipy looked at the watch, and it was 1:24.

"Tell me when it stops hurting."

Before the hand moved, Joyce said it was over.

"Well, that was less than a minute."

"It felt longer than a minute," Joyce snapped.

"Now it also says you feel pain in your lower back or abdomen. Where's your pain?"

"My back."

Nearly fifteen minutes passed, as Tipy and Joyce anxiously waited on pins and needles. It seemed like nothing else was going to happen, so Tipy hesitantly went to the restroom. Then suddenly, Joyce yelled out.

"It hurts again, Tipy!"

"It figures. Hold on, I'll be right there," Tipy yelled from the bathroom.

Walking back while pulling up her pants, she surmised that the contractions were about 20 minutes apart.

"Should we tell someone? Boppie and Veda won't be home for hours."

"Let me call my mom's house," Joyce said with a weak voice.

There was nobody home at the Sorrells, and the two didn't know what to do. So, Tipy decided to call Veda, the one person with all the answers.

"Newton Division, Veda speaking."

"Hi Veda"

"Hi, baby. What's going on?"

"I think Joyce is in labor. I timed it, and her contractions are 20 minutes apart."

"Are Howard or Marilyn home?"

"No, Joyce tried them already."

"Okay, just relax and stay calm. Labor can last a long time. I'll be there as soon as I can."

"Okay."

Tipy and Joyce waited, keeping track of the contractions. An hour had gone by, and they were still seventeen minutes apart. They tried entertaining themselves with comic books, but the pains were coming increasingly quicker.

It was 3 pm, and the contractions were only fifteen minutes apart now. Tipy worried about what would happen if the baby came before anyone arrived. What would she do?

Joyce was getting tired. She could only helplessly moan and grab her back as the pain radiated relentlessly. While beginning to break a sweat, she tried to remain calm. The cycles continued growing shorter, now only twelve minutes apart.

By 4 pm Joyce was dripping in sweat, and Tipy was frantic. What was taking Veda so long.? Right then, they heard an engine through the window and sighed with relief. Joyce had her bag packed, and they left for the hospital. She was going to deliver in North Hollywood, the only hospital in the Valley that accepted Negro births. Veda's first grandchild Tony Howard James was born December 18, 1958.

———————

Amidst Boppie's drama, Frenchie had proposed to Tipy after graduation. Following protocol, he asked for Veda's blessing first, and her reply was, "If you get a job."

Frenchy, a brilliant young man, who had graduated high school early, quickly began working at Los Angeles County Hospital. They scheduled the wedding for January 10, 1959, on Tipy's birthday. However, to make sure she was pure, Veda took her to the gynecologist to confirm her virginity. After the examination, Veda was ecstatic and spared no expense for the wedding.

Tipy left the planning to Veda, who booked the ceremony at First Methodist Church down the street on Glenoaks Blvd. She meticulously planned everything, picking out Tipy's dress and invitations with attention to detail. The photographer, cake, and flowers were all first-class. Tipy agreed with everything, giving minimal input.

Veda's only sadness was George's mission overseas would not allow him home for this significant event. He could not walk Tipy down the aisle, which put Veda in a dilemma. She thought about calling Romie but heard from Shalana his alcohol problem had gotten worse. He and Alicia now had five children, just what he always wanted. That idea was ruled out, so the logical person was her brother Pete. Yes, Uncle Pete would have to give Tipy away.

The wedding was full of laughs, food, family, and fun. The reception, held at Veda's house, included detectives and staff from Newton. Veda seemed to have more fun than Tipy, who disappeared to her room reading comic books with Frenchy while the family drank and danced.

Frenchy's grandfather Tom helped them buy a house a block away, on Montford Street. Boppie and Joyce moved in with them, and they split the $71.00 mortgage. Veda now had two married children, a grandson, and the house all to herself. At only 40, her time was now.

Veda stands proudly by Tipy on her wedding day, January 10, 1959, at First Methodist Church.

NEWTON ST.
1954

DETECTIVES
1954

LT. R.R. COPPAGE-CMMDR.

LT. A.A. M°BRIDE   LT. C.S. MITCHELL   VEDA JAMES STENO   SGT. H.B. DIMON DESK   LT. A.G. HERTEL

SGT. C.R. ROTHERT   SGT. W.E. TOOLE   SGT. R. BUCHANAN   SGT. E.D. HARMON   ORIN C. COX   SGT. E.M. KUDLAC   SGT. D.J. FURLONG   VIRGIL S. DeWITT

FRED R. BANKS   W™ C. BROADY   SGT. R.E. STEVENS   SGT. R.D. DAUGHTRY   LL. HIGHTOWER   SGT. F.J. COLLINS   SGT. R. HUTSON   OSIE R. WALTON

SGT. T.R. FIMPLE   SGT. W.E. GULDNER   M.J. BLANCH   M.L. M°MURTRY   SGT. R.W. WISE   W™ E. KEOGH   W.R. PINKSTON   C.R. STIDHAM

K.I. HARRIS   THOMAS J. DAVIS   SGT. H.W. SEAGER   J.H. WILLIAMS   E.H. BARR   GUY SALERNO   GEORGE HALL   R.E. SINDELAR

J.P. JOHNSON   D.F. CUNNINGHAM   SGT. K.A. BROWN   SGT. G.C. ROGERS   SGT. J.L. SCHOTT   SGT. R.P. BAUER

PHOTOS BY PHIL DUNHAM

Many thoughts cascaded through Veda's mind while sitting alone in her quiet house. Still disheartened that George didn't make it home for Tipy's wedding, she began feeling not married at all. He was always gone, and in her mind, life was passing right before her eyes. Yet, when she looked in the mirror, her appearance was intact. Her figure was the same, and she had no wrinkles, but the youth she once cherished was undeniably slipping away.

Despite loving her new grandson Tony, Veda never anticipated being a grandmother. Then Tipy announced she was pregnant and Joyce again as well. With things changing so fast, Veda had to quickly reprocess this phase of her life.

After learning that Foothill Station in Pacoima would be opening next year, Veda decided to give Coppage her transfer request. Although she knew he would have trouble without her, working closer to home was the priority. When she entered his office, he was shuffling through a pile of messy papers on the desk.

"Commander, I have something for you."

"Do you know where the board markers are?" Coppage responded, not really paying attention.

"Yes, I do."

"Where are they?"

"In your top right drawer."

Coppage opened the drawer and saw the marker.

"Thanks, Veda. I don't know what I'd do without you."

"Well, you're gonna have to figure that out. I'm requesting a transfer to Foothill Division. I'm sorry, commander, but I need to be closer to home."

"What?" he said, stunned. Coppage stopped what he was doing and looked at Veda.

"Here it is," she said, handing him the paperwork.

Coppage briefly looked, then set it down.

"Hmm, I'll take care of it," he said, returning to his task.

Veda went back to her desk, unable to read the commander's reaction. Part of her felt bad knowing how valuable she was, but at the same time, she deserved this. Detectives got promotions all the time and moved on. The department promoted Tom Bradley to lieutenant in 1958, but that was the highest he could go due to the LAPD policy. Because of that, he was already making plans to leave after graduating from law school and passing the bar exam. Veda realized she would never make detective nor go any higher in the department, so this move made sense.

After work, some detectives were going out to have a drink. Veda never joined them in the past because she had to get home. But, when Fred Ware, one of the detectives, invited her, she accepted. After all, she was one of them. Both Negros and whites from Newton frequented a bar on Jefferson Blvd, which was pretty much a hole in the wall. However, it gave the men time to unwind before heading home.

When Veda walked in, a plume of smoke hovered above the bar counter, pool tables, and booths. There was one long table in the center of the room where most of the force congregated. Veda went and found a seat. She kind of hoped Tom would come but knew he was not the type to hang out like that, being very faithful to his wife and family. But the other guys were flirting with waitresses and acting like they were not married. A few were shooting pool and drinking.

Veda knew how to play and was surprisingly good. She learned from her uncle Bubs at a young age, who had a table at his house, and they played whenever she visited. After having her first drink, Veda challenged the winner, a young sergeant named Hudson. He had a cocky demeanor but was always a pleasure to converse with.

"Ms. Veda, who knew you had pool playing skills? I would have never guessed," Hudson said.

"You've seen me at our picnics. I can hang with the best of them."

"I don't want to win too bad because you type up our reviews. So, I'll go easy on you," he boasted.

"That, my friend, is the wrong thing to do."

Veda picked out her pool stick carefully, not wanting one too heavy but needing it long. She grabbed the chalk and put it on the tip of her stick. Looking at Hudson's face, she noticed an air of confidence, all too familiar with people not knowing her.

"Are we playing eight-ball?" she asked.

"Uh, yeah," Hudson replied.

"Rack 'em up," Veda said as she pulled out a penny. "Heads or tails?"

"Heads."

Veda flipped the coin, and it was tails.

"My break."

Since Veda was short, shooting pool presented unique challenges, but still, she held her own. The other detectives started crowding around to watch. Veda noticed Pinkerton among them and wondered if he was going to say something out of line. She hit the cue ball and got a substantial break, sending a solid color in the right corner pocket as the others scattered around the table. The rules allowed her to shoot again. She saw an easy shot with the red three-ball.

"Three ball in the side pocket," Veda said.

She hit it right in with a soft tap.

Glancing at Hudson to read his expression, he recognized she knew how to play. However, her next shot was difficult, and she missed.

"Ten in the corner," Hudson barked out before sending a striped, blue ball hurling across the table into the pocket.

"That's how the boy's do it," he said.

His next shot was an easy one, but overly confident, he missed. Veda immediately saw her next opportunity. She marched around the table then decided the other side would be more accessible.

"Wow, Veda, you look like a pro," Detective Ware said.

She made the next two shots, a yellow and a blue, and the crowd began to cheer for her and talk smack to Hudson. After she missed, Hudson sunk two balls. Veda walked around the table and whispered in his ear.

"I thought you were going easy on me."

"Yeah, right," he said under his breath while studying his next shot.

"Thirteen in the side pocket."

Hudson hit the striped, orange ball directly in the pocket but scratched the white cue ball. Veda nailed the remaining solid balls with ease and only needed one last shot to win.

"Eight-ball side pocket," Veda said as she pointed with the stick. She carefully studied her shot as she remembered what Uncle Bubs had told her. 'Sometimes you need to hit it hard in the center and sometimes angle it and give it a soft touch.' This shot was a hard hit in the center, aiming to ricochet from the other end to the side pocket. She placed her stick across the table to get her spot; then boom, she hit it. The eight-ball headed towards the side pocket perfectly as it rolled in. It looked as though the cue ball might cost her the game for a second, but it rattled around the hole before victoriously bouncing back out.

"That's how the girls do it," she said, dropping her stick on the table.

The detectives cheered and bought Veda a drink.

Needing to use the toilet, she headed to the ladies room. There were two stalls, a sink, and a mirror. After finishing, she began washing her hands when someone came in. It was Pinkerton standing there with a lustful, ridiculous look in his eye. Veda recognized that goofy, crazy-eyed look that men got when they lusted after women.

"Veda, you look mighty sexy with that pool stick," he said, slurring.

"Don't mess with me, Pinkerton. In case you didn't know, this is the ladies restroom."

"Oh, it is?" Pinkerton slurred as he moved closer to Veda. "I know you like me. Can I get a kiss?"

"You're drunk and making a big mistake. I'm not the one!" Veda snapped.

"I like em rough. Something about a chocolate ass turns me on."

Pinkerton proceeded to grab Veda's breast, then tried to kiss her. They scuffled for a minute, then Veda forcefully pushed him back and stuck her foot around his ankle to trip him, an old tactic that always worked for her. Pinkerton fell with a loud thump as his head hit the wall, then slid down to the ground. Veda stepped over his leg to exit the room and looked back at him.

"So, you hate us and still try this? You're dumber than I thought you were."

Veda said her goodbyes to the detectives and gathered her things. Leave it to Pinkerton to ruin her good time. She wondered how his wife would react if she knew what had just happened. In general, Veda would have no problem reporting this incident but instinctively knew how things could get twisted. She had seen it too many times. If she went directly to Coppage, it could get ugly and possibly backfire. Men don't seem to care if females get harassed. Pinkerton would have to get fired without anyone knowing her involvement. He was not going to get away with this, she would make certain of that!

The next day at work, Veda avoided Pinkerton like the plague. Knowing his cowardness, she figured he would stay away too. Mounds of reports had piled up, so her plan was to knock them out first thing. Veda noticed James heading towards her. She appreciated they remained friends despite their rocky start. He always seemed to understand her, and she was amazed a good-looking man like him was still single.

"Good morning Mrs. James?"

"Top of the morning to you, Mr. Herndon," she answered playfully.

"I need to talk to you. Can we meet after work? It's kind of private."

"Ooh, sounds serious. Where?"

"The Dunbar?"

"Dunbar it is."

Veda finished up her reports as planned. The office air seemed thick, something she never felt before, even when things were chaotic. Foothill couldn't come fast enough after last night. Her thoughts kept drifting to all the highly suspect reports she typed for Pinkerton and processed without question. Now she was second-guessing herself. Perhaps exposing his blatant falsifications would have been the best way to go, but that would have presented problems of its own.

Dinner at the Dunbar sounded terrific. Veda wished she had the opportunity to dress a little fancier, but she always looked professional at work. She was wearing a black cardigan sweater with white trim and a peach-colored skirt. Her pearl earrings topped off her outfit enough to be appropriate for a place like the Dunbar. She thought of the fantastic time she had when George took her there a decade before.

She and James followed each other in their cars and walked in together, James wearing his uniform and Veda on his arm. Entering, they looked up at the white balconies on the top floor. The lobby had beautifully tiled walls made of flagstone as they headed toward the lounge.

"Did you by any chance make reservations?" Veda asked. Usually, she took care of stuff like that but not this time.

"Of course," James replied.

They were promptly seated, and Veda instantly recognized Lena Horne a few tables over. Knowing this would be a lovely evening, she smiled at the singer who was checking out James' police uniform.

"This is so nice," Veda said, remembering the fantastic ambiance of the place. "I can't believe I've only been here once, and that was at least ten years ago. George brought me here."

"I love this place. So much history," James said, glancing around the room. "It's the higher echelon of our folks coming here that I like."

"I saw Lena looking at you."

"Ha-ha," James laughed. "So, what made you get into law enforcement?"

"When I was very young, a white police officer helped my mother find us and get to California. That had an impact on me. His name was Officer Thomas Williams, and he encouraged me at an early age. I was a little girl with big dreams."

"And look at you now. I'd love to meet that Officer Williams and buy him a drink."

"He's a detective now and works downtown. You might just get that opportunity one day."

"So, how do you like living in the Valley? Seems kind of far from everything."

"I have a plan for that, but I love it there," Veda explained. "I just wish my husband wasn't gone so much."

"That must be hard on you."

"Sometimes, but the job keeps me busy. What about you? How did you get into law enforcement?"

"After my discharge from the Navy, law enforcement was the perfect field."

Veda thought it was nice to enjoy dinner with a handsome man. Her frustration with George had continued to grow and left her feeling cheated.

"So, you've got me here James, what did you want to talk about?"

"It's about Pinkerton."

Alarm bells raced through Veda's mind. Did James know something? How could he?

"What about Pinkerton?" she asked nervously.

"Did you hear about the young Negro that died while in custody?"

"Yes, what about it?" Veda sighed, relieved this was work-related.

"Well, Pinkerton did the arrest. Observers say he beat him for no reason. One person said they heard a gunshot, but he's afraid to come forward. How can they keep getting away with stuff like that? The poor kid is dead," James explained.

"I didn't read anything about a gunshot, but I wouldn't put anything past him. Pinkerton is a piece of shit."

"The reason I brought you here was that I was thinking about taking this to Coppage. What do you think about that?"

"I can't tell you what to do, but when it comes to color, it's a dead-end road with all of them. They all look out for each other. The man that inspired me to be a detective once said never to see color. What I learned, however, is most everybody else does, particularly LAPD."

"So, what are you saying, I should let it go?"

"They won't do anything, James. You just have to make things right in your own way and create your own justice. This department has a pecking order, and we're on the bottom."

James smiled, trying to ponder Veda's words, but found himself distracted. His attraction to her was difficult to resist as he gazed into her eyes from across the table.

"Is it okay for friends to dance when they are hanging out?" James asked.

"It's always okay to dance," Veda replied with charm.

The two got on the dance floor and finished out the evening. At that moment, Veda felt alive again. Being with a handsome man in a culturally attractive place was terrific. When they left and walked to the car, their connection was strong.

"So, what are you gonna do about Pinkerton?" Veda asked.

"I'm not sure. I'm going to give it some thought."

"James, just remember what I said about making your own justice. My mother is a God-fearing woman who doesn't have a dishonest bone in her body. Her justice as a housekeeper came listening to the things the other ladies did to their bosses. She listened to them talk about spitting in their beverages, chewing up the cooked chicken, and then putting it back in the pot when making soup. They did small things, but it made them feel better, and no one knew but them. Just keep that in mind."

"I hope I get to meet your mother one day."

"Well, she could never execute any of those things, but she liked listening to the stories. I hope you can meet her someday, too," Veda said as she opened her car door.

"Remember, small victories can do wonders. Don't see color. Just be smart."

Veda thought about it for a moment and decided she didn't want James to do anything too soon.

"James, give me a few days on this Pinkerton thing. Don't do anything just yet," she asked.

Veda drove off in her yellow 1959 Chevy impala with her mind leaving James and drifting to Pinkerton. His callous killing of a Black teenager did not surprise her, but it may have presented an opportunity. James said the witness heard a gunshot, but the internal report never mentioned that. The preliminary coroner's memo listed head trauma from ground impact as the cause of death. She needed the official statement to confirm, and that would be the first thing on her list tomorrow.

When Veda arrived at work, she immediately called Mr. Williams to see about his connections at the county coroner's office. Although Veda often received coroner reports, requesting them was rare, and she did not want to raise any suspicions or questions.

"Hi Mr. Williams, this is Veda."

"Hey Veda, how are you?"

"I'm good. I was wondering if you could do me a favor? I need to get a copy of a coroner's report, incognito. I'm doing some independent detective work."

"I might be able to do that," Williams said. "Who's the unlucky victim?

"Jeffrey Mills."

"I'll see what I can do."

Veda proceeded with her daily work. She knew Coppage would ask her to type a press release for City News Service, and like clockwork, he called her to his office.

"We need to get something out about the Mills death. I also need you to check with Yorty's gal Mrs. Bryant about his schedule."

"I'm still waiting on Pinkerton's revised report. Do you want me to release it as is?"

"No. I only want this story in once, if possible. So why is Pinkerton revising it?"

"You know how unorganized he is. It's probably something he left out. I'll follow up," Veda said. "And I'll give Ethyl a call to get the mayor's schedule."

"Stay on Pinkerton," Coppage barked.

Veda needed to handle this master plan with kid gloves, and she knew it. Everything depended on the coroner's report. She hoped Mr. Williams came through quickly, and it revealed what she suspected. Pinkerton would have a hard time explaining himself. As she walked back to her desk, she could see him in the room amongst all the tables and file cabinets. The key would be keeping her cool, especially after the other night. His breath was disgusting at the club, and it made her nauseous just thinking about it. She walked past her desk and over to him.

"Coppage needs the Mills report ASAP. Did you rewrite it?"

"I'll have it in 30 minutes," he said.

"Fine," Veda said as she walked off.

It was nearly noon, and she still didn't have Pinkerton's report, but she didn't have the coroner's report yet either. Then, a short, dark-haired man in a suit walked into the office and looked at Veda.

"I'm here for Veda James," he said.

"That's me."

"You? I spoke to you on the phone, but I didn't realize you were…."

"A woman." Veda interrupted sarcastically. "I know. I have a deep voice."

"I'm sorry, I have something for you," he continued as he pulled out a large manilla envelope and handed it to her.

"Thank you," she said with a professional smile.

Veda sat down and opened the envelope carefully, hoping this was it. The document was labeled Coroner's Report, and Veda scanned for the cause of death, which read a gunshot wound. Pinkerton walked up just then with his paper, dropped it on Veda's desk, and said nothing. She put down the report, looked at Pinkerton walking away, then picked up his memo and read what he wrote.

In an attempt to arrest the suspect, he resisted. We struggled, and he fell, hitting his head on the ground. He was unresponsive, so I attempted CPR, but he never regained consciousness.

"He's making himself to be a hero," Veda thought. The bullet shot was to the back of Mills' head, supposedly where he fell. There was no exit wound, which is why he thinks he can get away with it. She began typing it up as fast as she could, irritated that sleazy Pinkerton wanted to seem like a good guy.

Placing the police report in the file folder, Veda slipped the coroner's report right under it. Coppage better read them both, she thought, or this wouldn't work. He was usually thorough because he got questioned all the time and liked being well informed. People lying infuriated him. Veda went into the commander's office, but he was on the phone, so she put the file folder on his desk. With that mission completed, it was time for lunch.

Veda was gone for about an hour and did not know what to expect when she returned. Everything seemed normal as she sat at her desk and noticed Pinkerton was still chatting it up with the staff like he didn't have a care in the world.

Fearing her efforts might not result in justice, Veda disappointedly proceeded with the reports on her desk. Then

Coppage's door suddenly opened, and Chief of Police William Parker walked out. Veda was stunned, not recalling a scheduled meeting between the two. As Parker passed her desk, she casually smiled and said hello. Next, she glanced at Coppage's schedule, and nothing was logged with the chief.

Coppage then loudly called Pinkerton into his office. He motioned for Veda to come in as well.

While entering the room, her heart was beating fast. She brought her notepad, as usual, and Pinkerton arrived with an oddly proud look on his face expecting to get praised.

"Pinkerton, tell me exactly what happened with the Mills death," Coppage requested.

"Well, it's like I put in the report, Mills matched the description of a suspect in a robbery. He was stopped and questioned by Officer Kelly initially. I was investigating another case when I heard this one on the radio, so I went to see if I could help. Dispatch said there were no patrol cars in the vicinity. So, I took over for Kelly since he's a rookie, and the perp started resisting. We struggled, and he hit the ground pretty hard and lost consciousness. I tried to help him but nothing. That's about it."

"So, you think he died from his head hitting the ground?" Coppage asked.

"Absolutely," Pinkerton answered with confidence.

"I'm gonna ask you one more time. Are you sure?"

"Yes, sir, I'm sure."

Coppage pulled out the coroner's report and plopped it in front of Pinkerton.

"I work with all my officers and detectives and try to protect them. But not when they lie to me. You should know that

Pinkerton! Nobody makes a fool out of me. Turn in your badge and gun. I'm relieving you of duty!"

"What?" Pinkerton shouted in disbelief.

"You are out of here. It was a shot in the head, not a fall. You're officially suspended, pending a full investigation."

Pinkerton sat there stunned as he placed his badge and gun on the desk. He could not understand how Coppage knew. There was no bullet hole exit. The entry looked like it could be from the fall. His hands were visibly shaking as he stood up to leave. Veda kept her head down, continuing to write while showing no emotion as Pinkerton left.

"Did you read the coroner's report?" Coppage asked Veda.

"Of course, I did."

"Why didn't you say something?"

"Because I knew you would see it. That's why you're the commander," she said as she stood up.

"Can you take this Mills file back with you and order some duplicate photos for Pinkerton's records and process his paperwork too?"

"Sure."

"One more thing," he said. "Did you help him with that Burke serial murder case a long time ago? You know, the first murder case he solved?"

"Help him? I handed it to him on a silver platter with a pretty red bow."

"I knew it," Coppage said.

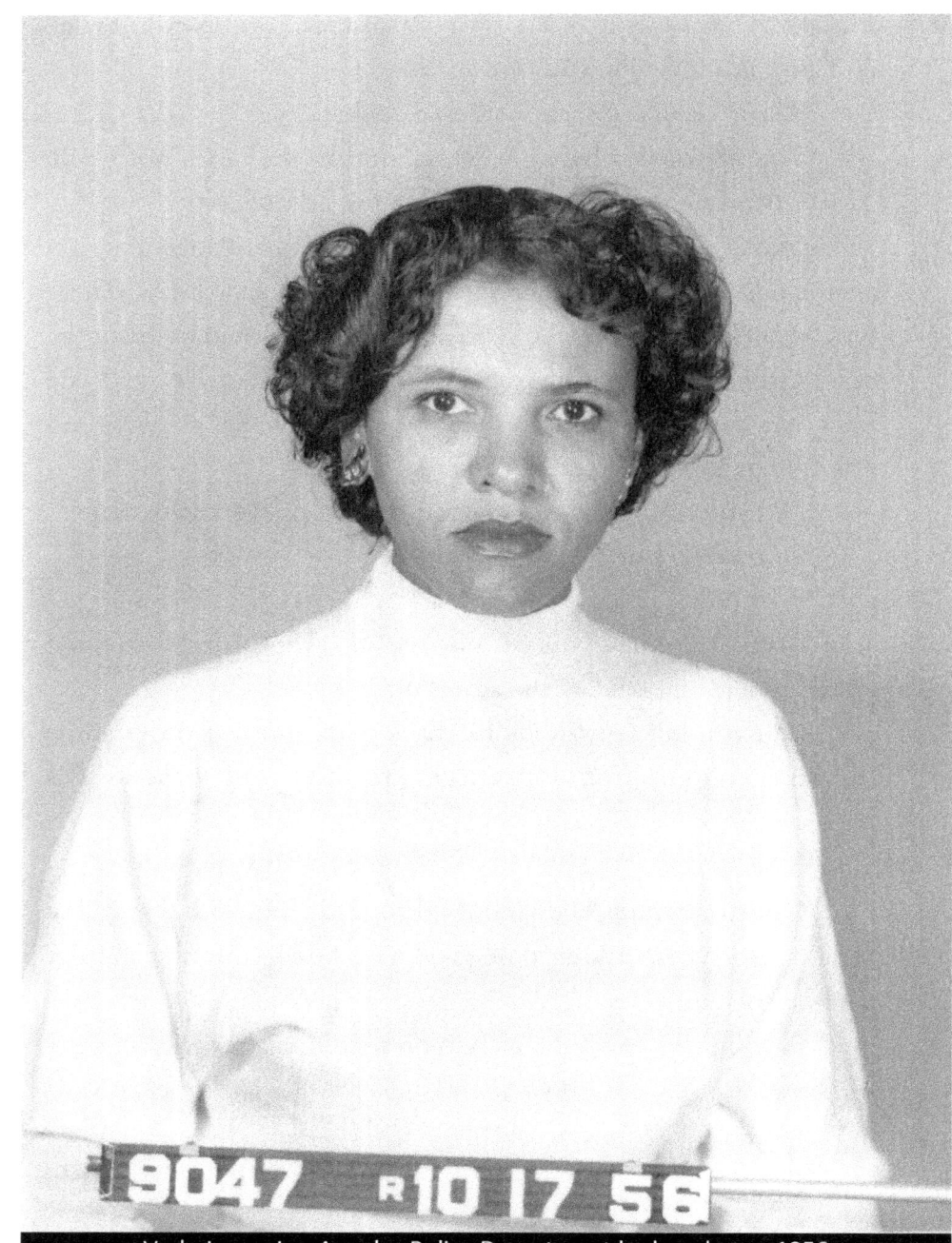

Veda James Los Angeles Police Department badge photo - 1956

The family continued to grow, and in November 1960, Tipy gave Veda her first granddaughter, Crystal. Over a 2 ½ year period, she gained a staggering total of five grandchildren. Feeling the strongest bonds with Tony and Crystal, she would babysit them individually. However, she cherished privacy, and her desire for order, neatness, and discipline didn't always work well with tots. But when the grandkids visited, Veda never had to yell because she had a look and tone that no kid and most adults ever challenged.

In September of 1961, Foothill Division in Pacoima opened, and Veda had yet to hear news about her transfer. Coppage always skirted the issue when she brought it up. Longing for a fresh start, her frustration began to mount, so she walked into his office looking for answers.

"Good morning, commander."

"Morning, Veda."

"You know, I hear Foothill is open now and I still haven't heard about my transfer. I need to know what's going on."

Coppage, who was shuffling through some papers, appeared disinterested in her concern, continued shuffling through his papers, and tried to downplay what she was saying.

"Oh, yeah?" he said, not bothering to look up. "I'll have to check and get back to you on that."

"You have told me that before. It's been months. What's the problem?"

"I've been busy and haven't heard back from them," Coppage snapped.

"This is ridiculous!"

"I'll get on it for you. Okay."

Still frustrated, Veda got up and went back to her desk. Something was not right. Why was he acting this way? Things just weren't adding up. So, she patiently waited until Coppage left for the day then decided to poke around. What a mess, she thought, scanning his office. It would be difficult finding anything, but she had to look. Grabbing the office keys, Veda went straight to his desk. 'How does he work in this?' she mumbled. Then, she opened the drawers and began sorting through them.

A few items caught her eye in the top drawer, including some gross crime scene photos with nude women, newspaper articles, a memo from the police chief, along with his markers. The middle one contained personal stuff with bills, home repair receipts, scissors, and tape. The bottom had stacks of papers, so Veda pulled them out. As she began flipping through, there it was—her transfer request, buried, unsigned, and not sent to Foothill. He never turned it in. She put everything back except her request and left. 'That snake,' she thought.

While sitting at her desk, James walked over.

"You look like you saw a ghost."

"I put in for my transfer, and Coppage never turned it in."

"You're too valuable here," James stated.

"That shouldn't stop me from getting what I want. I've served Newton for sixteen years and given my heart and soul to this department. The things I've done."

"You mean like getting Pinkerton fired? That was you, right?"

"You remember what I told you? We must do what we must do. It was best for the department."

"I'm afraid to ask how you pulled it off."

"As my mother once said. 'The truth will set you free.' What's done in the dark will come to light. I just made sure all the info was there. That's all."

"Well, thank you for the good advice to hold off," James said. "So, Coppage never turned in your transfer request?".

"No, he didn't. I've been making this drive all these years. Why would he do this to me?"

"Because you make his job easier. You run this place, Veda. I don't think Coppage could function without you, and he knows that."

"He's not gonna get away with it."

Veda picked up the phone and dialed Tom Bradley's number. They hadn't spoken in quite a while, but he could help her.

"Hello Tom, this is Veda. How are you?" she said, glad he answered the phone.

Tom was happy to hear from her. He had a lot of respect for Veda and was proud of how well she was doing in the department.

"Hi Veda, I'm fine, thank you. How are you?" he asked.

"I'm doing good. I know it's been a while, but I've been meaning to congratulate you on making lieutenant. How do you like downtown LA with upper brass?"

"Same but different. I miss the guys at Newton," he expressed. "And one particular lady."

"I've missed you too. Tom, I need a favor."

"What's that?"

"Can you get me a meeting with Chief Parker? I've met him before, but this needs to be formal."

"You know I'll do anything for you, Veda. Do you mind if I ask what it's about?"

"I can't explain it right now, but can you set it up? It's important."

"Of course, I'll talk to Parker's secretary tomorrow, and I'll let you know," he said. "Is everything alright?"

"Yes, it's something personal. You can be in on the meeting if you want."

"Okay. I will let you know."

"Thank you, Tom," she replied and hung up.

James looked at her with the utmost respect.

"You are like a dog with a bone when you get determined. The Pinkerton thing was impressive, but Coppage? You're going for the big guns now," James said admirably.

"I'm not going for him, per se. I'm doing what's right. Pinkerton killed that young boy and lied about it. Now Coppage is lying to me. I've been working with him too long for this bull, and I told him years ago to treat me with respect. Hiding my transfer request is not respect."

James felt empathy for Veda's dilemma. He wished he could do something to help but knew Veda was more than capable of handling this.

"Can I take you out for dinner? It's quitting time."

"Sure!" she replied, ready to get away from Newton.

Veda and James ended up at the Pantry Café off 9th and Figueroa. It wasn't the ambiance James wanted, but the food was good, and both needed to eat. They were able to get T-bone steaks, mashed potatoes, and green beans at this 24-hour establishment.

"What is your strategy with Chief Parker?"

"I'm just so fed up. The things I ignore, the butts I keep out of trouble, and the incompetence I deal with daily from white officers with half my intelligence. It's exhausting. I have no choice but to ask him to intervene."

"Well, everyone knows you're the best detective on the force."

"But I'm not a detective. I'm a clerk stenographer, a 'Girl Friday' that they want to box in doing the work of a detective."

"But you have more pull than the commander himself. Look at you now going to the chief of police."

"But they find a way to let me know I'm different. Not just being a Negro but being a woman too."

"I hate to tell you, but Negro men have it worse. We still can't even arrest white people. Imagine that, trying to do your job with your hands caught in the department's cuffs. Watching a criminal get away because you're Negro and they're white?

"Yeah, I know that is hard," she sympathized. "Years ago, Tom handcuffed a white perp suspected of stealing a cigarette truck. They said nothing about that, but his partner Hutch shot and killed the other suspect. They were the only Negro officers assigned guns, and all hell broke loose."

"What happened?"

"Hutch feared for his life from the white officers. After going on administrative leave, he left LAPD altogether and was never heard from again. I fear something bad happened to him, but we may never know. Needless to say, Negros were not issued firearms after that. So, believe me, I know how tough it is for Negro men. I have seen it firsthand."

"How did Tom escape harm?"

"Tom had a way with people. Everyone liked him, and they were so focused on the dead white man and Hutch; they never discussed his role. After the incident, LAPD transferred him to juvenile, where he was amazing with the youth."

"You have seen a lot."

"Yes, I have. But it's time for me to leave Newton. My kids are married and gone. I have grandchildren and need a break from that long drive."

"What makes you think Foothill will be any different?"

"I don't know how different it will be, but it's closer to home, and I love my job, James."

"So, where's your husband at these days?" he curiously asked.

"He's stationed somewhere. Actually, I don't know. I lost track."

No longer able to hide his feelings for Veda, James realized his illicit desire to cross the line. Her flawless face, pug nose, and captivating eyes were hypnotic. The sound of her voice alone triggered titillating sensations down his spine, but it was the smell of her Estee Lauder perfume he could not resist.

"I have to confess something," James said. "I've had a crush on you since I started with the police force. You are the most amazing woman I've ever known."

"I'm flattered," Veda replied. "Compliments get you everywhere."

He playfully laughed and pondered her inviting response with every bodily sense on heightened alert.

James' vibe was infectious, and Veda's thoughts drifted to a forbidden place. His deep voice mesmerized her while his kind ways and thoughtfulness warmed her soul. Witnessing so much death and deception on the force made her fear getting somewhat numb. Moreover, her nightmares were getting worse — a secret kept all to herself. She longed for someone to hold her, if only for one night. Should she, or shouldn't she? The thought was a little exciting.

"James, I know I'm married," Veda said. "But I don't feel like I am. I feel alone because George is never home. Sometimes I just want someone to hold me."

"Just say the word."

"Can you follow me home?"

Both made their way to Veda's house and her bedroom. She slowly undressed, not knowing if this was the right thing to do but felt safe in James' arms. His bronze skin, deep voice, and kindness were so attractive. When they kissed, Veda flashed back to the way she felt at the Dunbar Hotel with him. It just felt right. She was impressed when he undressed as his package was well endowed. He held her gently while running his hands through her thin hair.

"You're beautiful, Veda. I wish we would have met a long..."

"Shhhhhh," she said as she passionately kissed him. From there, they made love until the late hours, then fell asleep. When morning arrived, they both woke up at the same time.

"Why do I feel like a teenager?" James asked.

"You don't know how much I needed that. I wish I didn't have to go to work today. Otherwise, I would cook you some breakfast."

"You mean you can cook too?"

"I can bring home the bacon, fry it up in a pan, and never, never let you forget you're a man," Veda sang as they both fell out laughing.

When Veda got to the station, her phone was ringing. It was Tom Bradley, and he said to come downtown at noon and meet with Parker. She was ecstatic and told Coppage she had some errands to run.

The downtown Los Angeles Police Administration Building was an eight-story complex called the "Glass House." When Veda arrived, she went directly to Parker's office and was greeted by his secretary. Tom and Chief Parker were waiting in the office.

"How are things going for you, Mrs. James? You have been doing a wonderful job there at Newton. You've been there, what, 16 years?" Parker said.

"Yes, sir. Things are going well for me. My kids are grown, married, and out of the house, so I can't complain."

"What can I do for you, Mrs. James?"

"I'm having a problem transferring to Foothill."

"Did you submit your request for the transfer?"

Veda pulled out the form she got from Coppage's office and handed it to Parker.

"Months ago."

"What did they tell you?"

"That's the problem. Nothing. If you look at the request, it's not signed, nor has it been submitted."

Parker looked at the form and immediately picked up the phone and dialed.

"This is Chief Parker. Can you give me Captain Richards, please?"

"Hey Richards, how's it going?" he said...... "Good, okay, listen, did you ever get a transfer request for Veda James?"

Veda intently listened as Parker questioned the captain at Foothill.

"Hum. Well, have you ever heard of her?...... She was in the newspaper as the first woman to work at any LAPD detective unit...... Well, she lives there in Pacoima and wants to transfer to Foothill......Trust me, you won't regret it...... When can she start?...... I'll have my secretary send you a memo."

Parker hung up and looked at Veda with a smile.

"Done," he said. "So, you gave this request to Coppage?"

"Yes, I did. I was cleaning up his desk and saw he never submitted it. I've been asking about it for months."

"I'll handle this. I know how valuable you are to him. He'll be lost without you, but that's no excuse. You have been with us too long."

"I don't know how to thank you."

"Just keep up the good work."

Parker then turned to Bradley. "What's going on with you, lieutenant? I hear you're leaving us."

"Well, I just finished law school and have new ambitions. I plan to practice law, maybe run for city council. You know Veda helped me with some of my projects," Bradley said.

"Yeah, the Community Relations Department was useful. I'm sorry you are leaving. You've been a credit to the badge and all Negro officers. Good luck with everything."

"Thank you, Chief."

"I appreciate all your help Chief Parker," Veda said, feeling relieved her drive to Newton was finally coming to an end.

Tom gave her a hug of congratulations as they went their separate ways. Not surprised at Coppage's antics, he was pleased to help Veda, his long-time friend, before moving on.

Chief William Parker was the longest-serving L.A. Chief of Police, serving 39 years on the force. He died of a heart attack in 1966, and the Glass House complex headquarters was renamed the Parker Center after him.

FAREWELL PARTY honors Mrs. Veda James, Newton Division stenographer, whose transfer to Valley Division becomes effective this month. Co-workers at Newton sponsored the affair in recognition of Mrs. James 16 years of service in the department.

Veda was ecstatic about her first day at Foothill Station on Monday morning. After selecting a long-sleeved white cardigan sweater and black skirt to wear, with matching clip-on earrings, only her hair remained. She parted it to the side and heavily coated her curls with hairspray to make them hold. It was bothersome how much thinner her hair had become and the extra effort now required to make it look nice. Fortunately, she found a Remington hot roller set with small enough rollers. The curlers heated up on round metal stilts and had circular clips to hold them in place. Therefore, her morning routine required getting up early before work, putting the curlers on, then waiting for them to cool off.

However, the good news was she only had a ten-minute drive. She passed a Hostess Bakery Shop built of cobblestone on her way, and the aroma of fresh bread permeated the entire area. It instantly made her think of eating. Arriving, Veda wasn't sure where to park and chose Osborne Street in front of the station. She knew there probably was a back entrance but would ask after getting settled.

Foothill was a brand-new building, unlike the antiquated Newton facility, built in the 1930s. Newton had an old-fashioned appearance like many buildings in those days but never seemed outdated until seeing Foothill.

Walking through the front door, the newly opened station had modern furniture, including electric typewriters, and a freshly painted smell that further heightened her excitement. Veda saw a white lady with a blonde beehive hairdo and dark roots. The woman was dressed plainly and wore glasses that seemed a little big for her face. Veda approached feeling a little overdressed but always wanted to look her best at work, believing it commanded more respect.

"Hi there. I'm looking for Captain Richards."

"Are you Veda James?" the woman said, smiling while looking Veda over.

"Yes, I am," Veda replied, reaching her hand out to shake.

"Oh my God! I didn't know. I mean, I've heard so much about you. You're a legend. I'm sorry. I just didn't realize you were colored."

"What color am I?"

"I didn't mean anything by that. I'm just happy to meet you. My name is Midge. Come with me," she excitedly said as she escorted Veda to the captain's office.

Entering the detective's area, they approached the counter, which had a desk about 6 feet away and a large glass window looking into the room. Veda walked behind the counter, and Captain Richards' office was to the left. It was in stark contrast to Coppage. Everything was organized and neat, trays nicely stacked, with a holder for files so they couldn't get lost. I can work with this, Veda thought.

"Captain, this is Veda James," said Midge with an enthusiastic tone to her voice.

"Come in," Richards said.

"I'll show you around when you're finished here," Midge stated before closing the door.

Richards looked relatively young for a captain. He had combed-back brown hair, a clean-shaven face, and bags under his eyes that told Veda he was a hard worker. He was wearing a black long-sleeved uniform shirt and black tie with his badge shining loudly on his left side. His name plaque sat prominently on the desk with a few framed certificates on the wall.

"Well, I have heard a lot about you, Mrs. James."

"Thanks. I'm excited about joining the team."

"That's great. But, first, I want to get something straight right off the bat," Richards began. "Don't ever skip rank on me with the Chief of Police like you did, Coppage."

"Captain, Coppage left me no other choice," Veda said in her defense. "However, I have always and still do respect the chain of command."

They both sat there looking at each other with an awkward moment of silence.

"Let me also say this so we can be clear," Veda added. "There's nothing about LAPD that I don't know. The good, the bad, the ugly, and the truth. I'm here to work. And if you allow me, I'll turn Foothill into one of the best-run stations in the city."

"That's what I heard. You're the finest in the business. I'm sure that's why Coppage didn't want to let you go."

"Thank you, sir. There are only two things I require. One is that you treat me professionally, and two, don't label me. When you put people in a box, you don't get their true essence. View me as Veda James and nothing else."

Richards looked at her and smiled. Veda managed in minutes to gain his respect, and he instantly saw why she was successful. Despite knowing there were still challenges ahead, he felt she would fit in very well.

"Why do I already feel like you're the commander and I'm your assistant?"

Veda laughed, and he joined in. The vibe between them was good, a bit different than Coppage. Feeling very comfortable, she was ready for work and knew she would be running this place in no time.

"Where's my desk?"

Richards pointed to a desk in front, which was very well-stocked. The first thing she noticed was her electric typewriter. Veda couldn't help but think how things have changed from her first desk in 1945, buried in a closet, to this modern setup with a state-of-the-art intercom system. She loved the enormous glass window in front of her. It was the size of a sliding door and looked into the detective's room, which would make it easy to find people when transferring calls. To her right was the walk-up counter. This layout was much better than Newton.

The months passed quickly, with Veda learning everyone's name, phone number, and personal details. She got along excellent with Midge and the detectives. There were a few other females that worked in different departments that Veda befriended as well. While sitting at her desk, she noticed a white woman in her thirties standing at the counter. She had two black eyes, a swollen lip, and bruises all over. Veda got up and walked over to help.

"My God. Are you okay?"

"No. I don't know what to do. My husband gets drunk and goes crazy. He keeps beating me," the lady said.

"Do you want to press charges?"

"I do, but nothing ever happens. He always gets released, then beats me more," the woman said, distraught with tears running down her bruised face.

"What's your name, sweetie?"

"Madison...Patty Madison."

"Mrs. Madison. Can I get you some medical help?" Veda asked, concerned about the swelling and lacerations.

"No, that would just make him madder. He doesn't like to pay doctors."

"Do you have anybody you can go stay with?" Veda queried.

"No, I don't."

Veda reached down, pulled out a form, and grabbed a pen.

"Let's fill this out and arrest your husband."

"I can't take this anymore. I just hate him so much," Mrs. Madison screamed as she placed her hands over her ears.

"All I can tell you is to press charges," Veda pleaded.

"I have before. It doesn't work."

"Let's try again."

Mrs. Madison looked at Veda with a blank stare.

"If you're not going to press charges, then I suggest you save your money and just leave," Veda implored.

"He says if I leave him, he will kill me. Where would I even go?"

"If you don't make a plan to do something about this, it's going to keep happening over and over again," Veda explained. "You can't just do nothing. My rule is always to have a plan B."

"I'm sorry to bother you," she said with tears streaming down her swollen cheeks and her head down. She turned around slowly with a look of defeat and left the station.

Veda felt terrible for the confused lady. She thought about Edna, who got tossed out with nothing, nowhere to go, and ended up at a police station. Mr. Williams was her savior. Veda wondered if she could have helped Mrs. Madison more, but what? This lady was scared and dependent on her husband. Veda knew better and was always prepared for anything.

"Dammit, Mrs. Madison should have filed that report," she thought.

Arriving home that day, she appreciated her place even more. Veda had expanded the house in the front by about 10 feet with black and white tiles on the floor. A chandelier-type light above her new dining room table was added, along with a sparkling stucco ceiling. She had the wall knocked out from Boppie's old room and turned it into a den where she could relax and listen to the radio or read. There was a black and white television console in the living room she never used, so Boppie came over and moved it to the den.

Veda loved Cowboy and Indian shows such as "The Lone Ranger" and "Gunsmoke." She always listened to the Lone Ranger radio program and was thrilled about it becoming a television series. Home was comfortable until it was time for bed. Then her torture began after she fell asleep. Last night the skull with a cracked fracture terrorized her slumber. Once again, she woke up drenched, in a cold sweat, all alone.

Foothill Division was refreshing in many ways. Veda was included in a newspaper photo with Detective Bernie Garcia as she typed a burglary report on the theft of $4800 of dental gold and platinum bridges. Veda was no stranger to being in the paper but was excited to get her name out in the Pacoima community.

Captain Richards was easy to work with, and the detectives were becoming dependent on her.

It was a typical day when a baby donkey arrived at the precinct. The officers found it hilarious as it broke up the monotony of the day. When Veda came in to see what all the hoopla was about, she laughed wholeheartedly. Chief of Detectives, Tad Brown, who rarely smiled, found the situation funny as well.

"Veda, take a look at this. This ass just showed up," Brown said.

"Looks like Bowles," Bernie Garcia said, joking.

Bowles, the only Black detective at Foothill, was a large framed middle-aged man with a well-manicured mustache and kind face. He pushed for more people of color to join the force, and it pleased him that Veda was on board. In addition, Bowles gardened and mowed lawns for extra money on his off days, so he knew the community well.

"Looks like Brown has some competition. I always thought HE was the biggest jackass around," Bowles said as everyone got a good laugh.

"What on earth are we gonna do with it?" asked Veda.

"We were gonna see if you want to take him home, Veda?" Bowles said.

"Not me." Veda chuckled.

"So, who do we call on this one, Veda?" Brown asked.

"I guess I can try Animal Control or Humane Society," Veda said as she petted the donkey.

Veda went back to her desk and made the necessary phone calls. Captain Richards came to her desk and waited for her to get off the phone.

"Mornin Veda, did I see that you took crime scene pics at Newton?" he asked.

"Why yes, but…"

"Great. I need you. We have a crime scene that needs pics. Bowles is heading over there. Can you catch a ride with him? The camera is on my desk, and there's an extra roll of film in the supply cabinet."

"Okay," Veda reluctantly replied.

Crime scene photos were one thing she hoped to avoid, but the usual guy was on vacation. So, she left the station with Bowles and headed out. When they walked inside the house, a woman whose hair and clothes were covered in blood was in handcuffs. Veda instantly recognized her face. It was Mrs. Madison, who looked horrible and completely detached as she stared at Veda.

"This was my plan B," Mrs. Madison said to Veda as officers escorted her out of the house.

Veda could only imagine what happened and knew it was terrible based on all the blood. Her heart pounded as she stepped cautiously into the bedroom. Bowles froze, looking at the bed as drops of blood trickled slowly from the ceiling fan. Veda gasped as she saw a bloody sheet wrapped around a lifeless body. The face, savagely beaten, was unrecognizable. The sheet appeared to be sewed to the mattress, so the victim could not move.

"Do you know the suspect?" Bowles asked.

"She came in the station all beat up but didn't want to press charges."

Snapping photos, they placed numbers on the evidence, notably a bat covered in dark-red blood. Veda couldn't help but feel emotional, no matter how hard she tried. Not wanting to let detectives see her shed a tear, she painstakingly hid her face behind the camera. She took shots of the mutilated victim, bed, blood-spattered fan, and bat. It was incredibly gruesome, and Veda knew this would not go well for Mrs. Madison.

On their way back to the station, neither she nor Bowles spoke. That grisly scene would be hard to forget. The Madison home seemed so well kept, decorated in lovely earth tones with curtains that looked custom made. Everything looked normal from the outside, but behind closed doors was another story. This incident was a tragedy on so many levels.

As soon as Veda arrived at the station, she went to Mrs. Madison's cell, despite being against protocol.

"This was not a good plan B," Veda said.

"He came home drunk and was just punching me," Mrs. Madison said solemnly. "I just had it. When he passed out, I sewed and sewed. He never woke up. Once I started swinging, the bat kept striking him. I only wanted to teach him a lesson, but I just couldn't stop."

"They want to charge you with premeditated murder. You need to call a lawyer."

"I don't have one. Whatever happens, happens."

Veda sympathetically patted her back, wishing it was a hug, as Bowles and Garcia watched through the glass window. The moment revealed a vulnerable, sensitive side of Veda they had never experienced before.

She returned to her desk emotionally drained as Captain Richards walked over.

"Are you okay?"

"I'm fine. Here's the film. I put the camera back in your office. I'll have the report typed up as soon as possible."

"Sure you're okay?" Richards asked again.

"Yes. I'm fine."

When Veda got home that night, she poured herself a drink right away. That scene was horrifying, with brains smashed on the pillow and his eyeball dislodged from the socket. His murder was brutal, and he never had a chance. Wondering if he deserved this, she realized there were no winners in this situation, including herself.

Despite Mrs. Madison's abuse, Veda knew the system would make an example and throw the book at her. She hoped explaining the extenuating circumstances to the district attorney would help. That's the least she could do.

While sitting in her den, the phone rang, and it was James. He sensed instantly she wasn't okay by the way she answered. Since the day they met, he seemed to instinctively know when something was wrong as if he could read her soul.

"Are you okay?"

"I'm okay. Just had a tough day."

"I'm sorry, baby. Is there anything I can do?"

"No. It comes with the territory."

"When can I see you, Veda? I miss you."

"Why don't you come over tomorrow. I really need some company. Just call me before you leave."

"Alright, I can't wait. I have a surprise for you."

"I'll see you tomorrow," Veda said casually.

"You must surely be down. It isn't like you not reacting to a surprise," James said in a concerned tone.

"I'm pretty shaken, but I'll be okay. See you tomorrow."

"Good night, baby."

"Good night."

Despite feeling better after talking to James, Veda poured herself another drink. Sleep petrified her because of the nightmares, and today's murder scene was fresh in her mind. Even while awake, she saw Mr. Madison's disfigured face and could smell the body fluids that drenched the blankets and room. After her fourth drink, she was hammered and stumbled off to bed. Fortunately, she slept through the night.

Waking up the next morning, she realized it was a nightmare-free evening. Only a headache reminded her of how much she drank, but a few aspirins would solve that, and her Saturday could get started.

What to cook for James was Veda's first decision. She thought beef enchiladas would be tasty, which required a trip to Carrillo's in San Fernando for their homemade corn tortillas. A chubby Mexican lady worked behind the counter who hand patted the masa harina corn flour to perfection. She also made homemade flour tortillas and tamales. There was always a line on the weekends because folks brought their pots for menudo, which usually ran out by 1 pm. So, Veda got dressed and left for the taqueria. When she got there, the line was out the door. Carrillo's was a small storefront with a counter that had chicharrones (fried pork rinds) and salsa on display. She was always amazed at the diversity of the people, which included quite a few Caucasians, one or two Blacks, and the rest Mexican.

The workers at the counter were friendly, and Veda knew them by face but never learned the names. She ordered two dozen corn tortillas, a pint of fresh salsa, and a few tamales. She then stopped at Safeway on Glenoaks Blvd to get ground beef, cheese, and a bottle of Smirnoff Vodka before heading home.

After putting the groceries away, she made herself a drink and went outside to water the grass. All the houses on the block were well manicured and kept up. Most homes had children of various ages, and she enjoyed watching them play.

The Bridges across the street kept their house immaculate. Mr. Bridges was a flirt with all the ladies. He was a darker-skinned man who dressed in suits and drove a luxury car that he always kept clean. Mrs. Bridges was obsessed with catching him cheating and often piled the kids in her Volvo to find him. If found with someone, she would say, "See, see, I caught you!!" But she never left him or did anything about it, and he never changed his behavior.

After the Bridges kids were grown, she recruited the young Wilson boys down the street to ride with her and hunt him down. Jeff and Steve Wilson were her eyes as she continued her obsession with his cheating.

Still, she remained with her husband until passing away long before him. Veda tried to stay clear of that drama but was always friendly with both.

Down the street was the Millers, whose daughter Gwen was a big roller derby star for the Los Angeles Thunderbirds. Across from the Millers were the Jacksons, who lived next door to the Wilsons. All were hard-working middle-class families. Veda knew everyone on the block, and they knew her.

After watering the grass, Veda made a mental note to have Boppie cut it for her the next day. He still lived across Glenoaks Blvd on Montford Street with Tipy and Frenchy.

She began making her enchiladas, and after placing them in the oven, went to layout sexy lingerie in her room. Wanting to spice up the evening with James, she selected a see-through satin top with matching shorts. A bottle of champagne was placed on top for effect.

When the phone rang, she expected to hear James, but instead, it was Lita.

"Howdy doodie," Lita chirped in her usual happy demeanor.

"Hey, Lita. How are you?"

"I am fantastic. How are you doing, sis?"

"Oh, fair to middling."

"Frank and I wanted to invite you to dinner."

"So, you're done being newlyweds now?" Veda jabbed.

Lita had uncharacteristically slowed down hanging with the family after marrying a mysterious man named Frank McCrimmon. They recently bought a house together on Haas Avenue in Los Angeles, that anyone had yet to see.

"We're happy and we want you guys to come over and see our new house. Could you pick up Ednie and bring her with you?"

"I have plans today. Maybe next weekend."

"Awww. Okie dokie. I was gonna make lemon meringue pie too."

"Okay, rub it in."

"Alrighty. I'll talk to you soon."

While standing in the kitchen after taking the enchiladas out of the oven, Veda heard the front door close. She assumed it was Tipy or Boppie, who stopped by all the time but looked up, and to her surprise, it was George.

"Hey, sweetheart," he greeted her.

"What are you doing home?"

"What? You don't look happy to see me," George said with a frown.

Knowing this was a huge problem, Veda guardedly walked up and gave him a big hug. Disguising her disappointment in seeing him seemed impossible, no matter how hard she tried. Still, the need was dire to pretend everything was fine.

"Of course, I am. Don't be silly. I wish you would have called so that I could be ready."

George curiously looked at the tray of enchiladas and Spanish rice she had cooked.

"Smells good. Looks like you're ready for something."

"Oh. This is for Tipy and the kids." Veda lied.

"Lucky them," George said as he strolled through the kitchen.

Veda had extended the nook and put in a rectangular 6-foot bar-style counter with swivel stools, three on each side. She had a ceiling light above it, and that was where everyone ate, except for Thanksgiving and Christmas, when they used the formal dining room table. The kitchen wall phone had a long-coiled cord that allowed you to sit at the bar table and talk. As George walked back there, he passed by a trash can in the laundry room off to the left. He noticed vodka bottles in the garbage.

"You've been busy," he said.

Veda instantly knew what he was referring to as she sensed tension with his question.

"What?" she said.

"Liquor."

"Oh. Boppie and Tipy have been hanging out lately," Veda lied again.

Just then, the phone rang. Knowing it would be James, she couldn't grab it because George was standing next to the receiver.

"Hello," George said after picking up the phone. "Hello," he repeated, then hung up. "Hum, that was strange."

"Are you hungry?" Veda asked, acting like it was no big deal.

"No. I'm tired. I'm going to lay down for a minute."

"Are you sure you don't want some of my enchiladas?"

"I thought they were for Tipy."

"She'll survive. Sit down and try some."

"Nah, I'm going to the room."

George walked out of the kitchen. Veda knew this was going to be bad. She swiftly walked to the phone to call James and began dialing when George appeared back in the doorway. Veda instantly hung up the phone.

"Who were you calling?"

"Tipy. I wanted to tell her she can pick up the food."

George gave a perplexed look.

"I changed my mind. I want some enchiladas. Can you make me a plate?"

"Sure."

"I'm gonna go wash up."

Veda began making George's plate, hoping he would not go into the bedroom. Maybe she could get through this night after all.

"Who is this for Veda?" George yelled as he reappeared in the doorway. "I knew it. You're cheating on me. I can't believe you!!!"

George walked towards Veda, holding up her lingerie and bottle of champagne. Veda's expression never changed as she maintained her calm and tried to defuse this.

"Don't be silly. I was just feeling romantic."

"Romantic for who? I'm not a fool, Veda. First the phone call, then this? You're fucking some other man in our house while I'm making money for us. You're a whore! I never thought after Romie, you would ever cheat. Never. You know what it feels like, dammit, you know!" he screamed, with veins popping out the side of his head.

Veda felt a piercing sting on her cheek and saw stars as George slapped her.

"I could kill you," he exploded. "All I could think about was surprising you, and you happy to see me. All your letters made me miss you more, and all the time, you're hoeing around."

Just then, George snapped. He pulled his gun out and put it to Vedas' head. She could feel the metal on her temple as droplets hurled from his mouth when he yelled.

"I should put a bullet in your head right now," he said, clenching his teeth together.

"George! Put the gun down," she said calmly. "Put… The…Gun… Down… Now!" she firmly repeated as she twisted away from him.

 Looking at him she saw a hollowness in his crazed eyes. He did not look like the same man. There was a spooky dark difference in his entire facial structure that was almost satanic. She had to outthink him and somehow reach the rational side of his warped psyche. He's a career military man, so she opted to tap into that approach and go for broke. It was her only chance.

"Think of the headline. Senior sergeant convicted of murder. This is not how you want to go down, so put the goddamn gun down, George!"

He held the gun a bit higher and cocked the trigger.

"George this is how you protect and serve your country? This is how you want your mother to remember you? You will be a caged animal in jail for murder. Snap out of it."

Gradually George's face returned from its dark abyss, and he put the gun back in his pants. He glared at her intensely with sweat uncontrollably dripping down his face.

"Now leave!" Veda howled.

"This is my house too."

"Leave now, George."

He put his hand on his head and started erratically tapping it. It dawned on him she worked for LAPD and her obsession for justice. He stomped his right foot on the ground and hurled around at Veda.

"You gonna call your buddies like you did on Romie? You gonna have me locked up?"

"Not if you leave right now," Veda said, pointing at the door. "So, go! Go!"

George walked towards the door and turned around to Veda.

"Good thing I had my needs met without you overseas. I can do that here too. I don't need you, Veda!" George said as he picked up his bags from the floor.

She watched as he went outside the gate. Veda locked the door and deadbolt, then went straight to the kitchen phone.

"Hi, Midge. It's me. I need a squad car here right away. My husband just put a gun to my head. He's walking down my street right now."

Within minutes officers arrived and she gave a statement to Detective Bowles. George was apprehended moments later walking down the street.

Veda lit a cigarette. She was, in a way, relieved her twelve-year marriage was over. Afterward, she called James and explained what happened.

"Are you sure you don't want me to come over?" James asked.

"I'm sure. I'm just bothered by some of the things he called me."

"What did he say, baby?"

"Well, names you should never call a woman. I don't think of myself the way he described me. He implied I'm cold because I called the cops on Romie. He was afraid I would do it to him, and I did. I just have no patience for physical violence or abuse. We all have consequences for our actions. I've dealt with mine head-on since I can remember."

"What do you mean?"

"If I did something wrong or behaved badly, I accepted the consequences. So, I just think everyone should. Plus, every action has a reaction. When I was in the fourth grade, Edna got called weekly. I knew what I was doing would get me in trouble, and she made me pick my switch, and I got spanked. I dealt with it."

"He was hurt, Veda. You and I both know what happened," James said, comforting her. "George chose the military, and he chose it over you. You are a strong woman, but you're human too. I have never met anyone, ever, as strong as you."

"I love you, James, I really do. I realized that more today than ever. You understand me."

"We understand each other."

She hung up with James, feeling drained yet relieved. This has been the week from hell.

Veda pressed charges and George was initially hit with attempted murder but pled guilty to a lesser count of battery. This incident ended his 20-year military career and cost him his marriage.

Foothill detectives contemplating what to do with the donkey

Veda works at her Foothill Division desk in 1962 at Foothill. This modern facility was quite different than Newton station

Officer James Herndon in front of his Los Angeles home in 1961

Veda did not file for divorce right away. But, in retrospect, she realized George and her hadn't shared the same connection in years. The glam of having a husband overseas turned old, and even when they spoke, conversations were flat and superficial. She would tell stories from the station, and he would talk about the service, but their chemistry was gone. The distance was too much, and the loneliness even worse.

In the following months, things emerged that made Veda wonder if she ever knew George at all. Memories of Edna's warnings, all those years ago, rang loudly in her head. After getting dishonorably discharged, George shockingly began making obscene phone calls to neighborhood women.

Although she had experienced post-marital problems with Romie, nothing prepared her for George's deviant behavior. One of the victims he harassed was Frenchy's grandmother Minnie, who lived around the corner. A retired housekeeper, she was a light-skinned woman of color whose appearance resembled Granny on the hit television show "The Beverly Hillbillies." Minnie was incredibly kind with an extremely nervous personality. George would call, saying unimaginable vile things sending her into a panic. He was exposed when Frenchy visited one day and saw his grandmother in distress over a call. He took the phone and instantly recognized George's voice. After informing Veda, police arrested George and charged him with making obscene phone calls or telephone scatophilia, a class I misdemeanor. Subsequently, Veda officially filed for divorce, and the settlement allowed her to keep her Pacoima home.

Soon after, George disappeared for good. Veda later received a Christmas card from his mother saying he remarried after their divorce. 'Poor woman,' Veda thought. 'Too bad I couldn't warn her.'

On the weekends, James became a regular fixture at Veda's house. More than just lovers, they were best friends. Their relationship grew into a deep, profound bond, unlike her two husbands. She never imagined anyone could possess such pure, unadulterated insight into her bare essence. They were clearly soulmates.

On Sunday, August 5, 1962, James got off work and headed to Veda's as usual. It had been a long, bizarre day because Hollywood actress Marilyn Monroe had died, and crazy rumors circulated throughout the department. He loved sharing stories about Newton with Veda since they knew the same people, and this one would surely blow her away.

"Hey baby," James greeted her.

"Hi, sweetie. Guess what?" Veda said excitedly.

"What?"

"Marilyn Monroe died."

"How did you hear about that already?"

"It was on the news."

"Well, here's what you haven't heard, Mrs. know-it-all. This case has a whole lot of people talking. Big players are involved. It might reach all the way to the White House."

"Not a suicide? That's what the news is saying."

"Well, all I know is the secret service is involved, and the higher-ups are being very tight-lipped."

"You don't say? Be interesting to see what's circulating at Foothill tomorrow."

"Huh, you sure are a hard woman to scoop. Come over here into my arms and let me scoop you another way."

James gently picked Veda up like a ragdoll and gave her a big kiss. Then, he tenderly carried her to the bedroom while nibbling her ear.

On Monday, Tipy called Veda, saying she had something important to talk about regarding Frenchy and his job with the coroner's office. Since leaving the hospital, Frenchy, whose real name was Lionel Grandison, had become an LA County coroner's deputy. Mature and knowledgeable for his age, at 22-years-old he found himself in the center of Marilyn Monroe's death.

Tipy arrived at Veda's house uncharacteristically confused and looking for context from her mother.

"What's the problem, sweetie? You sounded worried."

"Frenchy came home last night with a book he was reading. He said it belonged to Marilyn Monroe."

"A book?" Veda asked.

"Well, it was a little red... I don't know... I guess diary."

"Frenchy came home with Marilyn Monroe's diary?"

"He talked about one of the deputies retrieving it from her house in Brentwood. It has some crazy stuff about Robert and Jack Kennedy."

"You saw this book, Tipy?"

"Yes! He was reading it to me. He said they assigned him the case, and protocols weren't being followed."

"Why was HE assigned the case? And why would he bring that diary home?"

"I have no idea. I didn't even understand the stuff he was reading. What is the Bay of Pigs?"

"Tipy, you realize this is serious stuff, right?"

"Yeah, it sounded like she was having affairs with both the Kennedys and wanted to expose it."

Veda recognized the implications of this immediately. She knew Tipy was unsophisticated and could not fully comprehend the significance of these people being the most prominent players in the country.

"You should be worried, sweetie. They're talking about the case at Foothill. It's major league. You need to tell him to leave that book alone. If they learn he has it, no telling what they'll do."

"Oh my God. It's that serious?"

"Tipy, he needs to pretend like he doesn't know anything. You know me, and I'm a finder of fact and always have been. But I don't want you to be a widow. People get killed over stuff like this."

"I'll tell him."

"I mean it, Tipy! This will be nothing but trouble for your family."

The diary was returned to the coroner's office and mysteriously disappeared shortly after. For Tipy and Frenchy's sake, Veda hoped it would end there. However, that was not the case. After being coerced into signing Marilyn Monroe's death certificate, Frenchy was set up for a blue-collar crime, forced to resign, and sentenced to jail.

Tipy took this embarrassing chain of events hard. No one believed somebody set him up except for her. She knew the pressure county officials had placed on him, but now that didn't matter. She had a different type of pressure — taking care of her family.

"Veda, I don't know what to do. Frenchy will be locked up for a year," Tipy solemnly confided after these events unfolded.

"Both Edna and me were faced with this exact situation. The women in our family don't have the luxury of being housewives."

"But that's what I always wanted."

Looking at Tipy so distraught, Veda wondered if she should have raised her tougher. Tipy was beautiful, graceful, funny, with a pleasant personality, and could converse with anyone. But she was not tough.

"Sweetie, it's sink or swim now. I told you all your life to only depend on yourself. I won't be your crutch, but I will help guide you. First, you must get a job, baby."

"A job?" Contorting her face.

"Yes. You have three young children. They need to eat."

Tipy pondered what her course of action could be.

"Well. Maybe I can work at Fantastic Fair. How hard can a department store be? But what will I do with the kids?"

"Lina down the street is doing daycare. Check with her."

"That's right. She's good with kids too. But I still can't cover the mortgage."

"The projects are affordable. You should apply there."

"The San Fernando Gardens? That's for poor folks."

"Tipy... You're poor. You need to set some goals. Take all the civil service tests you can and plan your future."

With reality settling in, Tipy felt both despair and determination. This was not her plan, but Veda was right, and she had to be up for the challenge. Although she did not have that same killer instinct as her mother, she somehow found her inner strength.

Since being a homemaker was no longer an option, Tipy landed the job at Fantastic Fair. She moved her family to the projects where they waited for Frenchy's release. Unfortunately, things were different when he got home, and she was not the same person. After a short while, Tipy filed for divorce, following the path of both Edna and Veda. She would be raising her children alone, bound by the Durr curse.

Tipy and her three children, (from left) Lionel, Lance, and Crystal take photos on Easter Sunday in 1965

Tipy and her husband, Lionel "Frenchy" Grandison, who became L.A. County's youngest coroner's deputy in 1961

Official copy of Marilyn Monroe's death certificate signed by Deputy Lionel Grandison on August 28, 1962

By 1970, Veda had been with LAPD for 25 years. The City of Los Angeles and the Board of Police Commissioners recognized her for this milestone with a formal ceremony and written citation that stated:

> *"During her 25 years with the police department, Mrs. James has consistently received exceptional ratings reflecting her abilities, efficiency, and loyalty. Because of her outstanding work with detective investigators, Mrs. James has been called upon many times to testify in court, for which she was highly commended by various Judges and Deputy District Attorneys."*

After reading these words of validation and receiving an engraved sterling silver platter, the recognition was overwhelming. Finally, Veda reached the pinnacle of her life-long dream with unprecedented acknowledgment from the highest echelon of peers. It felt simply incredible, but the price had taken its toll. The haunting terror of nightmares still plagued her, propelling alcohol as the dangerous remedy for numbing images. Sometimes it worked, and sometimes it did not.

Lying in bed at night became unbearable. There was no pathway to ridding her mind of Mr. Madison, the lone skull, the mutilated 16-year-old mother, or countless others. Vivid visions in intricate gory detail were getting the best of her senses. She still smelled the bodily fluids, and Mr. Madison eerily spoke out.

"You told her to have a plan B," his creepy voice said. "And look what happened."

His same smashed face and dislodged eyeball horrified her, and the images were unrelenting. At first, waking up in only a sweat, now she awoke confused and in terror, grappling to find reality.

As she lay in bed recovering from the trauma, thoughts of the Madison case naturally came to mind. It had been years since the trial, but of them all, this one stuck out the most. Shortly after the cell visit, Veda met with the District Attorney and told the story of Mrs. Madison coming to Foothill with lacerations and bruises on her face. As predicted, the DA had little interest in going easy, but Veda produced two of the previous abuse complaints filed. She argued the department had an element of responsibility for not protecting the victim.

Veda was relentless in making her case. She had testified for this DA many times on important cases, so he knew how valuable her expertise was. Finally, he dropped the charges from first-degree murder to manslaughter and allowed Veda to testify on what she saw when Mrs. Madison came to the station. The judge even appeared to have sympathy as he sentenced the least amount of time possible. That, to Veda, was a victory for women.

Now, if only she could get Mr. Madison out of her daunting dreams, life would be better. She closed her eyes with skepticism, hoping to sleep in peace.

Veda fulfilled her promise of making Foothill Division LA's most efficiently run station. She became a socialite, hosting numerous parties at her home that nearly everyone at Foothill attended. Not only had her social life expanded, but her family as well.

By this time, Veda had seven grandchildren and loved to flaunt her favorite, Crystal. Now ten, she was fair-skinned with beautiful brown hair and a charming personality. Most of the force knew her from the police picnics and, of course, Veda bragging.

During summer vacation, Crystal spent time at Veda's house and sometimes accompanied her to the station. Proud to show off her bright young granddaughter, Veda would put her to work purging old incident cards in the detective room. While going through the cards one day, she could hear some officers talking.

"You better get your story right. We might get some press. Don't want another Watts situation."

"This won't bring us down. Our story is airtight."

"But the security guard says he was pushed against the a/c unit before you shot him."

"Yeah, but we got witnesses too. It will be alright. That nigger won't bring us down."

Utterly shocked at what she heard, Crystal sat there quiet as a mouse. Feelings of discomfort shot through her body while suddenly absorbing the ugly side of policemen. Mostly attending all-white schools, sooner or later race came up, but rarely the N-word. How could these officers, people she looked up to, say that? Wanting to avoid eye contact, she kept her head down in disbelief.

One of the detectives put a file on Veda's desk.

"We got an important one for you to type up. We need you on our team for this," the detective said.

Veda opened the file and saw the photos of a young Black male riddled with bullets. Hearing the talk right after the incident, she knew something was sinister, just like with Pinkerton.

However, this situation was far more complicated, and she could do nothing about it. Crystal walked up to her desk.

"I'm hungry. Can we get something to eat?"

"Yes, of course, sweetie. Let's go get some lunch," Veda said, closing the file and placing it in the tray.

Leaving through the rear door, they passed by the jail cells, which were tiny rooms with glass windows. Crystal was always intrigued while walking past that area, curiously wondering why each person got arrested.

They jumped into Veda's burgundy 1968 Pontiac Bonneville and headed out. Crystal loved driving with Veda but hated that she always lit a cigarette. Fortunately, the car had corner vent windows allowing Crystal to shoo the waves of smoke seeming to follow her like a kite's tail in the wind.

"How come police use the N-word?" Crystal queried.

"Why? Did you hear somebody say that at the station?"

"Yes, I heard them talking when I was working on the incident cards."

Veda was upset about Crystal hearing those hurtful words and did not know what to think. She had known for years how officers talk and never took it personally. Police culture was part of her life, but she never expected her granddaughter to experience the racist nasty side. It wasn't right.

"I'm sorry, baby. That shouldn't have happened. But just remember, those ugly words can't ever change the beautiful young lady you are."

They went to a small drive-through restaurant in San Fernando called "Danny's Dogs." Instead of driving through, Veda parked, and they walked to the window. An older Mexican man took the order as Crystal asked for a hamburger with no onions and french fries. She really wanted a hot dog, but they only had pork. Her father had joined the Nation of Islam and forbid his kids from eating swine because the pig is unclean. Crystal wasn't happy about that, mostly because she loved making BLTs with the thick bacon they got from Roman's Market.

They took the food home, which was torture, smelling the flavorful aroma. Crystal knew not to say anything because Veda did not allow eating in her car, unlike her mom, who never cared. So, she remained quiet, her stomach growling uncontrollably the whole way.

Arriving at the house, Crystal got out to open the gate and stepped aside as Veda pulled in. Her black Labrador named Peppie greeted them with his silky dark coat and wagging tail. They sat at the bar counter in the kitchen and ate. The french fries were unique because they had seasoned salt on them, which no other place used. Crystal wolfed them down with joy.

"I'm gonna leave you here and go back to work. I'll be home a little later," Veda said.

"Okay."

Veda didn't go back to the station right away. She had an appointment with Dr. George Mason, one of the doctors in Pacoima who cared for almost everyone. He and Dr. Harvell were two prominent doctors in a town of Black professionals, including dentists, chiropractors, lawyers, and real estate executives.

The seventies presented Blacks with opportunities to move into other areas, and many took advantage. Red-lining still existed, but Tipy managed to get out of the projects and move to Panorama City, which was all white. During that time, she met a white man named George Louda, who she married, and they purchased a home in Granada Hills.

Entering Dr. Mason's office, Veda took a seat in the waiting room. She had heard he was moving his practice to Northridge, which saddened her. She trusted him, and after going her whole childhood without modern medicine, many mysteries finally made sense. Edna was angry with Veda for leaving the Christian Science religion and brought it up all the time. When Edna felt ill, which was rare, she reverted to its teachings. Pete and Lita remained faithful followers.

Dr. Mason's nurse called her in with a cheerful smile and sat Veda on the examination table. The doctor entered, a tall man around Veda's age. She felt comfortable sharing her whole story with him because he was so straightforward.

"I wish you would have come to me sooner about this," Dr. Mason said.

"What do you think?" she asked.

"You have a rare type of eidetic memory disorder. Your mind takes a snapshot, and it lingers. It's usually found in children and uncommon for adults, so I suspect you've had this for a long time."

"Yes, all my life. So, what can I do?"

"You need to talk to someone about it, Mrs. James. It's more mental than physical. And drop the Vodka. It only makes it worse."

"It's not just the images, but also my job has become more stressful."

"If you like, I can refer you to a psychiatrist."

"No. I don't want to do that. I really just need solid sleep."

"I'll give you something to help with that. If you need some time off, I can give you a note."

"No. I'll tough it out a little longer. Hopefully, the pills will help. Sleep is what I need. Thanks for everything, Dr. Mason. You're right. I should have come to you sooner."

Veda went back to work with a prescription in hand and high hopes of ending her longstanding sleep issue. Tackling the problem at Foothill was next. Fellow officers, who were also her friends, had killed an unarmed Black youth. This was different than Pinkerton, who shot his victim and blatantly lied on the report. These cops claimed reasonable cause because the 17-year-old kid was fighting them.

Pinkerton had attacked her in the restroom. Foothill guys were nice to her; she had welcomed them into her home, knew their families, and genuinely liked them. Should she just do her job and type up the report? Maybe color had nothing to do with it. Maybe?

Putting her doubts aside, she filed the report. The investigation would take a few weeks, and a few inconsistencies still existed. The deceased, six feet tall and 196 pounds, was a high school student with his whole life ahead of him. The tragedy of this case saddened Veda, but then her commonsense instincts sunk in. Why did he fight with the officers? Why didn't he comply?

Veda unequivocally knew that if you were Black in Los Angeles, there were different rules for engagement. She processed many reports where white suspects resisted arrest and did not end up riddled with bullets.

Meanwhile, complaints from parents about excessive use of force against their children were rising. Veda took grievance reports and turned them in, knowing they would go nowhere. When parents called for their status, it was usually a challenge.

Internal Affairs always produced the same answer, "it's under investigation," which is exactly what she told the parents.

Because the captain and white detectives treated her so well, it seemed the lines blurred whether she was Black or neutral. Veda just did her job, continued to help them solve cases, organized the unit, and made sure the station flowed smoothly. However, she was now seeing a disturbing trend, reminding her of the early years at Newton. Were things going backward in the world of color? The Watts Riots and Black Power Movement may have made things worse.

When Veda got home, she cooked spaghetti and garlic bread while Crystal watched TV. After dinner, they both sat in the den, polished their nails, and enjoyed the sitcom lineup of "Mary Tyler Moore" and "Here's Lucy" shows. After that, it was bedtime, so Veda took her new sleeping pills and slept like a baby.

Veda with LAPD Foothill Division detectives in 1965

Tom Bradley was elected Mayor of Los Angeles in 1973, and Veda could not have been prouder. In 1974, she arranged for Crystal and her friends to visit his office to interview him for a 9th-grade project. They had not spoken since the election, and she thought this was an excellent opportunity. Tom was happy to oblige, and the girls were thrilled.

"I can't wait to meet Mayor Bradley," Crystal said. "Sheri and Susan are excited too. They still can't believe my grandmother knows the mayor."

"No problem, baby. Do you have your questions for him ready?"

"Yep. It's about air pollution, littering, and what he's doing about it."

"Those are good topics. I know you'll do a great job."

Veda drove Crystal, Sheri, Susan, and Tipy who came along for the ride, to the interview. They walked up the long steps of city hall and found their way to Bradley's office. Tom greeted Veda with open arms and seemed genuinely glad to see her. Veda was thrilled to be able to arrange this for the girls and pleased that Tom took the time. Tipy and Veda stood aside while the girls took seats at Bradley's huge intimidating desk. He had photos of himself running track at UCLA and one wearing his LAPD uniform on the wall, along with his other accolades.

"So, what questions do you young ladies have for me," Bradley said.

"My generation is tired of breathing smog. Sometimes it makes my chest hurt. What is the city doing about it?" Crystal asked

"Right now, the city is doing what it can, but pollution is a problem that we all have to work together to fix."

"What about littering," Sheri softly queried.

"We currently fine people five-hundred dollars for littering."

"How many times have fines been imposed and collected?" Crystal jumped in.

"To date, unfortunately, there have been very few," the mayor honestly replied.

They took some photos, and all left with a feeling of achievement.

Los Angeles Times

LARGEST CIRCULATION IN THE WEST, 1,006,499 DAILY, 1,316,636 SUNDAY

| VOL XCII | 5† | SIX PARTS—PART ONE | CC | WEDNESDAY MORNING, MAY 30, 1973 | 100 PAGES | Copyright © 1973 Los Angeles Times | DAILY 10¢ |

BRADLEY DEFEATS YORTY IN LANDSLIDE

Pines Defeats Arnebergh for City Attorney

BY KENNETH REICH
Times Political Writer

Thirty-four-year-old Burt Pines—a political unknown when he announced his candidacy six months ago—swept by 20-year incumbent Roger Arnebergh Tuesday to be elected Los Angeles' new city attorney.

In nearly complete vote totals in the municipal election, Pines ran ahead of winning mayoral candidate Tom Bradley, and got 58.3% of the vote to Arnebergh's 41.7%.

Even though Pines had emerged as the favorite in the last days, the size of his triumph was a surprise. It marked a stunning first victory for a man who may one day aspire to an important role in state politics.

With 3,168 precincts of 3,163 reporting, the results were:

Pines   418,856
Arnebergh   200,213

Speaking from his election night

L.A. Becomes Largest U.S. City to Elect a Black Mayor

BY BILL BOYARSKY
Times Political Writer

City Councilman Tom Bradley, son of a black sharecropper, was elected mayor of Los Angeles by a landslide in Tuesday's election, driving Mayor Sam Yorty out of office after 12 tempestuous years.

Bradley's defeat of the 63-year-old Yorty exceeded the hopes of supporters who had been encouraged by favorable public opinion polls but remembered how Yorty came from behind to win four years ago. Bradley's victory margin was greater than Yorty's had been in 1969.

In the end, Yorty, who had survived scandals and the Watts riot, was a victim of his supporters' indifference. He said not enough voters in the white, blue-collar San Fernando Valley precincts that were Yorty strongholds showed up at the polls to vote.

But Pollster Mervin Field told The Times that even if Yorty's backers had turned out in the numbers they did in 1969, he would have had to get about 90% of their votes to win.

Helped by White Backlash

Bradley's aides said that the 55-

est city. Never before had a Negro been elected mayor of such a large city, one with a black population of only between 15% to 18% among 2.8 million residents.

In defeat, Yorty—always a hard scrapper—blamed his Valley supporters for his defeat and said of Bradley: "The change, if it takes place, will be a very radical one and there'll be a lot of people who wish they went out to vote. That's my prediction."

He did not concede, however, saying only "The trend at the moment doesn't look very good."

"We want Bradley. We want Bradley," the happy crowds shouted at the Bradley headquarters, at a party that overflowed a large room at the Los Angeles Hilton.

Smile Happily at Crowd

Bradley and his wife, Ethel, smiled happily at the crowd. Nearby was a key man in his victory, City Councilman Joel Wachs, whose revelations of how Mayor Yorty had misused an insurance policy financed by political funds was a major boost to the Bradley campaign in the last week.

Bradley seemed overcome with

FAMILY JOY—City Councilman Tom Bradley is hugged by daughters Phyllis, 28, left, Lorraine, 29, rear, and wife Ethel after returns showed him to be winner of mayor race over Sam Yorty.
Times photo by Rick Browne

Veda with her long-time friend, Mayor Tom Bradley in 1975

Veda's granddaughter Crystal (right) with friends Sheri Cornell (center) and Sue Fuller (left) at Mayor Bradley's office

The next day at the station, Veda bragged about her visit to the mayor's office. Detective Bowles was highly impressed. As a Black man, he knew the struggle but mostly stayed low-key among the white detectives, and they seemed to like him. He never wanted to appear militant.

"That's amazing, Veda. The mayor's office! We've come a long way," Bowles said.

"Yes, and I got VIP treatment."

Larry Scott, one of the lead detectives, walked by Veda's desk and stopped. He was a bald, middle-aged man who wore a white shirt and the same tie every day.

"What are you two gloating about?" Scott said.

"I was telling Bowles about my visit to Mayor Bradley's office," Veda explained.

"Oh, now you call him Mayor Bradley. What happened to Tom?" he said in a sarcastic tone.

"Don't be mad. We all know you voted for Yorty," Bowles interjected.

"You know he'll never make his full term. He won't be able to cut it."

"Why do you say that?" Veda asked.

"You know, his type can't stay at that level."

"What is his type?" Bowles snapped.

"That's a white man's job. Looks like he's giving special treatment to his own kind."

"You mean like you give to yours?" Veda said in an irritated voice.

Her blood began to boil. She couldn't believe Scott was like that. He was always pleasant when they worked cases together and had even been over her house. Never thinking of him as a racist, that attitude infuriated Veda and was a strong sign of Foothill's changing culture over the past decade.

After getting home, she ate some left-over chili and fed Nipper, her new dog. Peppie had died a few months earlier, and Veda was glad to have him. Nipper was a medium-sized sandy brown, long-haired mix of German shepherd and collie. Veda's nurturing nature worked well with taking care of a dog.

Still upset by Scott's callous attitude, Veda thought she was a better judge of character. This was a big blow and raised questions about people she called her friends. Never naïve about racists, she was dead wrong about Scott.

Even though Dr. Mason gave Veda sleeping pills, she did not stop drinking the "greyhounds" (Vodka and grapefruit juice). On weekends, Veda drank in the morning while watering the grass. Edna, who often spent time with her, became disturbed. She saw her father Wesley drink every day to drown out his pain. At times he was out of control and ultimately died from liver damage.

Edna did not want to see Veda suffer that dreadful fate. Never touching alcohol, it upset her one year when somebody secretly put rum in the eggnog. She became lightheaded and began stumbling, unaware of her intoxication. Edna was careful about drinking eggnog on the holidays from that point on. Unfortunately, Veda was going to do what she wanted, as always.

After going through a long week of back-to-back cases at work, the department assigned a new captain to Foothill, changing the dynamics of her job. Veda's entire career was reliant on her reputation, something the new boss seemed oblivious to.

Captain Karras was nothing like Richards. He had a big ego and little regard for women or people of color. Veda hoped he would understand her value, but instead, he overlooked it. His demeaning tone and attitude were not something Veda could easily accept.

"Hey, gal. Can I get some coffee?" he said on the intercom.

"My name is Veda."

"Can you hurry it up, Veda?"

Having been with LAPD for nearly 30 years, Veda could not tolerate disrespect, not at this juncture. She could accept never receiving the title "detective," but she wasn't just a secretary, and everyone knew that—everyone except the new man in charge. The job was changing, and Veda was feeling the stress. Surprisingly, things were more manageable in the forties because she knew what to expect. Now, when society is supposedly better, things are retreating.

The more Veda thought about the captain and Scott, the more it irritated her. Drinking a little more than usual, she took her pill and headed for the bedroom. Sitting on the bed, with an ashtray next to her, she watched a new cop show, "Get Christy Love." Liking all the police shows, Perry Mason and Adam 12 were her favorites. Having a television in her bedroom was great.

Later, while sitting there, Veda could not remember taking her sleeping pill. It was her first time failing to recall something. My God, she remembered everything, but staring at the pill bottle, it wouldn't come to her. Lighting her cigarette, she deducted she could not have forgotten to take the tablet and took another. Finally, Veda fell asleep with two fingers precariously wrapped around the burning tobacco stick and a long ash preparing to drop.

Having just dropped the kids off with Frenchy's grandmother, Tipy decided to stop by Veda's. Nipper was frantically barking when Tipy walked in, and the smell of smoke was ominously present. Running into Veda's bedroom, she instantly saw the bed smoldering with a small flame. Veda was sleeping next to it, so Tipy rushed to wake her up.

"Veda, Veda, the bed is on fire. GET UP!"

Veda tried to get up but was weak. Tipy moved her to the floor, then ran to the kitchen and got some water. She returned and threw it on the fire, which was growing bigger by the second. Then she grabbed a blanket and smothered it.

"I must have fallen asleep," Veda said in a groggy voice.

"Are you okay?" Tipy asked, helping her up from the floor. "Your cigarette started it. You could have died."

Tipy saw something in Veda's face she had never seen before. Fear. She looked dazed and afraid as the magnitude of what just happened sunk in.

"Did you see Dr. Mason?" Tipy asked.

Veda nodded her head, yes.

"What did he say?"

"He, he gave me these," she said as she picked up the bottle from the nightstand.

"Okay. We gotta do something. You can't drink and take these pills, Veda."

Tipy removed the bedding and placed it outside. She returned to examine the mattress, which had a huge burn hole and was usable.

"I just wanna sleep. I just wanna sleep and make them go away," Veda slurred.

"You're gonna have to sleep in the other room tonight. Come on."

Tipy tucked Veda into her old bedroom. It had changed a lot since she was a teen, now used for Edna when she visited. Veda immediately went back to sleep, and Tipy wondered if the sleeping pills were too strong or was it the alcohol combination? She picked up the phone and called James. Tipy knew James loved Veda unconditionally. The admiration on his face showed every time he looked at her. There was nothing he would not do for Veda.

"James, this is Tipy."

"Hi, Tipy. Is everything okay?" he immediately asked.

"Veda started a small fire in her room. I'm not sure what's going on, but I'm worried. I don't know if it's the Vodka or the new sleeping pills."

"She's been stressed about the job, and I think she's drinking more than usual. That may be why she wants me away. I can tell she's drunk when we talk. I'm coming over. Stay with her 'til I get there," James pleaded.

Tipy wondered the extent of Veda's problem and what would have happened had she not shown up. Her mother could be gone, and just thinking about that put a lump in her throat. She could not have asked for a better mother and walked back into the room to check on her; then Veda opened her eyes. She stared at Tipy for a minute, who took a seat on the bed next to her. Veda was groggy but wanted to talk.

"I have been strong all my life. I have always figured out a solution to any problem. I don't know how to get these images out of my head. Having this memory has been why I was successful. Now it's my demise. For once in my life, I don't know how to handle something. I thought I got help from Dr. Mason. But Tipy, I couldn't remember if I took the pill. I just couldn't find it in my brain," she said weeping.

"Drinking and taking pills is why you can't remember. It will make it worse. You think it numbs you, but it will only hide it for a while. For once, let me help you, mom."

"You called me mom," Veda said with a slight smile.

"I always wanted to call you mom," Tipy confessed.

Taking Veda's hand, she held it tight then kissed it, knowing something had to be done.

"Alcohol and pills are a crutch, not a cure," Tipy explained. "You have to clean that up. We need to clean it up."

"I'm not going in a facility Tipy."

"Then we will do it here. I'll stay with you through it."

"Alright," Veda said with a tear falling down her cheek.

"James is on his way over," Tipy announced, squeezing her hand tighter.

"You told him?"

"He loves you and wants to help."

Veda took a long deep breath. She was still groggy but understood the magnitude of her circumstances. It was a choice to live or die. She knew this would be hard, but those images could not defeat her. She was going to call Dr. Mason on Monday and get him to put her on temporary disability. She would beat this Vodka somehow.

"No one can know about this," she said, looking up at Tipy, her little girl. "I know you like to gossip, but please, please let me out of this with dignity. If I fail, you can blab to the world."

"You're asking a lot," Tipy said with a smirk.

"Not even Lita. She doesn't need to know."

"Veda, I hate to tell you, but everyone knows you drink a lot."

Veda turned her head to the side, away from Tipy, wondering how bad did she let this get?

"Does Crystal know?"

"She's with you a lot. We never talked about it, but you get silly when you drink. I'm sure she sees it. She loves you, though, and will not judge you. I won't mention it."

James came and stayed the night with Veda watching over her as she slept. Tipy went home to her husband and told him a fraction of the story, trying to honor Veda's wishes. Veda was right about Tipy's mouth. She always had a hard time keeping a secret, but this would be a first for her. James agreed to stay the weekend and knew what they were ultimately facing.

The following morning, Tipy and Boppie stopped by. Veda was okay at first, but as the day went on, her hand started shaking. Everyone could tell she was beginning to have withdrawals. She went to the liquor cabinet for Vodka, but it was empty. Not saying a word and fidgety, her only thought was getting some alcohol. By afternoon, it got worse.

"I'm going to the store to get us something for dinner," Veda said.

"I took out some chicken. We have broccoli and rice to go with it," Tipy responded.

Veda persisted.

"We don't have any bread. I could get some Bridgford Rolls to go with it."

"I'll go," Boppie replied. "Just relax."

Feeling something utterly foreign to her, Veda developed an awful pain in her stomach as nausea set in. She held her hand out and watched it shake violently, then looked helplessly at James.

"Let's go lay down and watch television. It will get your mind off it. You'll have a few really hard days." James said.

"Okay."

When Boppie returned from the store, Veda was vomiting in a bucket by her bed. James and Tipy were right there with her.

"This is gonna be a long night," Tipy said.

"How come nobody knew?" said Boppie.

"We all knew but just ignored it. Come on. This is Veda, and she never needs help."

"She was really good at hiding it," James said.

"I'm still here. You guys are talking like I don't speak English," Veda belted out, then spit up in the bucket again. It was all bile now as her stomach was empty. She was sweating and struggling but still knew what was going on.

The next day was worse. Veda could not get out of bed and was clutching her stomach. She rolled over on her back and stared at the ceiling like someone was there. Tipy noticed she was reaching for something in the air and began talking. She was now in a delusional state.

"Mrs. Madison, you have a lovely home... Mrs. Madison, you should have done things differently," Veda mumbled. "He talks to me, you know, but his face is pretty bad. His eyeballs are missing."

Then she started laughing. "I got you, Pinkerton. I got you. You lied."

Veda rolled over, facing Tipy with a muffled look in her eyes.

"Tipy, my pretty baby girl. You didn't clean the walls like you were supposed to. Get up and clean them."

As quickly as she said that she switched up and looked in the other direction as if someone else was there.

"Jimmy, I kicked your butt. Look at you now. Still a low life. That's what you get for messing with my brother."

Baffled by what Veda was saying, Tipy and Boppie walked out of the room.

"What is she talking about? I only remember getting in trouble for not cleaning the walls, but the rest. Who are Jimmy and Mrs. Madison? Tipy said.

"Got me?" Boppie replied. "How come she doesn't mention me?

"I guess you didn't register in her mind."

"I wonder how long this withdrawal will take?"

James walked out and heard the question.

"This part will be a few days, but it can take up a week or two to get it out of her system. The rest is mental."

Suddenly, they all heard Veda calling from the room.

"Tipy…Tipy!!!"

She ran to see what Veda wanted.

"Mr. Williams wants to meet you. Here she is, Mr. Williams, this is my daughter Tipy. Say hello, Tipy."

Not knowing how to respond, Tipy picked up the towel and wiped Veda's forehead. Her mother's fragile state was hard to watch. She never imagined Veda like this—helpless and powerless, now depending on a family that always relied on her.

"I'm here Veda, everything's going to be alright," Tipy soothed her, feeling awkward. "I need to check on dinner. I'll be right back."

Tipy never heard of Mr. Williams and wondered if he was real.

"Boppie, who is Mr. Williams?

"I have no idea."

"She knew him from her childhood, and he worked for LAPD," James said. "I think he had a big influence on her joining law enforcement. She told me Mr. Williams was sweet on Edna too."

"I wonder why she never mentioned him to us," Tipy reacted.

"Huh, I don't even remember ever seeing Edna with a man," Boppie reflected.

"This was when they were much younger," James said.

Veda felt physically better by Saturday, but she thought about liquor all the time. The worst of her gory images emerged during her withdrawals, but somehow, she wasn't afraid of them anymore. Dr. Mason recommended only taking sleeping pills if needed. It was ironic, but the only thing she ever feared was her nightmares. That, coupled with alcohol, was a lethal combination.

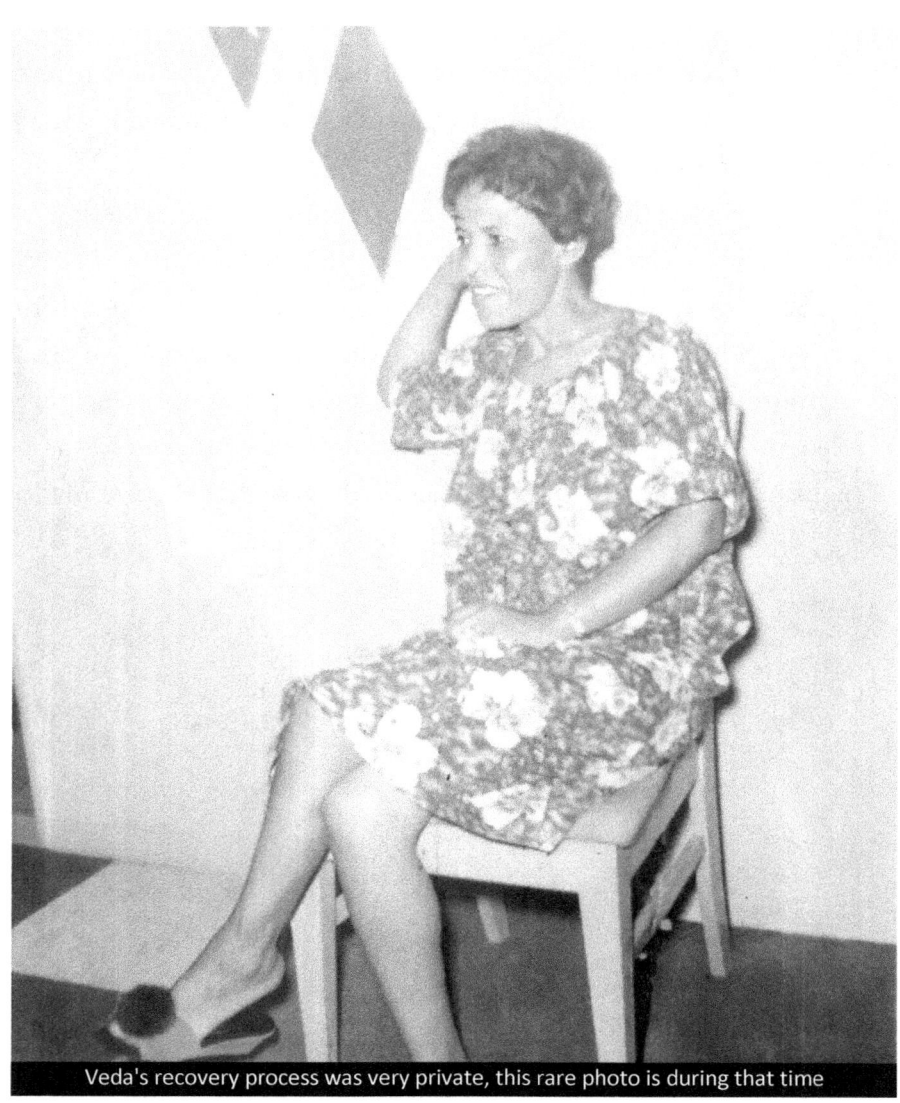

Veda's recovery process was very private, this rare photo is during that time

By the third week, Veda felt pretty good. She wasn't quite ready to go back to work, but her body was healing. A good Sunday dinner with the family and grandchildren would help. Although the kids were mostly teens now, their laughter was therapeutic.

She arranged for Pete to get Edna, informed Lita and Frank, and told Boppie and Tipy to bring their families. Tipy's husband never came to family affairs, presumably because he was uncomfortable around most Blacks. Although marrying a Black woman, he was raised in Chicago by a Bohemian racist father, and those values still reared their ugly head from time to time. He loved Tipy but was still a racist.

This dinner provided an opportunity to reflect on her family, which gave Veda joy. Although Lita and Frank had no children, they seemed happy. Always being a peacemaker and "go-with-the-flow" type of person, Lita's marriage had little visual turmoil. However, Veda had concerns about Frank's secretive lifestyle. Her natural instincts left her in a quandary because her sister was in complete bliss. So, Veda left it alone. Pete was divorced by this time and lived close to Edna. After building an enormous custom-style house on her property, he remodeled Annabelle's old place just down Sierra Hwy for himself.

Also invited were Pete's son, Rufus, his wife Deloris, and their daughter Delisa. It would be a packed house, which gave Veda something to plan and execute.

Veda cooked a traditional southern meal. Prime rib, ham, mashed potatoes, green beans, and yams. Everyone else brought a dish or dessert. Veda was nervous about alcohol because her house was notorious for liquor. The good news was Boppie and Tipy could discreetly curtail any issues that came up. She made a big punch bowl of raspberry lemonade with plastic cups lined up around it and served dinner at 5 pm. Everyone showed up, and James sat at the head of the table.

"I want everyone to join hands. It's been a while since we had a family dinner. I'm gonna ask Veda to lead us in prayer," James said.

Caught a little off guard, Veda looked down the long table at all the faces. Feeling emotional at that moment and blessed, she bowed her head.

"Dear Lord, thank you for bringing my family together. My mother, son and daughter, seven grandkids, brother, sister, and all the spouses. I am so grateful everyone is healthy and doing well. We pray you continue to bless us with each other's love and keep our family strong in times of need."

At that moment, Veda squeezed James' hand extra tight.

"Thank you, Lord, for the food we are about to receive in Jesus' name, Amen."

Everyone said Amen and proceeded to eat. The teens began their conversations about school and who was doing what in the neighborhood. Lita and Pete joked around while Frank and Boppie ate like it was their last meal. Joyce and Tipy reminisced about Tony's birth and how he was almost born at the house.

After dinner, they pulled out the Rummage Rummy game, and everyone dragged out their pennies. Pete was known for hiding how much he had, especially if he won. They laughed and played until 11 pm when everyone started to dispense. It was an excellent evening for Veda.

That night she slept without a pill or liquor, and it felt beautiful. James was by her side for the night, and she experienced a calmness that eluded her a long time. Some tough decisions loomed about her future, but she chose to enjoy the moment.

Dr. Mason concluded that work stress took its toll on Veda and filed for worker's compensation. She had to see state-appointed doctors weekly, but it gave her something to do. While out one afternoon, she decided to pick up some Uncle Ben's rice and pinto beans at Boys Market on Glenoaks and Hubbard. Walking through the aisles, she bumped into Marie Harris, a community leader and activist that made numerous visits to Foothill Division.

"Marie?" Veda said.

"Hi, Veda. What a surprise."

Marie was a Black woman and former fashion designer who dressed in lots of jewelry, makeup, and tailored clothes. Her hair and nails were always well-manicured, and people noticed when she entered a room.

"Yes, how are you doing?" Veda asked.

"I'm great. Staying busy. Are you still at Foothill?"

"Technically, yes, but I'm thinking of retiring."

"What are you gonna do with yourself in retirement?"

"I'll stay busy."

"If you want to get involved with community work, let me know."

"Well, I do volunteer at the voting polls, but I might be interested. Give me your number."

"Do you have a pen?"

"I don't need a pen. My expertise is memorizing addresses, names, faces, and phone numbers."

"You go head!! That's amazing. It's 896-2515. Call me tonight and give me your number."

"You got it!!" Veda said with enthusiasm.

When Veda got home, she put away her groceries and picked up the phone to call Marie. She went to dial the number, and it wasn't in her head. Veda froze in disbelief for a minute, then looked at the wall-mounted rotary phone as her mind continued to draw a blank.

"What was that number?" she thought while pounding her temple.

"Come on, Veda, what's the number, what's the number?"

There was nothing there, nothing. Veda couldn't even remember the first digits. Was it 899 or 896, the only two prefixes in Pacoima? She thought back to forgetting about that sleeping pill. It felt like she should retrieve the information but couldn't find it in her mind. It was gone. Veda put the phone down and got a notepad to document her memory loss. Wondering what this meant, she decided to ask Dr. Mason on her next visit.

Retirement stayed on Veda's mind. It was 1975, and she was mentally exhausted. Thirty years is a good number, she thought, and community work sounded appealing. So, Veda proceeded to research her retirement income and found out it was feasible.

Deciding to retire, she also quietly married her soulmate, James. They agreed to keep everything separate, including finances and residency. She never legally changed her name either. No one knew about the marriage except Tipy and Crystal.

Finally, October 9, 1975, was the big day, and the department planned a magnificent retirement dinner for Veda. They selected the Odyssey Restaurant in Granada Hills, which sat on top of a mountain with a great view of the San Fernando Valley. It was a venue ambiance Veda loved, and she had to look exactly right. Her search for the perfect dress led to Robinson's department store in Panorama City. There she found a sleeveless low-cut black cocktail dress and matching open-toed high heel pumps for the night.

That evening, Veda made an intentional fashionably late appearance, even though she was never late to anything. James looked handsome in his suit and tie and felt proud to be there with Veda. When she arrived, the ballroom was beautiful. Round tables, decorated in silver and white, each seating eight people and a head table with top LAPD officials. Veda and James sat with the family as prominent guests filled the venue.

All Veda's friends from Newton Division attended. To her surprise, Mr. Williams was the Master of Ceremonies. It was a pleasant shocker. Now in his seventies, he was still sharp as a tack. Midge organized the event, handling every detail, something Veda did at Newton and Foothill for many years.

Before things got started, Veda needed a quick restroom break to check her makeup and hair. She was pleased with her elegant look at age 58. While exiting the ladies room, she noticed a huge entourage of suits moving slowly towards the ballroom. In the center was a tall Negro man she quickly recognized. It was her long-time friend, Mayor Tom Bradley. As she stood there, their eyes locked when he subsequently noticed her. With a warm smile, Tom approached Veda.

"Looks like I found the star of the show," he said.

"Hi Tom, I wasn't sure you'd make it."

"I wouldn't have missed it for anything. There are only a few people I've been friends with longer than you."

Just then, an announcement was made informing everyone to take their seats.

"You were always there for me, Tom, and I will never forget it."

"You also taught me a few things," he said. "Both of us were forced to navigate the color game. Looks like we won."

"No, remember... we're not colored," Veda said jokingly.

She returned just in time for Mr. Williams to begin the program.

"Thank you, everyone, for being here tonight to celebrate Veda James's retirement after 30 years with LAPD," he began. "I've known Veda since she was a little girl, and it doesn't surprise me she made it this long in this capacity. She always wanted to be in law enforcement, and she actually profiled me from my wedding ring, mustache, and even a mole on my face, when I was a young rookie, still wet behind the ears. And she was only four at the time."

The crowd laughed.

"Then, at the age of seven, she remembered every last detail of our first meeting. She interrogated me relentlessly, embarrassing her poor mother."

There was laughter again.

"So, I wasn't surprised to find her working at Newton Division in the Detective unit. Not one bit. But her reputation preceded her. They said a colored woman was leading the charge there, and in the back of my mind, I wondered if it could be her. And it was. This woman remembered the smallest detail of everything she ever saw or experienced, which impressed me, amazed me, and made me proud to know her. Here to say a few words is Chief of Police Ed Davis."

The crowd applauded, some standing up. Mr. Williams went to Veda's family's table, sat next to Edna, and kissed her on the cheek. Edna blushed as they looked into each other's eyes and smiled.

Ed Davis took the stage. He was a middle-aged white male with gray spots in his hair, which he parted to the side. Nodding at Veda, he approached the microphone.

"Tonight, we are here to celebrate a woman who has worked tirelessly, consistently, and professionally in the detective unit for 30 years. She has put up with ugly crime scenes, foul-mouthed detectives, and officers but still greeted everyone with a smile and courtesy. Don't get me wrong. No one dared to say no to her for anything," Davis said as the audience chuckled.

"But she helped with and solved some of our highest-profile cases. If someone needed the history of something, the penal code number, the statute, even a case number from ten years ago, she was your person. That is something we can never replace. What Veda has you can't teach. It is a gift, and she shared that gift with both Newton and Foothill for many years. So, congratulations, Veda James, on your retirement."

The words from Chief Davis incredibly touched Veda as the crowd erupted.

"Now I want to call up someone who has known Veda since they worked together at Newton Division, our current mayor of the city of Los Angeles, Mayor Tom Bradley."

All the guests stood as they clapped for the first Black mayor of any major city in America. Proud beyond belief of Tom's achievement, Veda felt privileged by their career-long relationship.

"Thank you," he began. "Veda and I go back to, shall I dare say, the 1940's. She was essential in helping me with my projects and was always someone to depend on for answers. I saw what she went through as the only woman in the detective unit, and nothing ever stopped her. No hurdle was too high. No problem was unsolvable, and she never took no for an answer. Thirty years is a long time in this field, and you see a lot. But this woman dealt with it all. I'd like to read her official citation from the City of Los Angeles.

'Mrs. James began her career with the police department on April 3, 1945, as a clerk stenographer. During this time, she consistently received outstanding rating reports reflecting her adeptness at handling the public and maintaining excellent rapport with investigators. She has been complimented for her great assistance to homicide investigators in major homicide cases for her remarkable memory.'

"Congratulations on your retirement, Veda. I wish you happiness and the best of luck in your future endeavors. Now please come up and say a few words."

It was a proud moment for Veda, perhaps her proudest. She hugged Tom then stepped to the podium, quickly glancing behind her and smiling at the chief, captain, and all the department heads before beginning her speech.

"I'm never speechless, but I am today. Thank you all for the kind words tonight. It means a lot to me. I began this journey as a divorced parent with two small kids. It was my dream job to solve cases. I would have loved to be an actual detective but became the next best thing. I met some incredible people and made some incredible friends," she said, looking at the tables of people.

"Without my mother and sister, my early days would have been a disaster," she stated, gazing at Edna and Lita. "Those were some exhausting times. But I found my purpose through the department, and I fulfilled my dream. Thank you, everyone, for this incredible send-off, and I love you all."

Veda blew a kiss to the crowd as she turned around, shook hands, and hugged the speakers. She then looked to the family table and saw Mr. Williams and Edna talking and laughing. Imagine that after all these years.

The following week, Veda saw Dr. Mason, who performed a series of memory tests. She passed them all with flying colors. The doctor said he could not detect any problems, and her memory lapse could have been from the detox, but they will keep an eye on it.

Even though Veda felt a sense of relief, she knew a different kind of challenge awaited. Life after LAPD may represent her biggest test yet. Fiercely determined to be the same strong and resolute woman she always had been, a new chapter on the horizon, and there was no time for her to back down now.

C I T A T I O N

This Citation is Presented to

VEDA D. JAMES

on the Occasion of Her Attainment of
30 Years of City Service

The Board of Police Commissioners takes pleasure in commending Mrs. Veda D. James for 30 years of outstanding service.

Mrs. James began her career with the Police Department on April 3, 1945, as a Clerk Stenographer. During this time she has consistently received outstanding rating reports reflecting her adeptness at handling the public and maintaining excellent rapport with investigators. She has been complimented for her great assistance to homicide investigators in major homicide cases, and for her remarkable memory.

The Department is proud to have an employee with this dedication and loyalty.

BOARD OF POLICE COMMISSIONERS

_____   _____
President   Commissioner

_____   _____
Vice President   Commissioner

October 9, 1975
_____   _____
Date   Commissioner

LA Police Chief Ed Davis and Veda as she receives her 25-year citation

Veda is all smiles with the Chief of Detectives after receiving a historic citation from the City of Los Angeles Citation recognizing her 30 years with LAPD

Veda's defining moment with high-ranking LAPD officials looking on as she approaches podium at retirement dinner

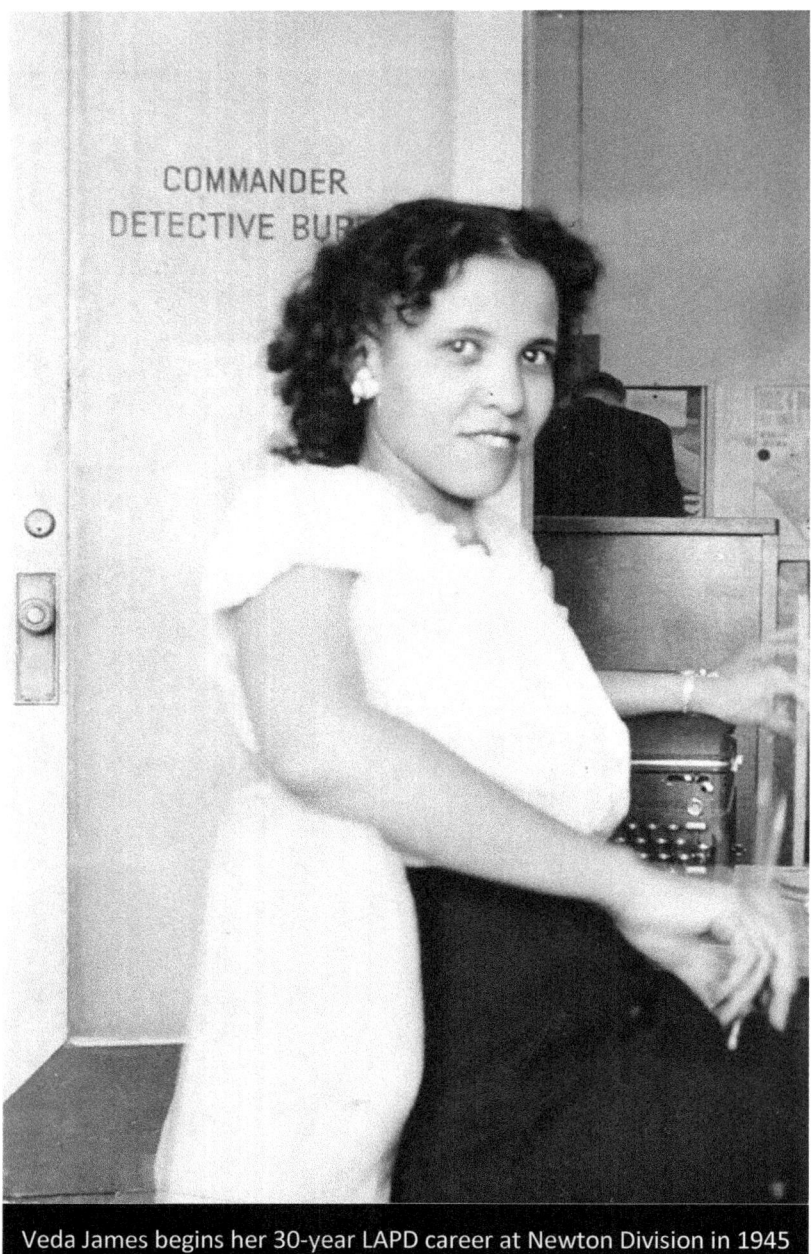

Veda James begins her 30-year LAPD career at Newton Division in 1945

Appendix

THE ETERNAL TRIANGLE with an angle of murder. Pensive Isabelle McGarry (top photo), sits in the kitchen of the home of Frank Valva and ponders over the events that led to the fatal shooting of Joseph Rhone (lower photo). At the right, Frank Valva tells a police official and a stenographer how he shot Rhone when the latter returned to his home for a book despite a warning to stay away. Isabelle McGarry has lived at Valva's home since 1944. Rhone was a friend of hers. A copy of the book for which Rhone returned and was killed is shown on the table in the lower right photo.

THE SCENE OF THE CRIME

"wrong man"!

...NG HOLMAN CASE

Story on page 5

$50,000 IN

5¢ *Tribune* **8**

LOS ANGELES

A MODEL OF JOURNALISM

Vol. 10, No. 41   Saturday, Dec. 2, 1950   Los Angeles 18, Calif.

...ST "MR. B" ECKSTINE

Story on page 2

...f the local community's princi-
...nd University, were made this
... Newton, going to University;
...le University captain, going to

...ex Newton commander is wel-
... oldest policemen in point of
...rvice: that he has 25 years to
... sleeve, one for each five years.
...dr is his secretary, Veda Craig.

...men's army,' which is rapidly
... Pvt. Allie D. McAdams, Los
... Allie is being presented the
...nd Certificate of Achievement
...or Margaret Wharton, for be-
...the 33rd leader's class, WAC
...nd she's pretty, too.

20-YEAR POLICE PIN

Detectives Turn Out as
Mrs. Veda James Honored

A 20-year service pin for "outstanding service" to the Los Angeles Police Dept. today had been awarded to Mrs. Veda James, secretary to the commander of the Foothill Division detective unit by L.A. Chief of Detectives Thad F. Brown.

Mrs. James, who entered the police department in March, 1945, has served in many of the numerous divisions of the department and has served in almost all secretarial classifications.

Det. Lt. Manuel S. Pena, to whom she has been secretary since 1961, said Mrs. James is "one of the top veteran secretary-stenographers who ever served in the Foothill detective bureau.

Turnout Watches

"She has served faithfully here for the past three years and we are proud to be able to work along with her," Pena said.

Brown came all the way from the downtown Los Angeles central police station to be able to present the pin to Mrs. James personally.

The presentation was made during a "coffee klatch" in the Foothill detective bureau with most detectives as-signed to the station in attendance.

Mrs. James, wife of Master Sgt. George E. James, U.S. Army (ret.), is a resident of Pacoima.

Serves Long in Army

They have a daughter, Alithra Grandison, employed by the Dept. of Motor Vehicles in San Fernando, and a son, Romie James, an employe of Western Carloading, Los Angeles.

Her husband recently completed 20 years of service in the Army in the administrative field. They have lived in the San Fernando Valley since 1952.

Mrs. James has worked in the Newton, Hollenbeck, the geographical detectives division in Los Angeles, and Foothill division.

Scores A 'First'

Beginning as a clerk-typist in the Records and Identification unit in Los Angeles, Mrs. James has earned the ranks of intermediate clerk, stenographer, clerk stenographer and secretary-stenographer.

She was the first stenographer ever to be appointed to the geographical detective division.

Police Honor Woman Clerk for Service

The first woman appointed to work in the detective bureau of the Los Angeles Police Dept. was honored this week by the Los Angeles Police Commission on the anniversary of her 25th year with the force.

Mrs. Veda James, detective clerk-stenographer with the department's Foothill Division, was appointed to the detective bureau of the Newton St. Station shortly after joining the force in April 1945.

She was the first woman to hold such a position and has worked primarily in the detective bureau, starting at Newton St. Division and taking over the job at Foothill Division, when that division opened in 1961.

Among those honoring Mrs. James were Police Chief Edward Davis, R. J. Carreon Jr., president of the police commission, deputy chief of police, Roger Murdock; deputy chief Noel McQuon and Capt. Deward Farmer, detective commander, Foothill Division.

Mrs. James said she began her career in 1945 and has worked with and watched as many of those honoring her advanced in the department.

She was presented a diamond-studded anniversary pin and certificate by commission president Carreon during ceremonies at the commission

NEW OFFICERS AT DISTRICT PARLEY

The California-Nevada-Hawaii district of Key Club International held its 24th annual convention at the International Hotel, Los Angeles.

Approximately 1500 Key Club members and Kiwanis advisers attended. Purpose of the convention was to elect new district officers and a sweetheart, and to approve amendments to the constitution.

New lieutenant governors also were installed. The new lieutenant Governor for Division 25, covering most of the Valley and containing 10 clubs, is James Mark D'Arrigo of North Hollywood, a junior at Notre Dame High School in Sherman Oaks, who has a 3.94 grade point average.

Anglea Mikelson, a junior at Corvallis High School in Studio City and the Division 25 sweetheart, was a finalist for district sweetheart at the convention.

Mrs. Veda James, detective clerk-stenographer with the department's Foothill Division, was appointed to the detective bureau of the Newton St. Station shortly after joining the force in April 1945.

She was the first woman to hold such a position and has worked primarily in the detective bureau, starting at Newton St. Division and taking over the job at Foothill Division, when that division opened in 1961.

Among those honoring Mrs. James were Police Chief Edward Davis; R. J. Carreon Jr., president of the police commission, deputy chief of police, Roger Murdock; deputy chief Noel McQuon and Capt. Deward Farmer, detective commander, Foothill Division.

Mrs. James said she began her career in 1945 and has worked with and watched as many of those honoring her advanced in the department.

She was presented a diamond-studded anniversary pin and certificate by commission president Carreon during ceremonies at the commission meeting.

VETERAN of Los Angeles Police Dept. civilian staff, Mrs. Veda James, is honored for 25 years service by Police Commission. In ceremony from left are R. J. Carreon Jr., commission president, and Mrs. James. She is detective bureau clerk at Foothill Division.

CITATION

This Citation is presented to

VEDA D. JAMES

on the occasion of her attainment of

25 years of City Service

The Board of Police Commissioners takes pleasure in commending Mrs. Veda D. James for her twenty-five years of outstanding service with the Los Angeles Police Department.

Mrs. James began her career with the Los Angeles Police Department April 3, 1945, as a War Emergency Clerk Stenographer, and was later appointed as a regular Clerk Stenographer on July 1, 1946.

During her twenty-five years with the Police Department, Mrs. James has consistently received exceptional ratings reflecting her abilities, efficiency, and loyalty. Because of her outstanding work with Detective Investigators, Mrs. James has been called upon many times to testify in court, for which she has been very highly commended by various Judges and Deputy District Attorneys.

BOARD OF POLICE COMMISSIONERS

President